WhipEye

BOOK ONE

of

WhipEye Chronicles

WhipEye Chronicles
BOOK ONE

WhipEye

Geoffrey Saign

KiraKu Press

First edition: July 2014

KiraKu Press
St Paul, MN

This is a work of fiction. Names, characters, places, and incidents are products of the author's imagination or used fictitiously. Any resemblance to actual events or persons, living or dead, is entirely coincidental.

Cover by Patrycja Ignaczak

Printed in the United States of America
ISBN: 978-0-9904013-0-8 (pbk.)
Library of Congress Control Number: 2014908901

www.geoffreysaign.net

For Mom, Dad, Craig, Connie, Kathy, Karin, & Jennifer

ONE

Stealing from a Monster

TODAY IS THE LAST DAY OF SCHOOL before summer vacation, and my twelfth birthday. So I should be crazy happy. Instead, this is the most messed up day of my life, except for the one I can't remember.

I have to talk to the parrot.

All day long, I sit through boring games and parties while the urge to see Charlie builds until it feels like my whole life depends on it. By the time school's out I'm going nuts. I race through town, park my bike, and enter the Endless Pet Store, hoping it'll be easy.

However, Plan A, walking right back to Charlie, is DOA—dead on arrival.

"Stay away from the parrot, girl." Magnar sounds angrier than usual and he glares at me from behind the front counter.

I lower my head and walk by fast. I don't like him. Mainly because of the way he treats Charlie. I've heard him shout at the parrot. Even his one-word name sounds harsh.

It's weird, but I think he hates me for talking to Charlie. As if it's a crime. I've never seen him show concern for the other pets here, either.

As always, he's rubbing his palms obsessively over his stupid nine gold rings. His left thumb is bare. I'm sure he has a ring fetish. They're probably on his toes too.

"Five minutes, then I want you out of here," he says. "We both know you don't have any money."

Hey, didn't you hear, Pug-face? I just won the lottery. I duck behind a horned toad aquarium, waiting for Magnar to return to punching keys in front of his supersized computer monitor.

Five minutes. I try to think of a Plan B, and imagine a moose charging through the front glass and barreling over the creep. It might improve his look. He's bald, short, and thin, and he always wears a dingy black suit and blood-red shirt. Deep wrinkles line his face and neck, which make him look like a pug.

"Sam's here, Sam's here."

Charlie. The parrot's voice is unusually soft. Puzzled how the bird saw me over the stacked aquariums, I risk a peek at Magnar. His beady eyes stare back. I flick my shoulder-length brown hair, pretending to be interested in a veiled chameleon. Any other day I would be.

Luckily, Plan B appears. Two customers take the creep's attention.

I crouch, murmuring, "Just do it, Sam," and shuffle awkwardly on my long, klutzy legs to the rear of the store.

Along the back wall, the stench of old cage litter fills my nostrils, and brightly colored Scarlet and Greenwing Macaws sit in large cages—a.k.a. Magnar's jail cells—watching me as I scurry past.

I slip on the dusty floor, my arms whirl, and I nearly nosedive into a pair of startled cockatiels. Regaining my footing, I hurry on.

At the back corner of the small store, I stop in front of a tall, open stand, where a twelve-inch gray parrot perches on a wood bar.

The red sign beneath the perch has four lines in black lettering:

Congo African Gray Parrot
Psittacus erithacus erithacus
NOT FOR SALE
Don't Touch The Parrot!

White rings circle the parrot's yellow eyes and he bobs excitedly when he sees me.

A small gold chain attached to the perch ends in a combination lock shackle that's fastened to the parrot's leg. It's a reminder of my life. I feel like I have a chain around me too, and I want to rip Charlie's off. I've always been able to sense what animals feel, and it's obvious the parrot is miserable.

I'm wheezing due to the animal dander, so I pull out my inhaler. Taking a quick puff, I glance over my shoulder to make sure Magnar isn't sneaking up on me. Nope. I turn back to the parrot.

"Look what I brought you, Charlie," I whisper. From my jacket pocket, I dig out a few organic raw almonds. "Fresh off the floor of the food co-op. I cleaned them for you, Charlie. I bet they're better than what Magnar feeds you."

The parrot pecks at the nuts with his black hooked bill, softly hitting my palm. "Nice girl. Nice manners." Bits of nuts fly everywhere.

"Thanks, Charlie. I took an online course." I brush strands of hair off my face. The parrot's presence relaxes me.

Nearly a year ago, after Mom died, I wandered into the Endless Pet Store after school one day, following a deep urge that kept my feet moving until I stood in front of the parrot. The bird noticed me too, and seemed interested in me. That first day I talked to Charlie for an hour, and after that I kept returning. The parrot seemed to enjoy my visits as much as I did. He was the one bright thing in my life over the last year.

I heave a deep breath, and the words spinning in my head all day long run off the tip of my tongue; "Charlie, Dad still isn't talking to me. I can't take it anymore. I miss Mom so much. I want my life back and—"

"Sorry, kid, but we don't have time for this." The parrot leans closer. "Make like double-O-seven and bust me out of here."

"What?" I look at him carefully. I've been visiting him four or five times a week over the last year, and he's never said those lines before. Maybe he watched a James Bond movie with Magnar. "Yeah, Charlie, I'll stuff you in my jacket pocket and skip out the door."

"I mean it." The parrot continues talking softly. "Right now. Let's fly the coop. Blow this pop stand. Make a jail break."

"Huh?" African grays are some of the smartest birds alive, but Charlie's eyes look different, as if he understands what he's saying. Or maybe Magnar scared the parrot with all his yelling, and Charlie strung together enough words so that he *sounds* smart.

For a moment, I consider running up to the front counter and screaming at the creep. But sanity quickly returns.

"Don't stare at me like a dumb bunny, Sam. For goodness sakes, let's go."

Panic. I can't be having a real conversation with a parrot, and a small voice in the back of my mind whispers that I've lost it. Instead of talking to a parrot over the last year, I should have been talking to the school counselor.

"Hey, kid, wake up already. Yoo-hoo, anyone in there?"

"I can't take you, Charlie. It's stealing. Grand theft parrot. Five years hard time."

"Take this, and don't lose it." With his beak, Charlie yanks a bright red feather out of his tail—the only place he has red feathers, and holds it down to me.

"Why?" I carefully slip the soft quill from his beak, worried the parrot hurt himself. Maybe he's lost it. If birds pull out their feathers, they're often depressed.

"We both need a change."

"What do you mean?" I ask.

"You're as miserable as I am. If you get any unhappier you could sell frowns for a living."

He's right. Change. I want it more than anything. "How can a feather change my life?"

He doesn't answer. My fingers find and rub the compass that's hanging around my neck on a leather string. I've told Charlie my problems all year long, but I never thought he actually understood me. "How did you learn to talk like this, Charlie?"

"We don't have time for explanations." His yellow eyes meet mine. "Are you a friend, or is all that sappy stuff you're always blabbing about freeing the animals in the pet store just nonsense?"

"C'mon, Charlie. Of course I want the animals free, but most of them can't survive in northern Minnesota."

The parrot cocks his head at me as if he doesn't believe me, as if I'm letting him down.

"It's not nonsense," I insist.

"Then prove it." He walks back and forth a few inches on his perch, his head bobbing.

"I don't know the combination, Charlie."

"I do. I pretended to be sleeping once."

"I must be nuts," I mutter. "Arguing with a parrot." Then a little louder, "Charlie, if I take you, Magnar will know it's me. They'll catch me and bring you back to him. End of story."

"Do you know how often I've wished I could fly through a real jungle? This pet store is a prison and Magnar's a monster. He wants me dead tomorrow. Now get me out of here, pronto, or this is the last time we'll ever talk, Sam." The parrot glares at me. "End of story."

Dead? Fire burns in my chest. Magnar is creepy scary. I've seen him get red-faced when he caught me talking to the parrot. He scares me too. I don't understand why he'd want the parrot dead, but it doesn't matter. I believe Charlie. And I can't risk coming back tomorrow and finding him gone.

Besides, the parrot deserves a life. So do I.

"Okay, Charlie."

"Seven, two, one," whispers the parrot.

My fingers tremble as I slide the feather into my blue flannel shirt pocket. With jittery hands, I shift the combination rings and unfasten the gold shackle. Gently, I grab Charlie and slide him under my jacket.

"What are you doing here?"

I lift my shoulders to my ears and turn, expecting Magnar's hands to curl around my neck like a boa constrictor and end my crappy life. But the creep is standing thirty feet away, his back to me. I have a few more seconds to live.

In front of Magnar, a massive hand slips between the door curtains separating the back supply room from the customer area. I should run, but my curiosity stops me. The fingers, five feet off the floor, are coarse and thick as a gorilla's.

"I lonely."

Even crazier, the voice behind the curtain is high-pitched, like a child's. I can relate to the loneliness, though.

"You have to leave." Magnar's tone is acid. "Now." He pushes the hand back through the curtains.

"But—"

"Go," snarls Magnar.

Magnar's fury sends me backpedaling into the nearest aisle, where I bend over and hurry past gerbil and hamster aquariums. I run my free hand along a shelf so I don't fall and make a parrot pancake. Sweat runs beneath my shirt and jeans, and my pulse pounds as if it's going to jump out of my skin.

At the end of the cages, I pause. I'm six feet from the front door and becoming a thief. Crouching, I peek sideways.

I'm so dead.

Tom, Magnar's assistant, stands at the checkout counter. Tall and lean, with spiked red hair and seven earring studs in his right ear, he's staring directly at me. He always lets me talk to Charlie when Magnar works in back, but I doubt his kindness means he'll let me steal the parrot.

I hold my breath, waiting for him to call Magnar, or at least ask why I'm crouching with my hand stuffed up my coat. *Just practicing CPR on myself.*

But he remains quiet and his eyes flash gold. *What?*

A deep, agonized groan, which doesn't sound human, fills the store. I'm in a freak show. I whip around.

Magnar stands at the back of the store, staring at Charlie's corner. His face darkens like a black cloud ready to spout lightning, while he rubs his right thumb ring with his other thumb.

If he moves his head a few inches, he'll see me, so I almost cheer when he takes another step toward the corner, out of sight.

Immediately, something gray, like a shadow, enters the far end of my aisle, hovering four feet off the floor. The shadow is so strange that I don't move. It's floating like a loop, a thin, scaled tendril that quickly thickens and lengthens, its two ends hidden by the aisle hiding Magnar. It's too solid to be smoke.

I've never seen anything like it before. On second thought, that isn't entirely true, because one end of the thick shadow slithers into the aisle, looking like the tapered tail of a snake. A very big snake.

Eyes wide, I crane my neck. When I do, the other end of the shadow appears. First, one head, then a second, swings into the aisle, both with flaring upper neck hoods.

Normally, I'd love to see the longest venomous snake in the world, even one with two heads, but this floating king cobra is fifty feet long and thick as a telephone pole. I'm not clear if it's real, my imagination, or some type of trick until its four dark eyes flick open and find mine.

Its eyes are full of hate. For some reason, it feels as if Magnar is staring at me.

I should run. Scream. Do anything. But the cobra's eyes lock on mine and I can't move. As if I'm hypnotized. I forget what I'm doing and just stare, lost in those dark orbs.

Opening both mouths, the snake hisses, showing eight-inch glistening fangs.

As it slithers toward me, its writhing body smashes into shelves on either side of the aisle, sending supplies, aquariums, and cages tumbling to the floor. I watch all the poor squeaking critters falling through the air until the crashing glass snaps me out of my stupor.

For once in my life I take three smooth steps, jerk open the door, and run.

TWO

The Chase

THE SNAKE'S TWO HEADS bump into the closed pet store door, then follow me along the inside of the window as I weave through shoppers on the sidewalk. I jump on my bike and take off, expecting to hear glass breaking behind me. It doesn't.

Squawk. "Free. Free! Let me out. I'm dying in here."

"Shh, Charlie. Almost there." I pedal my dirt bike down the sidewalk and across the street.

A car horn blares, and I swerve wildly.

Tires squeal and a car bumper stops inches away from my leg. The driver sticks his head out his window and yells, "Watch where you're going, kid!"

I swallow and keep pedaling. Cars always make me jittery, but other images in my mind are worse.

The afternoon spring sun forces me to squint at the city park ahead. A few more pumps on the pedals and thick trees will hide me.

Blood rushes to my ears. Why didn't the cobra bust through the glass? Maybe the people on the sidewalk saved me. Or the snake is some kind of 3-D magic trick. But how can a trick knock things over? Or hypnotize me? Really creepy.

The bell above the Endless Pet Store door jingles just as oak, birch, and aspen trees surround me.

Safe.

I hum the same song that always helps me relax. I'm unsure where I first heard it, and my father never answers my questions about it. However, a few months ago, in a rare moment of breaking The Silence, Dad said the tune was an old song about friendship. He wouldn't tell me anything else.

A muffled squawk beneath my jacket brings me back to the parrot. Charlie weighs less than a pound, and I relax my fingers around him so I don't choke the poor bird.

"Let me out."

"Just a little farther, Charlie." We're on a long, straight section of black pavement, and up ahead an elderly woman is walking toward us. I force a smile, pretending it's normal to ride a bike with an arm stuffed up your coat.

A vise clamps on my thumb and searing pain shoots through my hand.

"Ouch! All right, you." I bring the parrot out and set him on my shoulder.

The bird clutches my jacket, digging his feet into the fabric.

"You didn't have to bite me, Charlie." I shake my hand a few times. "You're welcome, by the way."

"Blue skies. Sunshine. Freedom!" Charlie flaps his wings, and then tilts his head at the passing woman. "What're you staring at?"

The woman stops and gapes as we keep going.

"Charlie, the woman's a witness." And I'm a criminal on the run.

But I've always thought animals would be excited to be set free from their cages. I'm happy about that.

"Relax, kid." Charlie fluffs his feathers and spreads his wings. "Everything is working out perfectly."

"A monster attacked me, Charlie." All I see are scary possibilities, most of them ending in misery, pain, or my death at the hands of Magnar. I have a growing list of questions for the parrot, but I ask, "What do we do now?"

"Bring me back my parrot, girl!"

The fury in those words hunches my shoulders. As I ride into the first curve in the path, I whip around and see a flash of black.

Magnar. On foot. Chasing me. My skin crawls.

I pedal harder. Pug-face sounds scary. Worse than scary. I clench the handlebars, the image of the two-headed king cobra in my brain again.

"I haven't flown for a hundred years," says Charlie. "Well, at least a few. I'll meet you at your place." He flies off my shoulder, his wings flapping hard.

Jamming the pedals, I skid to a stop. "Charlie!"

The parrot disappears immediately among the dense tree branches, the greenery hiding the bright red of his tail. I peer into the woods, disappointed and surprised he left me, and even more confused about what's going on.

"Girl."

Magnar's rounding the last curve, his feet floating a few inches off the ground. I rub my eyes and look again. Now the creep is walking along the path like a normal person, but he's still moving really fast.

I take off, my sweaty palms slippery on the bike grips. Standing on the pedals and riding fast, I keep searching for Charlie.

I must have talked to the parrot about my house. What else did

I tell him? Does he have any clue about how dangerous a northern Minnesota forest can be for a small bird?

In my peripheral vision, I glimpse something big moving silently through the woods. The hair on my forearms stands up. Trees and thick brush hide whatever it is.

Bears, cougars, or moose are unlikely in the small park. Has to be a deer. Please be a deer. All the shouting must have spooked it. I remember the giant hand and ride faster.

My foot slips off the pedal and my bike careens off the path into the grass. I'm staring at a tree trunk. There's a flash of movement farther ahead in the woods, but I can't quite make it out.

Yelling, I manage to swerve, but still clip the tree with the tip of my handlebar, bruising my pinky's knuckle. "Ow!"

Steering back onto the path, my lungs wheeze and my legs feel rubbery. I'm pedaling like a slug and shake my throbbing finger.

After the next curve, a long straight section of pavement appears. Far ahead, near the center of the forested park, a small walking bridge arches over a stream. Someone is sitting on the bridge bench. I'm saved. At least I'm not alone with Magnar in the woods.

"Charlieeee!" The parrot will easily beat me home, exactly what I don't need. Dad always talks about the importance of honesty. If he finds out I stole Charlie, he'll be really upset.

Closer to the bridge, I recognize the bench-sitter. It's Rose, an old woman who rents Dad's cabin in the woods. The tension in my chest eases a little. I figure not even Magnar will hurt me with another adult present.

Pond water glints blue-green through the trees to either side of the path, and the scent of humus on the forest floor fills the air. Usually that would calm me and I'd stop to look for interesting critters near the water, like Tiger salamanders and American toads. Today I barely notice.

A sixth sense causes me to look back. Magnar has cut the distance between us in half, his legs blurs of motion. Cold shock hits me. Even though I'm riding a bike, he's going to catch me. *How is this possible?*

Familiar noises break me out of my trance. A score of croaking frogs are scattered across the path ahead of me, hopping between the ponds on either side. I don't want to hit one and try to steer around them.

"Girl."

I glance over my shoulder. Magnar's twenty yards away, stampeding like a bull elephant.

Footsteps—from the bridge.

I whirl. Rose is racing at me, wild-eyed, her left hand holding a walking stick, her right arm extended toward me with a small ball of golden light in her raised palm. *What?*

My head jerks back to Magnar, then to Rose, then to Magnar almost on top of me, then to Rose about to run me over.

Breaking hard, I lean sideways on the bike and put a foot out to brace myself on the pavement.

The light in Rose's palm flashes into Magnar's chest, and she stops at my bike, her arm dropping.

Magnar stands three feet away, suspended in mid-stride, one foot off the ground, one hand an inch from my neck.

THREE

Rose

AT FIRST, IT SEEMS LIKE AN ACT. Magnar pretending to be stiff, so he can scare the life out of me, which he's doing. I inch my neck away from his pale, veined hand. I'm aware of Rose breathing hard beside me, but she doesn't look surprised, just tired.

I get off my bike and lightly kick Magnar's shin. I want to kick him again, harder, but light flashes near the toe of his raised foot, expanding into a thin gold ring of crackling electricity that slowly circles his shoe and moves along it. Bizarre.

Magnar's dark eyes shift, burning into me, and his pupils are replaced by a vertical sliver of gold. Like the flash of gold I saw in Tom's eyes. I want to run, but I'm panting.

Worse, the green and black skin of a leopard frog twists like a bedsheet under my front wheel. My eyes mist over.

Rose rests her free hand on my shoulder and leans on me. I slump under the added strain.

"Help me to the bench, Samantha."

"Sure, why not," I say hoarsely.

We wobble together, carefully picking our way around the frogs, then up the gently arching bridge. Rose teeters as if she might fall over. I drop my bike to catch her elbow. Luckily, she falls onto the wood bench. I follow.

If I don't get more air into my lungs, I'm going to die. Which would be pretty lame, given all that's happened today. *Yeah, she escaped monsters, but then she ran out of air.*

I drag my inhaler from my jeans and depress the cartridge. Rescue medicine flies into my airways. I close my mouth a few seconds, then gasp. After using the inhaler once more, I'm able to hold my breath longer.

Releasing a deep sigh, I sit back.

Rose gives a tired smile. "Magnar didn't think I had anything left in me."

"Hey, I'm glad you did. Nice job with Pug-face." I barge forward. "Okay, what's this all about?"

Rose has a warm, wrinkled face and could easily be as old as Magnar. I wonder how they know each other. Probably through the weird magic they both seem to have.

"A battle has been fought for centuries, Samantha, between ancient creatures and Magnar." Her voice softens. "Charlie's in the middle of it, and Magnar is winning."

"Huh." She's freaking me out as much as Magnar. And I'm surprised she knows Charlie.

Nearly a year ago, Rose showed up at our door and asked to rent the old cabin on Dad's property. Dad felt sorry for her and let her have it cheap, but we only see her a few minutes every month when she comes to the house to pay rent.

She's harmless and always smiling, but I never talk to her. Dad tried on several occasions, but each time she mumbled nonsense and walked away. I always thought she was a little crazy. Now she's also a mystery. A big one.

I roll my head sideways. Magnar stands like carved stone, but his creepy gaze finds me. The crackling ring of light is moving up his ankle.

Shivers run down my back, and I turn to Rose. "Are you a witch?"

She chuckles. "No, just a friend."

"Yeah, right. You just froze Magnar like a popsicle." And why call me a friend when we've never talked? I'm sweating beneath my jacket and pull it off, stuffing it behind me.

Every time I've seen Rose, her long, silver hair is in a braid with a flower tucked in it. Today it's a small red rose. Faded jeans, a white blouse frayed at the sleeves, and beat-up canvas tennis shoes make her appear homeless. Not that I dress any better.

"You didn't mean to kill the frog, Samantha."

"A.k.a. *Rana pipiens*." My gut wrenches. I never want to kill any animal. Worse, anything dying reminds me of mom. "Stupid Magnar scared me."

"Fear makes us do things we shouldn't." She bends closer. "What happened to your thumb?"

I study its black-and-blue tip. "Charlie bit me."

Water splashes.

I lift my head, expecting to see bushes rustling along the side of the brook. But everything is still. Something big just raced across the stream, and Rose doesn't even bother to look, her face calm. After the last fifteen minutes, I rule out a deer.

Magnar is a chunk of clay with moving eyeballs, but he probably hears us talking. So weird. The wiggly line of light is circling his thigh.

I grip my knees. "How long will he stay like that? Hopefully at least a few hours."

"Charlie gave you a feather."

"How do you know that?" I look down. "Oh." The feather is visible in my pocket, and I pull it out. It shines like a thin ruby in the sunlight.

"You're lucky." Rose's eyes brighten. "Charlie trusts you."

"He's my friend." Her interest in the parrot nags at my brain. What's her connection to him? But concern for Charlie crowds out my curiosity. I'm anxious to get going. I hold the feather out to her. "You can have it."

Rose shakes her head and gives a vehement, "No."

Wary, I lean away from her.

Her face relaxes. Slowly, gently, with one gnarled hand she closes my fingers around the feather. "Charlie's a methuselah parrot." Her hand drops to her lap.

"Methuselah?" I know the word means a man who lived a long time; it was a bonus vocabulary word in English last month. But why would she use it for a parrot?

"Every thousand years, a long-lived animal—a methuselah, is born on the planet to gather wisdom. You've been given a great honor."

My brow wrinkles. "How old is Charlie?"

Rose rests a palm lightly on my shoulder. "Charlie needs your help and protection. So does the world. Everything is at stake, Samantha. Trust Charlie. He chose to give you some of his wisdom with his feather."

"I don't feel any smarter." I also have enough problems without having to play Wonder Woman. Besides, none of what she's saying makes sense. How can I help the world? I'm not even brave enough to start a conversation with my father.

But Rose is right about one thing: I have to help Charlie. My lungs are breathing easier. Time to go.

Before I can move, she says, "You might see scary things, Samantha."

"Like a giant two-headed king cobra?" Definitely scary.

Rose's voice softens, full of sadness. "Magnar and I have been around a long time. He used to be different. Long ago, he was guided by goodness and was a true guardian, not a keeper of shadow monsters."

"Monsters? As in plural?" My stomach knots.

"Does your compass work, Samantha?"

Surprised by her question, I lift the compass off my chest and inspect it. Set in a gold ring, glass covers a gold needle hovering over a black face. All the numbers and directional marks are gold and the outer crystal rim sparkles. On the rim of the black face, inscribed in gold cursive letters, are the words, *Trust, Love, Trust,* and *Mom*. *Trust* lies at east and west, *Love* at north, and *Mom* at south.

"Mom gave it to me on my eleventh birthday," I say quietly. "She said it was in her family for hundreds of years, and her mother gave it to her." I screw my eyes shut, pushing memories away. "What does my compass have to do with anything?"

"If you can't find north, you'll never know where you are. Most people have forgotten how to find their way through life."

I understand what Rose is talking about, because most of the time I'm lost, drifting through the days like plankton floating in a big ocean with nothing to hang onto. Sometimes it seems like I'll just float away forever.

I pocket the feather, stand, and pick up my bike. "I have to go. Appointment with a parrot." The blue circle of light is crackling around Magnar's waist, sending adrenaline into my limbs.

Rose tries, but she can't quite stand up.

I grab her arm, thin and weak in my grip, and pull her to her feet. She wobbles, leans on her walking stick, and hobbles along the bridge away from Magnar. I walk my bike at her side.

"We both have a few parlor tricks," she says. "But I can't stop him again. Long ago, I could do more. Now I'm too old and tired."

"Bummer. Because I don't have *any* tricks." I glance back. The blue light flows over Magnar's head and vanishes. Immediately, his raised foot drops to the ground and he bends over, resting his hands on his thighs.

Slowly, he straightens, lifting a fist. Purple veins line his haggard face. "I want my parrot, girl." Walking slowly, he steps onto the bridge.

I jump on my bike, but Rose doesn't look worried. Maybe she's too old to care about dying. She's barely shuffling. She'll never outwalk Magnar. I want to shout at her, but she's probably moving as fast as she can. I consider giving her a ride on my handlebars. Yikes.

When we reach the pavement, Rose swings around to face Magnar. He's stumbling over the top of the bridge.

I want to turn, but can't. Like a hand against my head, something pushes my gaze toward the six-foot walking stick in Rose's hand. For the first time I really see it. She never brought it to the house before. I would have noticed.

Spaced along the staff are several dozen small, lifelike animal faces carved into the chestnut wood. Predators, herbivores, birds, amphibians, and reptiles. Their fur, teeth, ears, and eyes are captured in flawless detail, as if someone took real animal heads, shrunk them, and stuck them into the wood. It's beautiful.

Strangely, I sense it calling to me. Burrowing into my mind and heart and asking me to join it. Dreamlike, I reach for it.

"Samantha!" Rose's voice is sharp. "Don't touch WhipEye."

I wake up from my daze, my cheeks burning. "Sorry. It's . . . I've never seen anything like . . . it's so . . . perfect." Even the staff's name is beautiful and beckons to me, deep down, as if it's somehow touching a part of me that can't resist. It's all I can do to keep my hands on my bike.

"You're a good girl, Samantha Green." She pats my shoulder. "You have a good heart. Never doubt it."

No one has said something that nice to me in a year. No matter how scared I am, there's no way I'll leave her now. Besides, I owe her.

The creep stops a few yards away on the bridge, rubbing his thumb ring and glaring at Rose. His thin lips twist as if he wants to scream.

Rose lifts the staff with both hands and thumps it against the path, sending a deep echo—*boom!*—into the distance. Confused by the strength of it, I cock my head to listen.

"Are you ready to risk it all, Magnar?" Rose grimaces, as if she's prepared to fight.

Magnar bares his teeth like a rabid dog. "Are you, Rose?"

A shudder runs through me. Rose doesn't stand a chance against him.

I blurt, "Leave her alone, you bully."

Magnar doesn't look at me as he snarls, "You'll pay for this with your life, girl."

Shock flutters down my core. I've never had anyone tell me he'll kill me. Not seriously, anyway. And never an adult. It's freakier that he said it in front of a witness.

I try to sound confident. "The police might be interested in what you said."

His hard eyes flick at me as if he could care less about the police, which frays my nerves even more. *What have I gotten myself into?*

Rose whispers something and moves the bottom of the staff in some kind of pattern in front of her legs. I'm staring at Magnar, my arms rigid, and barely pay attention to what she's doing.

She glances over her shoulder. "Go home, Samantha, and remember the gift Charlie gave you." Her eyes have the same sliver of gold as Magnar's.

I hesitate, wanting to leave but feeling guilty about it. "Are you sure?"

"Go." Her tone is stern.

Confused, I ride away, afraid for her.

Boom!

The staff echoes again far into the distance, and on the third echo, I check back.

Magnar is striding along the path, following me, and Rose is gone.

Chills sweep my skin. I imagine the creep breaking Rose's neck and throwing her body into the woods. He's capable of it. That would explain why he threatened me in front of her. He planned to kill the witness.

I pump my legs as images of Rose, Magnar, and Charlie swirl through my mind. And in my peripheral vision, something large moves silently through the woods, keeping pace with me.

I don't look.

FOUR

A Promise

OUR SOMEWHAT SECLUDED DIRT ROAD only has a few houses on either side of it, with more grass fields than homes. I don't mind the lack of neighbors.

At the end of the street is a wooded lot. To the east of it sits our two-story green house, with its peeling paint and tilted shutters. A tall, rusty metal fence surrounds the front yard.

Whatever moved through the trees in the park remained in the woods when I left, slowing my pounding pulse one notch.

I pull up to the gate, panting, and rest my arms on the bike's handlebars. Mom's lilac bushes fill the air with a sweet scent, bringing back memories I try to ignore. As usual, Dad's old blue pickup sits in the dirt driveway. I'm glad he's home, because I can't get Magnar's threat out of my head.

Thinking about Dad reminds me of my jacket. We don't have money to go out and buy another one, and he'll be upset if he finds out I left it on the park bench. Stupid. It's my only coat, but no way am I returning for it.

After catching my breath, I call softly, "Charlie." He doesn't

22

reply, but the parrot might be hiding in the backyard, where Dad tends the animals. I hope Charlie won't go to him, but the crazy bird seems capable of anything. I figure I have only minutes to find him and get him somewhere safe before Magnar arrives.

Wheeling my bike through the broken gate, I stand it against the lilacs. In the overgrown grass, a white sign with hand-painted green letters advertises GREEN'S WILDLIFE SANCTUARY AND SHELTER. Guests pay to view the wild animals my father rescues from traps or car accidents.

Located in a small town in northern Minnesota, near Superior National Forest, the shelter doesn't earn much money. So Dad takes on odd jobs, like carpentry and plumbing. He can fix anything. He says we have to be thrifty in what we buy, but that we're rich in other ways. I never complain about the lack of money, because I love the animals and I know they need help to recover.

But today I had to listen to kids in school talk about summer plans like road trips, swimming, camping, and sports, while all I have to look forward to is avoiding my silent father all day long.

I hate The Silence. Dad says *Hi,* or *Do your chores,* or other necessary words, but he never *talks* to me. It's like living with a zombie, someone just going through the motions every day.

A soft grating sound comes from behind me, and I jerk my head around. Not Magnar.

Across the street, in front of a yellow, well-kept house and yard, Jake Morris is riding his skateboard in his driveway. He moved in a few weeks ago and is two months younger than me. A group of kids always circles him at school. Mr. Popular.

I, on the other hand, stopped talking to everyone a year ago. My friends lost interest. It's my fault, but if I talk to people, they ask questions, and all questions eventually lead back to Mom. So it's better not talking to anyone.

Sometimes, Jake wanders over to chat with Dad and watch the animals, but I avoid him.

"Yo, Sam." He skates down his paved driveway, flipping his board onto the grass before he reaches the dirt road.

I ignore him and hustle toward the front door in my sluggish gait.

His feet beat across the street in swift pats. Before I reach the front steps he jumps in front of me, blocking my path. One hand moves like an animated puppet as he talks, which I find annoying, and he pokes a finger lightly against my shoulder—which I find even more irritating.

"What're you doing?" he asks.

The usual. Stole a parrot. Met a witch. Running from a monster. "Seeing the sights."

Stuffing my hands in my pockets, I scan the street. The road is empty, but it feels like spiders are crawling along my spine. I don't have time for this, but if I don't act normal, Jake will never leave me alone.

Sturdy and a little shorter than me, he wears glasses, which make him appear a little dorky, especially if he scrunches up his face as he sometimes does. But he has nice blue eyes. Today's outfit is a new sleeveless red T-shirt, black shorts, and black tennis shoes.

My flannel shirt, old jeans, and beat-up sneakers are grungy by comparison.

He shoves his arms in front of me. "New tattoos. Do you like them?" Temporary lion and tiger images circle his forearms.

"Cool." And I mean it. "I'd love to hang, but I have chores to do." Now go home.

"I could help." He adjusts an elbow pad, then hitches up his shorts.

"I don't need help. But thanks, anyway."

"Someone's in your house and it sounds like they're sick. Is that the Charlie you were calling?"

"You should get your hearing checked." What if a raptor attacked Charlie? Or dad heard the parrot? "Great talking to you. Have a nice day."

I run around him with the speed of a tired turtle and head for the front steps.

Jake whirls. "Then it's a new animal."

"Wrong again." Stumbling up the rickety front stairs, I yank open the screen door and push in the weathered wood door. Once through, I shove the inside door to close it, and keep going. When it bangs against something solid, I turn.

"Ow!" Jake is holding his head, bent over.

I blurt, "Sorry, I didn't see you coming in."

He groans and bends lower, then drops his hand and straightens with a smile. "Just kidding. The door hit my shoe."

Under different circumstances I might have found this funny, but not today.

His hand does a flourish. "Bryon said I'm always welcome if he's home. He's out back, feeding the animals."

Bothered over his use of my father's first name, and that he came in without an invitation from me, I frown and grab the knob. "Well today we're busy, so . . ."

He squeezes past me into the large, wood floor entryway, stopping with his hands on his hips.

My face is hot because he's ignoring me, and also because of the piles of magazines, books, and recyclables lining the hallway to the back door, all layered with dust. The adjacent dining and living rooms aren't any better.

The whole house smells musty, and my cheeks burn when I think about how clean his home probably is. But he has a mom.

A muted clucking comes from the second floor. Yep. Sounds like a sick person. How did Charlie get inside?

"What's that?" Jake looks up the stairs, then at me. "Weird." He's like a bloodhound on a trail.

"It's a bird recording I made." I avoid his eyes. I don't like lying, but I'm imagining Magnar at my front door. Controlling the urge to bolt upstairs, I casually shuffle toward the stairway.

He shrugs. "If you're busy, I'll go talk to Bryon about the new animal."

"He's busy too." I step in front of him to block the hallway to the back door. The last thing I need is Jake helping Dad discover that I stole Charlie from the pet store. "Ever heard of breaking and entering?"

He spreads his hands, actually looking worried. "Hey, I walked through an open door."

"And now you can back out through it." I consider shoving him, but he's strong.

He's on the track team at school, and every day he sprints the road in front of our house. I'd like to race him for the fun of it. Once my legs get moving, I'm not such a klutz. But with my asthma I wouldn't have a chance to win, anyway.

We've experimented with all kinds of medication, but nothing helps. Sometimes I think I'd be more coordinated if I could breathe normally, like everyone else.

I inch forward. His blond hair, always trimmed and neat, is too short to pull. But I'm desperate.

His eyes narrow. "I'm a black belt in kung fu."

No way will I touch him now. "That would be assault and battery on top of breaking and entering. I could call the cops." But it's the last thing I want to do.

He looks disappointed and flaps a hand at me. "All right, Sam, you win. I'll leave." He grabs the doorknob, then gives a sly smile. "I'll go around to your outside fence and ask Bryon if I can come over to talk about the new animal."

He starts to leave.

"No, wait!" I'm beyond annoyed with him now. And more than a little worried.

He flips a palm. "C'mon, Sam, I just want to see it."

"Dang, you're pushy." I've run out of ideas to get rid of him and can't waste any more time talking.

I spin and run up the wooden steps between piles of wildlife magazines. The railing creaks under my weight, and I slip on a magazine and bang my knee. My face is hot again as I keep going.

Jake follows. "What kind of animal is it?"

"I never said there was one."

"I bet it's cool."

Taking a right at the top of the landing, I hurry down the hallway to the first open door on the left.

Gulp. Crumpled sheets cover my bed and dirty laundry is scattered across the dusty wood floor. Magazines, photos, a pair of scissors, and coins lay strewn across my dresser, and heaps of stuffed birds, plastic and rubber lizards, and other animal figures litter my small desk—all equally dusty. Even my desktop computer screen needs cleaning.

"Wait a minute," I throw over my shoulder. "The maid has the day off."

Jake rolls his eyes, but stops in the hallway. I kick dirty clothes under my bed, bury the underwear, and then stop. Charlie is sitting on a bedpost at the foot of my mattress.

I jump in front of the parrot as Jake rounds the corner.

He eyes the walls. "Wow. I like your room. Very cool."

Hundreds of animal photos and paintings create a beautiful mosaic, which covers all four walls and most of the faded white paint. A large painting of a leaping spinner dolphin hangs on the wall by my bed.

Scattered amidst the animal photos are pictures of giant redwoods, giant sequoias, baobabs, and bristle cone pine. Mom loved the ancient trees. It took us years to do the walls. I don't pay attention to them anymore, since they always remind me of her.

I think Jake will make fun of the small stuffed animals, but instead he squeezes a loon, which gives its haunting call, and then quickly presses the cardinal, blue jay, and catbird, which all sing.

He chuckles. "Neat." Moving on to the bookshelf near the window, he stares at my collection of four dozen animal books. "You're an animal nerd."

I wonder how he means that until he adds, "Awesome."

"Yeah, I watch every TV and Internet program I can find." Casually, I slide along the side of the bed, hiding Charlie. "And anything on YouTube. I'm an expert." It's actually nice to say that to someone, since Dad is one of the few people who know it. I don't tell Jake we had to discontinue internet service a year ago.

"I read a lot of comic books. *Wolverine* and *Spider-Man* are my favorites, and *Avengers* and *Justice League*." He trails his fingers over the book spines. "But I love animals too."

"Great." I bet he doesn't know anything about wild animals.

Jake reaches my dresser and picks up a framed photograph lying facedown. "Is this your mom?"

"Leave it alone." I rush over and grab it from him, my breath catching.

"I wasn't going to drop it."

"It's none of your business." My eyes move past my image in the photo to Dad's smile, then to Mom's hazel eyes—soft and inviting.

Her face was young, full of energy, framed with long, brown hair. Dad called her perfect. I agree. My chest heaves.

Jake crosses his arms. "All right, I get it."

"Will you kids stop with the crazy talk already? And something's ripe, Sam. You should do your laundry before you have guests over."

"What?" Jake peeks around me. "A talking parrot."

Charlie swivels his head toward him. "A talking human."

Jake gasps.

I replace the photo facedown on the dresser, then notice the open bedroom window. The thin screen has a large tear in it. "Great, Charlie. Just great. How am I going to explain this to Dad?"

I walk over to inspect it, and something large, black, and yellow, flashes past the window. "Whoa." I yank my hand away.

A buzzing accompanies the flying shape, which recedes in the distance with a drone like a bumblebee. A six-foot bumble. No animal I can think of even comes close to that description.

Jake's eyebrows lift, but I ignore him and step back from the window. Too many unexplained things crowd my brain and I want to scream. Pushing all of it to a corner of my mind, I try to focus. Magnar will be here any minute and I have to hide Charlie. Heck, I have to hide *myself*. But where?

"Sorry about the screen, but I had to bust in." Charlie shivers. "A hawk was circling me. I was so excited to fly I forgot how risky it might be for a nice sweet parrot like me."

"You'd be on the snack list for most raptors, Charlie." I walk closer to him. "We also have eagles, osprey, and owls." And monsters.

"Thanks for the nightmares, Sam."

"Anytime."

Jake gapes, his hands quiet for once. "You're a real talking parrot."

"Can we change the subject, please?" Charlie turns away.

"Wow." Jake pushes up his glasses. "Did you train him? How can he talk like that?"

I shrug and look at Charlie. "Good question."

"I read a book, kids. *English for Idiots.*"

"Crows might be smarter than chimpanzees, but even they can't read," I say.

His jaw slack, Jake's eyes widen further as he watches the parrot.

"It's not polite to show your teeth, kiddo. Sign of aggression." Charlie preens a feather.

Jake's hands go crazy. "Hey, aren't you the parrot in the pet store? The one that's not for sale?"

I search for an excuse to explain why Charlie's in my bedroom. "I don't have a clue how he got here. I—"

"Sam rescued me. By the way, great job, kid."

I'm exasperated, but also pleased with the compliment. "Thanks, Charlie."

"Amazing." Jake gazes at Charlie. "I don't like birds sold as pets, either. Mom says they should outlaw caged birds."

Squawk. Charlie puts out one wing. "I second the motion."

"Your mother," I murmur. Jake's mom, Cynthia Morris, is a special agent for the US Fish and Wildlife Service and arrests people who import illegal exotic pets. She's the last person I want to find out I stole Charlie. I imagine myself handcuffed and taken away, while Dad gives me his perpetual look of disapproval.

"Don't worry, Sam, I won't rat you out." Jake grins. "Unless there's a reward." He reaches toward Charlie.

The parrot ducks his fingers. "I'm not a stuffed animal from the carnival."

"Sorry." Jake throws a hand wide. "You're brave, Sam. No wonder you didn't want me up here. You could go to jail for this. Charlie has to be worth a fortune. A real talking parrot."

"You're repeating yourself, kid."

The prospect of prison dries my mouth, but Jake's praise raises my spirits.

An idea pops into my mind. Charlie can stay with Aunt Sue, Dad's sister. She visited us a few times when mom was alive, and she loves animals. Plus, she lives in Florida. Magnar would never find the parrot there.

The image of Pug-face at the front door stampedes my thoughts, but something else bothers me. "Why does Magnar want you dead, Charlie?"

"Who's Magnar?" asks Jake.

"The pet store owner."

Jake glances from me to the parrot. "It's illegal to kill a parrot. At least animal abuse."

When Charlie remains silent, I ask, "And what about the two-headed snake and the giant hand?"

"Giant hand?" asks Jake. "What are you talking about? I hate snakes, and two-headed snakes are extra creepy. I saw one on the Internet."

I don't think the Internet snake was fifty feet long, but I don't want to get into that. "How come you won't answer my questions, Charlie?"

The parrot looks at Jake. "Are you a friend of Samantha's?"

He shrugs. "Sure."

I grip a bedpost, not believing him. He doesn't even know me. "Charlie, we have to get out of here. Magnar's coming and—"

"Did someone see you take Charlie?" Jake frowns.

I avoid his eyes. "Not really."

Charlie looks at me. "Do you like being alone, Sam? Or do you want some company?"

My lips clamp shut. Living in The Silence with Dad is like living

31

alone, and I hate it. But I don't want Jake's company. I don't understand why the parrot's asking me this.

Charlie ruffles his neck feathers. "Life's a journey, Sam, and you need help. We all do." He cocks his head. "In fact, I'd like you to take a little trip with me."

The way Charlie says that raises the hairs on my arms. I haven't gone anywhere during the last year, except to school and the pet store. "I don't have a passport." When he doesn't respond, I ask, "Okay, Charlie, where?"

"You have to keep me out of Magnar's hands for the next twenty-four hours. Then he can't hurt me." The parrot eyes me. "Will you help me, kid?"

The way he looks at me melts any resistance, but images of the giant cobra and Magnar's angry face flash through me. "Does Magnar want your feathers?" The fact that Charlie gave me one gnaws at me, as if it's important in some way.

Charlie shakes his wings. "Something like that."

"He can't do that." Jake cuts the air sharply with a hand.

The image of the creep plucking Charlie's feathers one by one tightens my fists. "Rose said you're a methuselah."

"A methusa what?" asks Jake.

"We don't have time for this, kids. Sam's right, Magnar's coming. I can sense him."

"Really?" I open the bedroom door and take a quick peek, but it's quiet downstairs.

"In or out, Sam?" asks Charlie.

I close the door and rest against it. I have more questions than answers, but I can't abandon Charlie. Keeping him from Magnar for one day should be doable. I'm freaking out, but a jolt of energy runs through me. After spending every evening alone in my bedroom for the last year, I finally have something to do. "Yeah, Charlie, I'm in."

"I knew I could count on you, kid."

The way the parrot says that warms me. Like we're a team. Like I was with Mom. "I'm a sucker for crazy parrots."

Charlie locks eyes with Jake. "What about you, kiddo? Will you help us?"

I wait, annoyed Jake bulldozed his way into this.

"Of course I'm in. I don't want Magnar to hurt you."

I stare at him. He just met Charlie minutes ago and yet he doesn't hesitate. He has guts. Of course, I haven't told him about the snake. I feel a little guilty over that. However, all the crazy stuff is more real with his joining us.

"You're Jake, right?" asks Charlie. "Sam mentioned you a few times."

"She did?" He looks at me, but I gaze elsewhere.

"Nice to meet you, Jake. Now hold up your mitt."

Jake raises a hand, but hesitates. "What's Charlie going to do, Sam?"

I shrug. "It won't hurt too much." The parrot is right about one thing, it will be nice to have help, even if it has to be Jake.

"A little closer, kiddo."

Cautiously, Jake moves his hand beneath Charlie's mouth. "You're not going to bite me, are you?" He eyes Charlie's beak.

"This isn't *Twilight*, Jake. I'm a parrot, not a vampire."

Charlie cranes his neck, pulls another crimson feather from his tail, and releases it. Jake watches it float to his palm.

I wince when Charlie pulls the feather, but that's not as bad as Jake's yell when the feather lands. Jake's eyes roll up into his head and he swoons onto the bed.

The doorbell rings.

FIVE

Magnar's Monster

I CRACK OPEN THE DOOR.

Soft footsteps pad along the first floor hallway and Dad's back comes into view. He opens the front door, but I can't see who it is. It has to be Magnar, which knots my stomach.

I quietly close my door, waiting.

"Samantha! Please come down. Mr. Magnar from the pet store wants to talk to you."

My skin goes clammy. "Jake. Get up."

He sits up, smiling. "You made it sound like something scary would happen, so I played along."

I barely listen, my attention bouncing all over the room as I try to think of a hiding place for Charlie. For a moment, my eyes rest on the bird. Although he's a fairly large parrot, Charlie appears small and fragile, his feathers like soft wisps. I can't let Magnar find him.

Jake strokes the feather Charlie gave him. "So, what does it do, Charlie?"

"It's not going to get up and dance, kid. Just don't lose it."

He blushes. "I won't, Charlie. Thanks."

"You're welcome. It's nice to be appreciated."

"Enough about the feather already." I hustle over to my open closet, which has a tangle of gear on the floor. The shelves are crammed too. No place to stuff a parrot. I whirl around.

"Charlie, you have to hide. I'll run downstairs and try to convince Dad to stay out of my room." I'll have to lie. The problem is I never lie to Dad and I'm uncertain I can pull it off. The bigger problem is that Magnar will definitely rat me out. Or worse.

"Samantha."

Dad sounds upset.

"In case you haven't noticed, Sam, your father's waltzing up the stairs and you have a stolen parrot in your bedroom."

I rush to the door, snapping at Jake, "Hide Charlie."

"Stall Bryon," he hisses.

I stick my head out just when Dad reaches the top of the stairs. My hands are sweating.

Dad's wearing his zombie mask. At least that's what I call it when he looks this tired. Circles underline his eyes, as if he isn't sleeping much, and he's wearing the usual jeans and rumpled brown flannel shirt. A stubble beard darkens his face.

He takes a few steps toward my room and stops, keeping his distance. His forehead furrows and his eyebrows arch. He's perfected his look of disapproval over the last year, and he almost *never* smiles anymore. Neither do I. Mom always smiled.

"Didn't you hear me?" he asks.

The Silence is rarely broken between us, so things are serious.

I'm unable to meet his eyes with my next words. "No, I had music on." My fingers clamp on the doorframe.

"You never listen to music." He pauses. "Is anyone in there with you?"

I shrug casually. "Just Jake." Sweat streams down my back.

The stairs creak and the top of Magnar's bald head appears. I swallow. But I'm not surprised. Dad would let a drifter in, so I'm guessing old Pug-face didn't faze him one bit. Dad is friendly to everyone, and anyone can get help at our house. Except me.

Magnar moves stiffly, but something about the way he carries himself makes him seem strong in a way that doesn't match his appearance. When he reaches the top of the stairs, he glares at me while rubbing his right thumb ring with his other thumb. He seems to have recovered from whatever Rose did to him in the park.

Even so, Dad stands a half-foot taller than Magnar, and I've seen him throw hundred-pound sacks of corn over his shoulders without straining. Also, I don't believe Magnar will unleash his shadow snake in front of another grownup.

Dad motions to the creep. "Mr. Magnar from the Endless Pet Store says you stole his parrot."

I'm unable to take my gaze off Pug-face's thumb ring. "Why would I steal a parrot?" What will they do to me for stealing Charlie? My nails dig into the oak wood and my ears strain for police sirens.

Dad runs a hand through his sandy hair, which is always a mess, and studies me. I'm hoping he'll believe me, since I've never been in trouble at school.

"The girl's a thief and a liar." Magnar's acid tone tightens my jaw.

"Now just a minute." Dad frowns. "Samantha never lies, and if she says she didn't steal your parrot, she didn't."

My face grows hot when Dad defends me, but better to lie than to give up Charlie.

"The girl didn't say she doesn't have the parrot." Magnar sneers. "She asked a question. Search her room."

Dad hesitates. "Sam, if we have a quick look we can get this over with."

"Ugh." I flinch when Jake jabs my back.

He breathes in my ear, "It's safe."

For Charlie's sake, he better be right. "Okay, Dad, check it out."

Jake swings the bedroom door wide open and stands beside me. "Hi, Bryon. I hope you're not upset I'm in Sam's room." The way he says it, as if he's both guilty and sorry, is believable.

"Hello, Jake." Dad steps forward. He's tall enough to peek over our heads, and he inspects the room.

"Ask Magnar what he did to Rose," I blurt.

"Rose?" Dad's frown deepens as he regards Magnar. "Our renter?"

Magnar raises his palms, his eyes steady. "That crazy lady on the bridge? She left as soon as you did."

Maybe Rose did escape. But how? As slow moving as she was, I should have seen her walking away. "I don't believe you."

Dad turns back to me. "What happened, Samantha?"

Magnar's eyes flash victory.

I shrug. What can I say that Dad will believe? "Magnar said he was going to hurt me."

"They're both lying about the parrot." Magnar sounds smug.

"Now hold on." Dad's voice is steel and he looks alive. "You threatened my daughter?"

Go, zombie man!

"Why would I do that?" Magnar sounds innocent, but his eyes are hard.

"You need to go, Mr. Magnar."

Magnar doesn't flinch. "Not without my parrot."

"I could call the police." Dad walks back to the top of the stairs. "I allowed you into my home, but now I'm asking you to leave."

I think I've won, but Magnar doesn't budge. Instead, a tiny stream of gray rises from his thumb ring, like a genie coming out of a lamp. My eyes clamp on it.

The gray stream quickly lengthens, expanding until it's thick as a small tree trunk, while the front end of it splits in two, shifting and flattening to form the two heads of the giant king cobra. The monster appears even bigger crammed into our second-floor hallway.

When its four gray eyes blink open, my hand slips on the door-jamb. I want to slam my door shut and hide beneath my bed.

Jake turns pale, so I know he sees it. But Dad shows no awareness of the snake. Maybe Magnar decides who can see his monster.

Winding back and forth three feet off the floor, the snake fills the hallway with its thick torso, its tail separating from Magnar's ring. The two heads of the massive shadow beast rise to the ten-foot ceiling, arching back as if to strike.

Anger fills its baseball-sized eyes again, as if it carries Magnar's hatred. Those eyes bore into mine, and just like in the pet store I find I can't move.

"I asked you to leave, Mr. Magnar." Dad still shows no reaction to the snake, and he'd never believe me if I told him.

One of the snake heads hisses in a slippery cadence, "You sss-tole my parrot, girl."

The other head hisses, "Do you want me to kill your father?"

"No," I whisper. My knees wobble. Magnar's talking to me through the snake. I'm certain of it. The man not only has monsters hidden in his rings, but he's a monster too. No way will I hand Charlie over to him, but I can't lose Dad, either.

Dad stiffens. "It's okay, Sam."

I don't know what to tell him as the snake weaves back and forth, its thick tongues flicking in and out. Jake starts to shake. I'm squeezing the door frame so hard my knuckles hurt.

"Jake?" A feminine voice comes from outside the front door.

"Mom!" shouts Jake.

The outer screen door opens and feet pound stairs until Cynthia Morris stands a few steps below Magnar.

Both snake heads swivel to her, freeing me from their spell.

Cynthia doesn't seem to see the snake, but her calm blue eyes give me a spark of hope. Tall and slender, with long blond hair, she wears a blue suit with a white blouse. Her sculpted face shows confidence.

I read somewhere that Fish and Wildlife field agents are armed. Maybe she carries a gun under her coat. I want to yell at her to empty it into Magnar's back before the snake attacks.

"What's going on?" Cynthia looks at each of us.

Magnar ignores her.

Dad's tone hardens. "Mr. Magnar was about to leave."

"I want my parrot." Magnar's face clouds.

"You're leaving now." Fists form at Dad's sides and his stance shifts.

I'm proud of my father, something I haven't felt for a year. But the cobra heads rear back, eyeing Dad again, opening their mouths to reveal their curved fangs. I hold my breath.

"Everyone needs to calm down." Cynthia sounds neutral.

"I'm warning all of you." Magnar turns to me, his eyes glowing.

The shadow snake inches forward.

A scream forms in my throat.

"Mom." Jake's face is pinched and he bites his lip.

Cynthia's voice hardens. "Mr. Magnar, you should step outside. We can talk there."

"It's none of your business, woman." The man's words crack like a whip. "I'd advise you to leave before you get hurt."

One of the snake's heads swivels to her.

Cynthia frowns and unbuttons her coat, revealing a gun.

I want to yell, *Shoot him!* But I'm afraid the snake will kill her before she can draw her weapon.

Quietly, she says, "I'm a US Fish and Wildlife agent. You've been asked to leave this house and I'd advise you to do so now."

I almost cheer, thinking it's enough to convince Magnar to leave.

But instead he spits, "You have no idea who you're talking to, woman."

Cynthia drops her hand onto her gun grip. "You need to leave or you will be arrested."

"Is that a threat?" Magnar's face is eerily calm, and he looks satisfied, as if he's been waiting for this. Wants her to pull her gun.

The cobra head staring at Cynthia lowers, arching over Magnar's head, slowly inching toward her.

I finally get it. Magnar won't hesitate to kill all of us. He doesn't care what he has to do to get Charlie back. It sends a wave of panic through me and my thoughts spin.

The cobra heads float closer. Dad tenses and Cynthia clenches her gun.

I blurt, "You won't get away with it, Magnar. People saw you chase me through the park, and someone in the neighborhood must have seen you on our street. They'll know it's you."

Dad's forehead furrows, but he doesn't take his eyes off Magnar.

Cynthia pulls her gun a few inches from its holster. "This is your last warning."

Magnar's face is red. Clutching the stair railing, veins popping out of his forehead, he shakes his head back and forth as if to tell me he's going to do it anyway, kill all of us.

Both cobra heads jerk back, facing me. They swerve past Dad in a flash, coming fast.

Gasping, I stiffen and Jake leans back.

At the last moment the monster's heads sweep up and over us. Just past the door, the beast pauses to study my room, finally gazing toward my open bedroom window. Charlie must have left.

Retreating into the hallway, the throat of the snake floats past me until one head slowly lowers in front of my face, the other in front of Jake's, their neck hoods flaring out.

Dizzy and unblinking, I stare into the cobra's shiny gray eyes. Its breath smells like dead rats and its fangs are long enough to punch through my chest. The snake's eyes burn into mine.

The monster wants to bite my head off. I can feel it. Magnar is begging for an excuse to do it.

In its slippery voice the head in front of me says, "I'll be watching you, girl and boy." The one in front of Jake says, "Sssoon you'll both be a nicsse little sssnack."

They snap open their mouths and two gray tongues caress our faces with quick swipes. Cold and slimy. My stomach convulses and I almost puke.

The head in front of me comes closer, nearly touching my lips. "A pathetic nobody like you can't sssteal my parrot and get away with it, girl."

I wobble. Jake grabs my wrist, steadying me. Or maybe he's just trying to stay upright.

Abruptly, Magnar's shadow shrinks like a deflating balloon, thinning and slithering back into the ring. Pug-face bares his teeth, then pivots and walks past Cynthia and out the front door, without so much as a word or a glance back.

My hands tremble and no one moves for several breaths. Dad stares at Cynthia, as if seeing her for the first time.

Jake takes off his glasses and wipes his face with his palm, then rubs his hand on his shorts. After quickly cleaning his lenses with his shirt, he replaces them on his nose.

He taps my shoulder. "Later." Bounding past my father, he says, "Thanks, Bryon." He flies down the stairs to Cynthia and kisses her cheek. "Mom, you're awesome." She stares at him.

"We need to talk." Dad gives a limp gesture. "All of us."

Cynthia turns. "Jake."

Jake pauses on the bottom stair, looking up at his mother.

"I'd like to hear what this was about too," she says.

He shrugs. "Sure."

"That includes you, Sam." Dad sounds tired, as if I've disappointed him again, as I have for the last year.

When Cynthia turns to Dad, Jake zips his lips with his fingers. He won't tell our parents about Charlie.

Grateful, I give a tiny nod. "Bathroom break."

"We'll be waiting." Dad follows Cynthia down the stairs.

I close the bedroom door and rush to the window. "Charlie."

Muffled gurgles dribble from a small laundry pile near the dresser. The parrot pokes his head out. "Your clothing stinks. Yuck. The nerve of that boy."

"Better than a giant cobra licking your face." I shuffle over, dig him out, and set him on the bed. Using the corner of my bed sheet, I wipe my face. "Charlie, how long have you known Magnar?"

"That monster kept me prisoner for almost a thousand years, Sam."

Charlie and Magnar are ancient. Parrots in captivity can live to be seventy or more, yet Charlie appears young. Twenty years, max. "Rose said she and Magnar are guardians. What are they guarding?"

Charlie bobs his head. "Methuselahs. Magnar and Rose aren't human. More like old spirits with a little magic thrown in. Rose is trying to do what's right, but Magnar changed a long time ago. He's nothing like Rose anymore, and he'll do anything to get me back in chains."

"Do you think he would have murdered us?" I need to hear Charlie say it.

"Of course. The brute surprised me and almost lost control. But four bodies would attract too much attention. He doesn't want police swarming him."

"I nearly got everyone killed," I murmur. "That's why the cobra didn't break through the pet store glass and chase me. Magnar didn't want to be noticed. How many monsters does he have, Charlie?"

Dad's voice interrupts us. "Samantha!"

"I'm coming!" There are so many unanswered questions it unnerves me. "Charlie, after I talk with Dad, you have to tell me everything."

"Sure." He flutters to the dresser. "I'm going out. I need some fresh air."

"You'll be safer inside."

"Not if your dad decides to search your room."

"What if Magnar's snake is outside?"

"I'd know if it was, kid."

I don't see how that's possible, but I walk over to the window. Nothing flits past and there's no buzzing. Gingerly, I push the flimsy piece of torn screen out to make it easier for the parrot.

He jumps to the desk and then the windowsill.

"Charlie, do you know anything about a big bumblebee?"

"Weird."

"Yeah. No kidding."

"For the record, Sam, you did a brilliant job standing up to Magnar. You outplayed him. That took guts."

"Temporary insanity." I let the praise soak in. "Where will you go?"

"Meet me out back right away."

"Dad wants to talk to me."

"Make up some excuse. We have to sort things out before Magnar returns."

I swallow. "Returns?"

"You can count on it, kid. And I'm talking minutes, not hours."

SIX

Secrets

AT THE BOTTOM OF THE STAIRS, the sound of voices pulls my jittery legs toward the dining room. The deadbolt is drawn on the front door, though I doubt a measly door will stop Magnar or his snake.

"Sam." Dad sounds weary.

I pause at the edge of the room, trying to find an excuse to stall the talk.

Mom used to fill vases with exotic orchids, which she sold online, scenting the whole room. The woodwork in here used to sparkle. Now papers cover the antique oak table and buffet, and only the scent of musty dust fills the air.

I never eat here anymore. There are too many memories. Usually I make a sandwich and eat in my room.

Jake sits on the opposite side of the table, his lips pursed. Behind him, on top of the buffet, rests the red phone book with Aunt Sue's phone number.

I don't want Charlie to go. He's my best and only friend and he *gets* me, which excites and scares me at the same time. Mom always understood me. But for the parrot's safety, and ours, Charlie has to leave.

Dad sits at the far end of the table. I suddenly realize Cynthia is sitting at the end near me. My eyes blur.

Dad lifts his head from his hands. "Sam, we're waiting."

"It's our house." I look at Cynthia.

"What's wrong?" She brushes blond bangs from her forehead, glancing in confusion from me to Dad.

Dad says, "Sam."

"It's Mom's chair. She shouldn't sit in it."

Cynthia stiffens, but Dad raises a palm. "It's all right, Cynthia."

"No, it isn't." I grasp my compass.

Dad sighs. "Mr. Magnar said his parrot disappeared when you left the store."

Words erupt from my throat. "How would you like to be a parrot and never fly in the jungle your whole life and spend it chained up in a stupid, crappy pet store?" Something breaks loose inside. "Or if no one ever talked to you and you were ignored all the time?"

Dad's eyes widen.

"Or you spent all your time in a cage?" Jake outlines one with his hands.

Dad gestures to Cynthia. "It's Samantha's twelfth birthday, and her mother passed away a year ago today." More to himself, he adds, "Nothing has been the same without Faith. She was always bright and happy."

Hearing Mom's name brings a deep pain to my chest. How can Dad talk about her now? He hasn't mentioned her once during The Silence of the last year, so why do it now in front of strangers?

"It's none of her business," I say.

Jake's forehead creases.

Cynthia's face softens. "I'm sorry, Samantha. I had no idea."

"I'll be out back." I storm away as my father calls my name again.

Footsteps follow me.

Jake.

Pushing open the back door, I step onto the wooden deck, examining the fenced acres. The shed and greenhouse are the only places that could hide a monster snake. But it's enough to make me hesitate.

Jake barges through the door. "Way to go in getting creepy Magnar to back off."

His compliment throws me off guard, and I bite back angry words about his mother. "Thanks for hiding Charlie."

"No problem." He snaps my shoulder with a finger.

"What's that for?" I hurry down the steps, annoyed again.

"Are you kidding me? We just got face-licked by a monster cobra. I told you I hate snakes. No more secrets." His face scrunches into that dorky look. He's as scared as I am.

"Okay. Charlie's a thousand years old, and Rose and Magnar aren't human. Rose said a war has been going on for centuries between ancient creatures and Magnar, and Magnar's winning. Charlie's involved somehow. That's all I know."

Jake's mouth hangs open while he registers this. "I told our parents I'd talk to you. We could have dinner together and celebrate your birthday. Mom could help us with Magnar."

"We don't need your mom around." I keep walking. I bet his mother is pushy too. "And celebrating my birthday is the last thing I want to do."

"Really?" Jake's hands loop in arcs. "And by the way, Mom already helped us with Magnar."

"We can't tell them about Magnar without telling them about Charlie, and then they'll make us return the parrot." I pause on the grass, scanning the woods beyond the fence. "We're thieves, and they'll never believe us about the cobra. We have no proof. Besides, if we keep Charlie safe for a day, it'll all be over."

I expect him to object to being called a thief, since technically I'm the one who stole the parrot. But he doesn't.

He stops beside me, studying the back acres. "So what are we going to do?"

"Find the parrot." I wish Jake wasn't here, wish Cynthia wasn't here, and wish I were alone. But I've had that for a whole year, and it was miserable.

I walk toward the greenhouse, which blocks our path to the rear gate. Enclosed by heavy opaque plastic, it's twenty feet wide, twice as long, and ten feet high.

"The feathers allow us to see the snake, right?" Jake glances around. "You knew that before Charlie gave mine to me, didn't you?"

"No, I didn't." But now that he says it, I think he's right about the feathers.

"I don't believe you."

"The snake attacked me in the pet store, but I wasn't sure where it came from or that the feather allowed me to see it." I pause. "Charlie said Magnar's coming back."

His face pales. "When?"

He has to be thinking the same thing I am. *Next time, we're snake bait.* "Magnar has to walk back into the park, then cut through the woods so he can cross into the rear of the properties without anyone seeing him. I'm hoping he's too tired to do any speed walking."

"Speed walking?"

"Oh, yeah, I forgot. He walks fast."

"How fast?"

"Faster than I can ride a bike. I'm guessing we have ten minutes, max."

His hands shake emphatically. "We've already used half that. So where's Charlie?"

"He said to meet him here."

"Where?" he whispers.

"Shh."

"You shh." His hands do somersaults.

"Very mature." He makes a face, which I ignore.

To the left of us are grassy acres with a few trees, a dozen grazing deer, and no snake. To the far right is our fenced garden, which is also empty of monsters.

When I can see behind the garden shed, there's nothing to worry about there, either. I stop at the greenhouse and peek inside the half-open door.

Mom's orchids used to perfume the building, filling it with bright splashes of color, but weeds have overtaken everything and clay pots lie scattered on the dirt. Like other things, I've avoided Mom's flower garden over the last year, not ready for its memories.

A shadow moves behind the rear wall and there's a soft rustling.

I edge back from the door, panic sweeping me.

Jake raises his arms like a martial artist. It looks crazy, but it gives me courage.

Taking a deep breath, I round the corner and creep along the side of the greenhouse, my attention on the far end. When we near the back, I see a vague shape moving behind the plastic.

A foot from the corner, Jake presses his shoulder against mine. I want to yell. Inch-by-inch I bend forward.

A dark figure rushes around the edge.

I jerk my arms up and Jake gasps.

Jake's face is red as he steps away from me. "A deer."

"A.k.a. *Odocoileus virginianus*." I sheepishly lower my hands.

Jake flicks my shoulder, but softly this time. "What a geek."

"It's not my fault. I was born that way." The doe nuzzles my fingers. Our deer are tame, due to all the time we spend with them. I stroke its warm neck, loving the color of its reddish-brown coat.

"Deer can jump a twelve-foot fence, run forty miles an hour, and they have four stomachs." I stop. Jake probably thinks I'm stupid.

But his eyes are sincere when he says, "Neat." He scratches the head of another doe, which followed the first around the corner.

"Come on." I keep walking. We have to cross an open acre of grass to the high chain-link fence running along the back of the property. "Maybe Charlie's in the woods."

"What's the 'a.k.a.' thing about?" asks Jake.

At first I don't want to answer, but I surprise myself again. "Mom played the 'also known as' game with me every day. She'd name an animal followed by a.k.a., and I'd give the scientific name and some fun facts. Eventually we got more creative." I pause. "She was always doing fun stuff with me."

I'm immediately annoyed I've told him any of this. Annoyed and a little sad.

He just looks at me with a tilted smile, probably thinking I'm weird. I hurry toward the fence.

"I used to cook with my dad." His cheeks turn pink. "I love to cook."

"Huh. That could be fun." I can't remember the last time Dad cooked anything.

His hands spin. "Cakes, pies, homemade bread, and lots of Italian stuff like spaghetti and lasagna."

"I like lasagna. Mom used to make bread."

"Neat." He looks over his shoulder. "You're lucky to have animals. Mom doesn't want me to have a pet. Says they're emotional slaves to humans."

"Dad says people don't care about wild animals because they don't need humans like pets do." Of course, Dad doesn't need me, either.

Against the fence, two large enclosures contain a lynx and bobcat. Other cages hold a bald eagle, a flightless crow, and smaller animals. The rear gate is between the cat cages and I stride toward it, the dry grass crunching beneath my feet.

The resting cats lift their heads off the ground as we pass by, ears alert, their fur shining in the late sunlight. "Hey, you two, any giant snakes around?"

When the cats flick their tails, it eases my hunched shoulders. Somehow I think they'd know if a monster snake was nearby, even if they couldn't see it.

"I love cats." Jake sucks in a big breath. "Hey, sorry about your mom, Sam." He pauses. "At least your dad didn't leave you."

"I have a zombie dad who never talks to me. You probably talk to him more than I do." I pretend to look elsewhere.

He does the same. "So where's Charlie, anyway?"

"I'm not psychic. He said he'd be here." My words have an edge to them, because there's no sign of the parrot past the twelve-foot fence, either.

Undoing the latch, I pull the wood gate open, glancing back into the yard once more.

"Why don't you like my mom?" Jake squeezes past me.

"Geez, I just met her." My ears burn. "It doesn't matter."

"I bet I would have liked your mom."

"So?" I want him to stop talking. After a year of The Silence, I'm not used to all this jabbering.

I close the gate and take a dozen steps into the trees, stopping near some big pines. I scan the woods farther in. Where the heck is Charlie?

"Well, I like Bryon." Jake studies his feet. "We don't visit anyone, and most of the time I'm home by myself. Mom's always working."

"Invite friends over."

"Why bother? We keep moving every few years. We just moved here, and Mom's already talking about a job in Washington State that's opening up this summer."

"That's rough." I can't imagine leaving the animal shelter.

"Besides, she won't let me have anyone over when she isn't around, and she's never around." He taps my shoulder. "You and your dad are cool."

"Do your glasses work? Dad and I dress as if we're going camping."

"It's cool you help animals."

"Oh." I can't disagree.

Scattered sugar maple, birch, and brush fill in between the tall pine, which scent the gentle breeze. I listen carefully. No blue jays, crows, or warblers are calling. It's too quiet. I hum until Jake frowns at me.

Leaves rustle above us. Charlie's perched on a high branch. He floats down in slow spirals until he lands on my shoulder, clutching it tightly with his talons.

I like that he picks my shoulder. "I was going nuts worrying about you, Charlie."

"We both were," says Jake.

"Whew, kids. That was close. Big ugly birds were flying everywhere I looked. I had to hide until the coast was clear."

The parrot's presence relaxes me. "Come on," I say.

Glancing around, I walk a few more steps into the woods, stopping in the center of a clump of birch so we're mostly hidden. I rest my shoulder against a tree trunk. "I've found a safe place for you, Charlie. I have an aunt in Florida, but I'm not sure how to get you there. Maybe she'll come here."

"No thanks, Sam."

"She's nice and—"

"Save it, kid. Old single women scare me."

The parrot's refusal surprises me. "I don't have a Plan B, Charlie."

"I have grandparents in Chicago." Jake spreads his hands. "They might like a parrot."

Charlie bobs his head. "Great. Two old people talking nonsense every day. Polly want a cracker? Is Polly a cute birdie? I've had my fill of that garbage. And humans think they're the intelligent species."

"Where can you go, Charlie?" I ask. "You can't stay with me or Jake, so . . ."

"Snake-face is back," murmurs the parrot.

Jake puts a finger to his lips and points to the back of the house.

I peek around the tree. Five feet off the ground, the serpent is winding through the back acres.

The lynx and bobcat stand, heads lowered, staring out their cages.

At first I worry the snake will head for the deer, but the two-headed cobra whips past the animal pens, around the greenhouse, and bolts to the rear of the house. There it stares into each window before moving to the next. Eventually it climbs to my bedroom window, then crawls over the roof, its tail sliding from sight.

Concerned for Dad, I take a step forward, my hands clenched. I don't see Magnar, but he could be hiding.

"Magnar doesn't want your father, kid. But the more distance we put between your dad and us, the safer he'll be. Take me to Rosey's cabin."

"Why?" Rose's cabin is in the deepest part of the woods, and I haven't gone there for a year. Our family used to go for walks in the forest all the time, but now the woods look foreign.

Everything is getting more complicated. More dangerous. How many more surprises is the darn parrot going to throw at me?

"The old lady?" Jake's forehead wrinkles. "What if the snake follows us?"

Charlie ruffles his wings. "Rosey can help us, kids."

"Magnar might have hurt her." I remember the park.

"I heard three echoes from the staff," says Charlie. "She's okay."

"How do you know that?" Charlie doesn't answer. Another secret. But I'm glad he thinks Rose is alive. I finger my compass and retreat with Jake behind the tree again.

"Why me, Charlie?"

Charlie rubs his beak against my cheek. "Because you care, Sam."

"Yeah." I do care. But helping him feels like I'm walking along the edge of a cliff with my eyes closed. "Why did you wait until today to talk to me?"

"Timing is everything, Sam. You had to trust me and I had to trust you. And I figured we had a better chance to avoid Magnar for one day than for anything longer. I didn't want to put you at risk for more than that."

"What about the big hand in the pet store?"

"Never met the owner."

"Big hand?" Jake looks quizzically at the parrot. "Why does Magnar want you, Charlie?"

"My birthday's tomorrow. That's when a methuselah releases its energy, on its one-thousandth birthday. And that's the only time Magnar can get my power. Power is all he cares about anymore."

I study the parrot, waiting. "I'm tired of secrets, Charlie. Rose told me about the battle. What's it all about?"

He clucks. "Look, kids, giant creatures called Great Ones have fought Magnar for centuries. The Great Ones sent nine methuselahs to your world to help humans. The methuselahs were supposed to gather energy over their lifetimes and release it to your world, but Magnar turned traitor and enslaved them in his rings as shadow monsters. I'm the last methuselah. Magnar has waited ten thousand years for this. If he gets me tomorrow, nothing will stop him. With the power of ten methuselahs trapped in his rings, he'll be a thousand times more powerful. He'll easily take over your world."

The world keeps changing, making my voice tremble. "Great. So every one of Magnar's nine rings holds a monster?"

"That's right." Charlie doesn't sound worried. "And they're all cute, like the cobra."

"Crap." I don't even want to know what the other monsters are.

"So the cobra used to be a methuselah?" Jake regards the parrot with a wrinkled brow.

"Yes," says Charlie.

I wince. "And Magnar was planning on putting you into a ring tomorrow, to trap you as one of his shadow monsters?"

"Yes. I'd end up looking like a giant parrot on steroids." Charlie fluffs his feathers. "Parrotzilla."

I have too many questions, but the parrot adds, "We have to go or snake-face will find us. And it won't be pretty."

Jake presses his palms into the tree trunk. "How far is the cabin, Sam?"

"About an hour's walk."

"That's a long hike." His face tightens. "I don't want to be stuck in the woods with Magnar's snake on the loose."

Charlie stares at me. "What's it going to be, kid?"

I'm trapped without any good solutions. But if Rose is alive, maybe she can take Charlie somewhere safe. She wasn't afraid of Magnar. Besides, no matter how scared I am, I can't let the parrot down. "Rose has to explain everything, Charlie. No more secrets."

"Everything, kiddos. I promise."

I look at Jake, suddenly hoping he won't back out. I don't want to be alone in the woods with Charlie. "Jake?"

He taps the side of his fist against the tree several times, then says, "All right.

"Hang on." Relieved, I level my compass.

The general direction of the cabin is east, but I want to get a bearing. The needle points north, so I sight where east is, but then something strange happens. The needle slowly moves off north until it's pointing due east for a few moments, before it pops back to north. "Weird." It's never done this before and I hope it isn't broken. For a moment, it reminds me of Rose and her magic. I don't know what to make of it.

I peek around the tree and freeze. Both the lynx and bobcat are pacing their cages, fur bristling. The snake must be close by.

"Let's go." I crouch and run into the forest, trying to keep trees between us and the back fence.

Charlie flies off my shoulder and Jake sprints beside me.

After a minute, I look back and nearly trip.

The cobra heads are rising above the rear gate, weaving in the air. At least they're looking north, away from us.

The lynx and bobcat yowl, and the snake whips sideways, both heads ducking for a moment.

Hoping the monster didn't see us, I jump with Jake behind a large fallen tree. We huddle with our backs to it. Charlie lands near my feet.

Jake adjusts his glasses, staring straight ahead into the forest, his eyes wide.

"Cobras can see three hundred feet," I whisper. "And crawl ten miles an hour." Jake pales, so I add, "But they have poor hearing."

"Great." After a minute, Jake nudges my shoulder, his voice barely a whisper. "Is it still there?"

I swivel to my knees, then edge my head above the top of the trunk.

The snake is staring at me from the fence. I can't turn away from its wavering heads. Even this far away, it's hypnotizing me again.

"Come here, girl and boy, or I'll have your daddy and mommy for a sssnack."

"He's lying, kids. He's trying to trick you."

"Mom," whispers Jake.

I try to move my lips. I want to tell Jake to hit me or pull me or do anything, but I can't.

The snake glides over the back fence, its heads held high.

"Ow!" My ankle suddenly stings, but I'm able to escape the serpent's gaze. Charlie's standing next to my leg, his beak near my skin.

"That hurt, Charlie."

"No kidding. That was the idea." The parrot cocks his head at me. "Shadow monsters have to remain near their ring, so Magnar's not far from here. Running would be a good idea."

I scramble to my feet.

The snake's crawling toward us. Fast.

Jake remains sitting, his back against the tree trunk, his eyes closed.

"Jake, let's go!"

"I hate snakes," he mutters.

I grab his wrist, pull hard, and we run.

SEVEN

Trapping a Snake

J AKE RUNS LIKE A CHEETAH, while I'm moving more like an injured penguin.

My weak lungs make it impossible to keep up with him. Dodging dogwood and honeysuckle, and sometimes crashing through sticker bushes and tripping over low brush, my goal is just to stay on my feet.

Charlie flies beside me. He could fly away and leave me, and I'm grateful he doesn't.

When I glance over my shoulder, I see the snake weaving around trees and gaining on me.

Jake pulls farther ahead, yelling as he runs. "Faster, Sam."

Even with his speed, the snake will catch him too. I doubt Magnar plans on leaving witnesses.

Looking north, I recognize something. "Jake!"

I swerve, and he follows my lead, running in a line to intersect my path.

The monster slithers a dozen yards away, coming fast, both heads reared back. I want to scream.

Ten steps ahead is a big birch. Jake reaches the east side of it, finds a rock, and throws it. He hits one of the cobra heads in the snout, and the beast hisses and veers toward him. Yelling, he bolts.

Squawk! "Jump, kid!" says Charlie.

The other snake head strikes at me.

I leap sideways and the snake misses my legs, catching a mouthful of dirt instead. I'm inches from its long fangs and wrinkled mouth. It gives me a burst of adrenaline.

Gasping, I spurt around the west side of the tree. The snake's heads chase us on opposite sides of the trunk, one after Jake and one after me. Its body smacks into the tree trunk, the two heads twisting, trying to force the other around its side. Stupid monster. It buys us a few seconds.

Not far ahead, a massive rotting log is leaning against another big tree, its high end four feet off the ground. It's a natural deadfall in front of a small opening at the base of a pile of boulders. Dad showed it to me several years ago, explaining how dangerous it could be and warning me never to go near it. He said just bumping into it could knock it over.

"Under the tree," I yell. I watch Jake and trip over a tree root, my legs flying too far out as I try to remain upright. "Don't touch it," I croak.

Jake dives beneath it and Charlie flies in low after him.

I stumble to the slanted log off balance and bend over at the waist. The back of my head bangs against the wood when I try to duck beneath it. "Umph."

Dropping to my knees, I roll to the side several times, ending up on my back. Little rocks and sticks jab through my flannel shirt into my skin.

Behind me, Jake scrambles into the opening in the rocks, shouting, "Sam."

I tilt my head to see beneath the crack under the log. The cobra is racing toward us, inches above the ground. Feeling exposed, I slide over farther to hide behind the low end of the deadfall.

"Here I am, you stupid worm!" Charlie perches on a rock near Jake, trying to take the snake's attention away from me. *Squawk!* "Do something, kid."

Bringing my knees to my chest, trying to time the snake's speed, I kick the deadfall with both feet. It's like hitting a boulder. It doesn't budge. Huge disappointment. The way Dad described it, a big mosquito flying into it would topple it.

The hissing cobra slides beneath the dead tree five feet from me, and stops abruptly, slowly raising its heads and eyeing Jake and Charlie.

I go rigid while staring at the monster. *Please don't see me.*

Using his feet to shove himself farther into the opening, Jake pants, "Sam."

I kick again, hard as I can. Then again, fast.

The cobra heads whip sideways, their dagger-sized fangs gleaming. This time all four eyes find mine and I freeze.

The trunk slams the snake into the dirt, crushing the creature's thick necks.

I hastily wriggle on my back toward the small cave. Hissing, its tail writhing, the monster snaps at my feet, just missing my toes. Once in the cave, I flip over and follow Jake.

When I look back, the cobra's large eyes shine in the entrance, its body squirming wildly on the other side of the log. I doubt the trap will hold it long.

A short ways in, the small cave narrows and quickly dead-ends at a rock wall. But light shines from above through a hole that looks just big enough to squeeze through.

Jake starts climbing. I follow, with Charlie on my shoulder. In minutes, I'm pulling myself out the opening at the top.

Jake's standing, watching the monster's tail writhing below. "Stupid snake," he says. "I hope it rots there."

"That went well, kids."

"We were almost snake bait, Charlie," I gasp.

"Stay positive," says the parrot.

Jake flicks my shoulder. "Let's get out of here."

"Yeah."

He scrambles down the back side of the pile of boulders.

I go slower, trying not to bang my elbows and knees into rocks. Charlie flies off my shoulder. It takes a few minutes to carefully pick my way through the chunks of stone to the bottom, but I'm still scraped and bruised.

Hurrying up to Jake, I check my compass. It does its odd thing again, moving off north to point in the direction we need to go. Jake waits until I lead the way in a jog.

After a minute, he sails past me. I work hard to keep up with him. When I look back, the snake's tail is curling in the air. Farther beyond the serpent, something black is moving through the forest. Magnar. And when he reaches the snake, he'll easily free it by calling it back to his ring.

I keep looking back long after the forest hides him and his beast from view. Then I'm glancing everywhere for monsters.

EIGHT

A New Monster

WE KEEP RUNNING.

I haven't visited the cabin for a year, but it isn't hard to find the way again. Small red marks appear on tree trunks along the trail. I'd forgotten them. Dad painted the slashes on the trees years ago, so I could easily find my way home if I ever got lost.

The faded marks appear every hundred feet, bringing back memories of running through the woods. Old logs, a few scarred trees, and other natural markings are also familiar. It's nice to recognize the landmarks after a year, but I don't have time to enjoy the scenery.

Every time I check it, the compass needle points due east, toward *Trust*, but I don't trust anything. Any moment, I expect Magnar's snake to crawl out from behind a tree.

My legs tire, and soon I have to stop and use my inhaler.

Ahead of me, Jake's face is flushed. "We can't stop."

"All right." I use the inhaler while walking, exhaling loudly a few seconds later. It's hard to fill my lungs. Charlie returns to my shoulder. I'm glad he's there.

Sunlight breaks through the treetops, but none of it warms me. Several times I correct Jake on his direction when he misses a red slash.

Finally he stops, his blue eyes showing frustration. "Why don't you give me the compass?"

I keep trudging. "No."

"What's the big deal?" He wipes sweat from his face.

I look away. "Mom gave it to me on my last birthday."

"Oh." His eyes soften and he continues walking.

I don't tell him that the urge to keep the compass around my neck is nearly overwhelming, as if parting from it would be painful. As if it's the last connection I have to Mom.

We walk and run for half an hour without talking. Jake slows the pace for me, but I'm still working hard to keep up with him. Except for my feet crunching pine needles, the woods are strangely silent, as though everything is in hiding. It makes me jittery, so I start talking.

"Charlie, when we were in my bedroom, how did you know Magnar was coming? And how did you sense the cobra was in the backyard?"

Jake glances back, listening.

"I sense when methuselahs are around, Sam, since I'm one myself."

"Then why didn't the snake know you were hiding in my bedroom?"

"Magnar's shadow monsters follow his will, not their own, so they've lost our connection. They aren't the same creatures they once were."

I'm glad about that, but I wonder if Rose will be at the cabin or if Charlie's going to surprise me again with some new twist in all this.

As if reading my mind, the parrot says, "All for one and one for all, kids." When Jake and I stare at him, he says, "What? It's from *The Three Musketeers* movie. I didn't get out a lot with Magnar, but after enough squawking he broke down and allowed me to watch movies with him. I think he just wanted me to stay healthy long enough to reach my one-thousandth birthday. What a nice guy, huh?" He adds, "We're in this together. I won't let you down."

"Thanks, Charlie," I say.

"Back at you. And don't worry about snake-face. Rosey can handle him."

"I hope so." Charlie's confidence doesn't calm me, but it does push me to reach Rose as fast as possible.

Clouds fill the sky, creating more shadows on the forest floor. Eventually, Jake slows and walks beside me.

I continually swat mosquitoes and try to avoid sticker bushes. Twice I brush off my lower legs in case ticks are on me. Jake does the same, and I see scratches on his bare calves.

He flicks my shoulder with the back of his hand. "That was pretty smart back there with the snake."

"Brilliant move," Charlie adds.

Their praise warms me. "Yeah, and it looked like he enjoyed it. Thanks for throwing the rock. You should play baseball."

"I like ping pong." Jake pretends he has a paddle in his hand and whips the air. Then he flashes a smile. Something about that is even nicer.

A distant roar prickles the hairs on my neck.

"What's that?" Jake looks back, his face pale. "Walk faster."

I hustle to keep up with him. After a few minutes of waiting for another roar, I need to get my mind off monsters. "Why do you hate snakes, Jake?"

He curls two fingers like fangs and taps his wrist. "I was bitten once when I was five. In Florida. A baby boa, but it scared me."

"I love snakes, but not Magnar's." Then something occurs to me. "Charlie, how can Magnar take over the world with methuselahs? As scary as they are, they can't defeat armies with high tech weapons."

"Magnar has a plan, but he didn't tell me what it is. He kept me close, but he never talked about his endgame."

"How much farther, Sam?" asks Jake.

"We're over halfway there."

"There must be a million bugs in here." He beats his thighs and back with his hands, as if he's playing a drum set.

"In fall the frost kills mosquitoes and ticks. Dad says fall is like talking to a good friend. It clears out the yucky stuff."

"Cool."

"Yeah, Dad used to say a lot of neat things to me."

I hum softly. This time Jake doesn't frown.

After a while, I voice the question that's been nagging me. "Why did your father leave?" I can't believe I'm asking this.

Jake stiffens. "Mom says Dad left because of her and it has nothing to do with me." He lowers his head. "I used to think he'd come back, but I don't anymore. It's been three years."

Charlie clicks his beak. "Your father probably loves you, Jake. He just couldn't stay with your mom. Some people get married too young, or they change and don't match anymore. It has nothing to do with you."

The parrot nudges my cheek. "Kind of like your dad, Sam. It's not that he doesn't love you, but he has a broken heart and doesn't know how to fix it."

Jake and I regard Charlie in silence, and then Jake gives me a thumbs up. "By the way, happy birthday, Sam."

Charlie nods. "Quite the day you're having, kid."

"Yeah, it's been a riot," I say. Jake looks disappointed, so I add, "Thanks anyway," and his face brightens.

"I've had lots of birthdays," says Charlie. "None of them too sweet, either. Magnar wasn't much for baking cakes or singing songs to me. Most of my time was spent in a cage or shackled in the dark."

I feel bad for the parrot. "I can't imagine a thousand birthdays spent with Magnar. Ugh. We can celebrate all your birthdays when we lose the creep."

"Yeah, we'll have a big parrot party." Jake's arms spread wide.

"Sounds wonderful, kids."

Strangely enough, even though I'm running from Magnar and his monster, I feel alive. I have friends again, and something to do besides avoiding The Silence with Dad or thinking about Mom.

In a moment of craziness, I blurt, "When Mom died on my eleventh birthday, I was with her, but I can't remember it."

Jake's mouth drops open. I immediately wish I were invisible.

"No wonder you don't want to celebrate your birthday." His voice softens. "Why can't you remember?"

I shrug. "Amnesia."

"Wow." Jake swats mosquitoes. "Do you want to remember it?"

"Sure." I avoid his gaze, my cheeks hot. "Why wouldn't I?" But I've never asked Dad to tell me about the day Mom died.

Our conversation is interrupted by a faint buzzing to the north. It quickly becomes louder. We stop and peer into the forest, but thick trees hide whatever it is.

"What is it?" Jake's face scrunches.

Magnar's monsters fill my thoughts. "Charlie?"

"Not a methuselah, kid."

I step around a tree to get a better view. "I heard it before, outside my bedroom window."

Jake flicks my shoulder. "How come you didn't tell me?"

"I forgot."

"Shouldn't we run?"

The noise ends abruptly. Someone appears in the distance, running toward us and wearing a white T-shirt and jeans.

I recognize the red spiked hair. "It's Tom, from the pet store. Over the last year he let me talk to Charlie for hours when Magnar was in the back room."

Jake waves dismissively. "Yeah, I've seen him around. I don't like him. He never says hello, as if he's better than everyone else. Let's keep going."

I relax a little. "He sees us, and he'll catch us, anyway, Jake. Might as well wait." I wonder what Tom is doing here and how he found us. And why isn't Charlie saying anything?

The young man runs with unbelievable agility, using his long arms to push off logs, swing around trunks, or pull himself under higher branches. All in complete silence. Amazingly, not even clusters of bushes and undergrowth slow him. He maneuvers through the woods faster than anyone should be able to.

Jake gapes. "No one moves like that."

"Maybe an Olympic gymnast on fairy dust," I suggest.

The way Tom moves reminds me of Magnar's fast walk. And the gold I saw in his eyes means he's somehow related to Magnar and Rose. Since he didn't try to stop me when I stole Charlie, maybe he's on Rose's side. Unless he wants Charlie for himself. That idea tenses me.

Pushing off a low tree branch, he hurtles thirty feet through the air and lands silently in front of me. His feet are bare. He's not even sweating. Three silver canteens hang from leather straps around his neck, crisscrossing his chest.

Before I can say a word he starts talking, his voice urgent. "Magnar's after you, Samantha. Raging. Thinks you stole Charlie." He looks at the parrot. "Guess you have. Hi, Charlie."

Charlie cocks his head at Tom, but remains silent.

Tom faces Jake. "Hi, uh . . ."

"Jake." Jake doesn't extend his hand.

I motion to Tom. "Tom helped me when I took Charlie. He's a friend." I hope it's true, but I say it more as a question.

Jake scowls.

Tom stands there, waiting, wanting something from us.

I shove my hands in my pockets. "How did you learn to move like that?"

He shrugs. "Born that way."

I decide to follow Charlie's cue. "Well, thanks for warning us, Tom. We're kind of in a hurry."

"Can I come with?" His forehead wrinkles. "I'll help. Please, Charlie?"

Tom knows something about the parrot, but Charlie doesn't appear to trust him. And why does Tom want to help? Does he realize how dangerous things are? Maybe he cares about the parrot. He was always gentle with the pet store animals.

Charlie clicks softly. "Are you Samantha's friend?"

"Yes." Tom leans over, his seven earring studs close to my face. "And yours."

My cheeks get hot. Tom sounds desperate and his eyes are pleading.

Charlie fluffs his feathers. "It's up to Sam."

Jake crosses his arms. "We should talk about this in private, Sam."

Tom straightens, his head bowed. "Begging you, Samantha. Please. Let me come."

It's awkward, since he's older than I am. "Were you following me through the woods, when Magnar chased me in the park?"

"Wanted to keep you safe."

He doesn't strike me as the bodyguard type. "Magnar's monster is chasing us."

"Scary."

Yet he doesn't seem frightened. That's a good thing. And it might be useful to have someone with his abilities with us. I also owe him for all the times he let me talk to Charlie. Besides, if he wants to follow us, we can't stop him.

I shrug. "All right, you can join the fun."

Jake's jaw tightens and he shakes his head.

Tom drops to a knee in front of me. "Thank you, thank you, thank you, Samantha and Charlie."

"Don't thank me, yet," I mutter. Tom's odd display of gratefulness is confusing, as are his three canteens. "Did you hear that buzzing in the woods?"

His eyebrows arch. He doesn't answer, adding to the tension in my limbs. "Did you see Magnar's snake in the pet store?" I ask.

He stands and nods. "Monster."

That raises more questions. I doubt Charlie gave him a feather, so how did he see the cobra? Maybe it has something to do with his golden eyes. Also, his clipped way of talking makes me curious.

A chilly wind blows and gray clouds block the sun. Another roar floats through the forest and I look west.

"See something." Tom's speaking above us.

Astonished, I look up. "What the heck?"

Jake stares up too. "That's impossible."

The young man climbed or jumped twenty feet up an eight-inch-thick birch tree. He's hanging onto the trunk with one arm wrapped around it like a monkey as he leans out, his bare feet pressed against the bark. Gold flashes in his eyes.

"Is it the snake?" Jake shuffles back.

"No." Tom stretches out farther from the tree. "Bigger."

"Bigger?" I look west. What could be larger than the cobra?

"Run, kids!" Charlie flies off my shoulder, heading east.

I finally spot something lumbering through the trees in the distance, and Tom's right, it's not the cobra. It's *much* bigger.

NINE

fighting Magnar

I RUN AFTER JAKE AND CHARLIE.

Tom jumps off the tree, landing quietly behind me.

With the appearance of Tom-the-super-athlete, the world as I know it continues to change, raising more questions about what's going on. How does Tom fit into the battle between the ancient creatures and Magnar? And what does he really want?

Charlie calls to us, "Run, you landlubbers. Run. We need to get to Rosie."

Arms pumping, I glance back. But I stare too long, then stumble and yell, my limbs flailing.

Tom runs around Jake and me in a blur, chasing after Charlie.

"Hey," I yell. My upper body is curving forward off balance and I'm staring at dirt.

Jake slows and grabs my wrist, steadying me before I fall on my face. "That idiot," he says. "You shouldn't have let him come with us."

"How could we stop him?" I gasp between breaths as we run. "And maybe he can help."

"He's only interested in helping himself." Jakes glares after him.

"Why do you say that?"

"Some kids were picking on me in town when I first moved here, and he could have stopped it. But all he did was walk by, as if nothing was happening." Jake runs ahead.

Tom has no problem catching up to the parrot, and they quickly outdistance us, disappearing in the woods.

"Charlie," I shout. Why would the parrot leave us? I want to call to him again, but I'm out of air.

Jake continues to check on me over his shoulder, which reduces my panic to a low boil.

The wind blows stronger at our backs, whistling loudly, while leaves and small branches tumble by on the ground. Pine trees tilt sideways while more clouds sweep across the sky.

The next time I look back, I wish I hadn't. Something dark, the color of Magnar's shadow snake, lurches after us, but it must be twenty-five feet tall. Branches snap off trees and the ground crunches under heavy footsteps.

I stumble into a thick stand of birch. Once through, I glimpse the monster, which is forced to slow down to squeeze its thick body between the close-growing trees. It buys us a few more moments. But it doesn't matter, I'm finished.

"I can't make it, Jake." My voice is weak, but he hears me.

"You have to." He slows and puts an arm beneath one of mine, taking some of my weight as we run.

I want to hug him. Instead, I manage a hoarse, "Thanks."

In a minute, I'm mostly dragged by him out of the trees and into a clearing next to a small lake. Near the lakeshore sits Dad's small wooden cabin, its windows boarded up, moss and vines covering its walls. Tom is banging on the door.

A large circle of waist-high grass surrounds the building, growing higher than the nearby meadow. I don't recall it being here a year ago. We plunge into it.

"Rosey." Charlie stands on the ground near Tom, his feathers brighter, a faint aura of gold outlining his body. It has to be the sunlight, but the sky's mostly cloudy.

Tom yanks on the wooden handle. When it doesn't budge, he continues to pound on the door with big fists. "Help. Help. Let us in!"

Jake leaves me and runs for the door.

I fall to my knees a dozen steps from the cabin, unable to go farther.

Jake grabs the door handle, but Tom pushes him to the side. Moving into a martial arts stance, Jake looks ready to attack him.

Ignoring him, Tom continues to smack the door. "Open up!"

I pull my inhaler from my pocket. After taking a puff, I hold my breath as long as I can, then exhale loudly and plant both palms on the ground while watching the woods.

Surrounded by darkness, the shadow monster runs up to the tall grass.

Massive, stunning, and horrible, it resembles an upright buffalo on two feet. The creature has thick legs and a horned head, but its two raised legs are more like arms, and instead of hooves, all four limbs end in sharp claws. Dagger-size teeth fill its mouth. Thick shaggy fur covers its limbs and thick torso, and it rocks side-to-side, glaring with shiny black eyes. It's a buffalo freak.

I know we should hide or run, but there's nowhere to go. We're so dead.

However, the beast doesn't move forward. Maybe it's waiting for its master.

Jake tries his cell phone. "It's not working." He keeps tapping keys. "Charlie, where's Rose?" Lips quivering, he pockets the phone and watches the monster.

Tom quits pounding on the door and stands with his back against it, gaping at the shadow beast.

What if everything the parrot told me is a lie and I trusted a friend who betrayed me? I toss that aside. But Charlie might have it wrong. Maybe Magnar killed Rose in the park and there's no hope for any of us.

"Charlie?" I say, hating the way my voice cracks.

The parrot faces the cabin. "Rosey, dear. Yoo-hoo. Get your butt out here."

Breathing hard, I push myself to my feet, not wanting to die without even knowing why.

The cabin door bursts open, throwing Tom hard to the side, but even then he moves gracefully, regaining his balance with ease.

The wind bangs the door against the outer wall and Rose steps out, her long silver hair blowing wildly. A dozen red flowers wind through her locks, garlands of them around her waist. In one gnarled hand is her staff, WhipEye. As she strides through the grass, the wind plasters her blouse to her thin frame.

My trust in her and Charlie is instantly restored. "Rose!" I shout.

Ignoring me, she stares at Magnar's monster, her face taut.

Tom sidles toward the open cabin door. Jake edges closer too.

I panic they'll leave me behind. "Hey, you guys."

Tom's eyes flash gold, and then he leaps through the door and vanishes. Why would he expect to be safe inside the puny cabin?

Jake doesn't move, his hand on the doorframe. His eyes show

he won't leave without me, but he hurriedly waves me toward him. "Get Charlie."

Before I can move, Rose grips my wrist. "You have a gift, Samantha. That's why Charlie picked you. You can save him."

"I can't fight Magnar's monsters." I look at Charlie, expecting him to back me up.

But the parrot cocks his head at me. "I'm counting on you, kid."

His words startle me and I stare at him. Something inside won't allow me to disappoint him, and I get the strange feeling that I'm putting him at risk if I don't help.

"Just do it, Sam," I murmur.

I walk stiffly with Rose to the edge of the tall grass. The buffalo shadow towers over us. It's hard to imagine it used to be a buffalo methuselah.

Above the howling wind, Rose says, "Hold WhipEye, Samantha."

"Why?" Earlier she didn't want me to touch it, now she's demanding I do. I glance at the perfectly carved wood, and just like before, the urge to grasp it is so strong I can't refuse Rose's request. My clammy hand curls around the staff, beneath hers, and my fingers tighten reflexively, as if forced to do so by WhipEye.

Three times, Rose lifts and thumps the staff against the ground, sending heavy echoes into the distance. Vibrations from the wood reverberate through me. Something about that seems different, as if the staff isn't just joined to my hand, but also reaching deep into my body and mind.

Rose shouts, "Great buffalo shadow, you're not welcome here."

Her voice is stronger this time, giving me hope.

Magnar floats out of the black air beside his creature. Hovering a few feet above the ground, he rubs his rings over and over, his eyes as dark as the sky except for the gold in his pupils.

Compared to Magnar and his beast, Rose looks small and weak. Magnar glares at me, as if he wants to kill me. "Girl," he spits.

Adrenaline shoots through my limbs. I check to make sure Jake hasn't left, reassured when I see him by the door. He pales as he stares at Magnar and his monster.

Oddly, Magnar's face softens and he extends a hand. "Join me, Rose. We can save the planet together. End technology and the era of machines, and return the planet to its state ten thousand years ago. Let nature rule again, and be vibrant, healthy."

Strangely, his concern over the world's problems reminds me of talks Dad and I have about humans destroying nature. But Dad wants cleaner, safer technology for the planet, not an end to all machines.

"Do you really want everyone living in caves and huts again?" Charlie hops closer.

Magnar scowls at the parrot, then turns to Rose and speaks gently. "We once loved each other, Rose."

It's hard to believe there was ever anything lovable about Magnar. I've never heard him speak kindly to anyone. All of it is at odds with the creepy buffalo shadow.

Rose's face shows hope. "We did love each other, and it's not too late, Magnar. Everything can be like before."

"Yes, it can." He smiles. "We'll be young and beautiful again, Rose. One more ring and everything will be in place. Join me. The largest trees will witness our new beginning."

Rose's voice hardens. "Free the methuselahs and work beside me again as a guardian." A flash of sadness fills her eyes.

Magnar's eyes narrow, his tone harsh. "You're following the weak plan of the Great Ones. They want control too. Don't you care about what's happening to this world, Rose?"

"If you care for the planet and me, you'll stop this," says Rose.

In the blackness behind Magnar something stirs, floating in the air, vague and half-hidden. I crane my neck, gaping at its size. It's larger than the buffalo shadow.

"What have you brought with you?" Rose stares beyond Magnar.

"The Great Ones gave me more than they realized with the methuselahs." Magnar's eyes shine. "It's possible to join the essence of animals. Humans will bow to my power." The gleam in his eyes is crazier than his hulking monster.

"Darth Vader, Hitler, and Napoleon all wanted to be dictators." Charlie clucks. "We know how they ended up."

"We'll see, parrot."

Rose stiffens. "What have you done, Magnar?"

"Give me WhipEye, Rose, and let's end our fighting." When she doesn't reply, he says, "You've failed nine methuselahs, and you'll fail this one too. I can't believe you pinned your hopes on a stupid girl." His eyes blaze at me again and I shrink back.

I look at Rose. What does she expect me to do?

Magnar's face hardens. "I don't want to hurt you, Rose, but I won't allow you to interfere."

"I won't let you harm Charlie or the children."

Rose looks calm, so I'm hoping she has a backup to me. I'm definitely not a Plan B.

Magnar raises a fist. "In less than a day it's all mine."

His body drifts forward, floating over the ground. Keeping pace with him, the buffalo shadow steps into the tall grass.

I try to release WhipEye, but my fingers remain curled around the wood. "I can't let go," I murmur, jerking my hand.

Charlie chatters, "Rosey, Rosey, Rosey."

Lifting the staff and striking it against the ground, Rose shouts, "Caracal!"

Warmth sweeps into my palm from the wood, cozy and powerful. It feels so good I want more of it. At the same time, the African cat's carved face on the staff glows brightly. Gaping, I watch its eyes open, the head changing color. The caracal's lips and head move like a live animal as it hisses loudly.

I have to shield my eyes when golden light streaks from the caracal's head to a spot fifteen yards away, expanding until it outlines a monstrous cat whose shoulder reaches far above Rose. Its reddish brown fur shines in the dim light.

Caracals are usually the size of a medium dog, not an elephant. Its back legs are longer, and the tips of its triangular-shaped, black ears have tuffs of black fur. Its vertical pupils are gold. It has to be one of the Great Ones Charlie mentioned.

"Beautiful," I murmur. No wonder Rose is confident. Dozens of Great Ones are carved into the staff.

My free hand forms a fist. Magnar's monsters won't stand a chance against all these creatures. The caracal alone can probably defeat the buffalo shadow. When I look, the same hope fills Jake's eyes. Charlie hasn't moved, watching silently.

Baring its four canines at Magnar, the muscular cat snarls.

Magnar stops moving forward and regards the cat calmly. The buffalo shadow twists and growls.

Crouching, its powerful hind legs bunched, the cat springs up twenty feet, its claws blurring as it slashes the buffalo shadow's chest, leaving gashes in the gray beast. In mid-air, it pushes off the monster's torso, somersaulting and escaping the beast's swinging arms.

Compared to the cat, the buffalo freak is clumsy and slow.

"Yeah!" Jake shakes his fist in the air.

"Go caracal," I yell. I become more subdued when I see the buffalo creature's wounds quickly healing.

When the cat lands on the ground, it pivots and jumps forward, slashing the legs of the roaring monster. Without pause, it leaps straight up at it.

This time the buffalo shadow moves faster and swings a forearm into the cat, sending it flying end-over-end past Magnar, where it disappears into the black air.

Magnar's eyes narrow and his growling beast stares after the cat.

My pulse throbs on the wood as I strain to see the feline. Rose must believe in the cat, because she isn't calling more animals from the staff.

There's a deep hiss from the pitch air. Running full tilt, the cat flashes into view again, canines bared. It leaps high at the buffalo shadow, slashing and ripping gouges in the shadow's neck.

Moving even faster this time, Magnar's beast catches the caracal with its meaty limbs. With a flurry of strikes the cat tries to break free, but the shadow squeezes the hissing feline until it's motionless.

Ears pinned back, the helpless cat looks at Rose.

My limbs tense. Why isn't she doing anything? "Call more animals, Rose." But she ignores me.

Magnar smirks and Rose backs up.

I shuffle back with her, my legs stiff, the wind screaming in my ears. "Rose," I plead. I'm unable to loosen my grip on the staff and have no idea why she wanted me to hold it. I knew I couldn't help her fight Magnar.

She finally thumps WhipEye into the ground again, sending another echo, while calling, "Gorilla, bear, wolverine!"

I watch the staff, but the wood turns cold in my hand, chilling my limbs and expectations. Something's wrong, but Rose doesn't look surprised.

"No more Great Ones will come, will they Rose?" Magnar

sounds triumphant. "And why should they? I was a fool to think they ever would. What have humans done for any of them?"

My palm becomes clammy with Magnar's words. Rose's drawn face shows he's telling the truth. Time to run. "Rose . . ."

"Into the cabin, children," she shouts.

The staff finally releases my hand. My fingers slide off the wood and I'm running for the building, knowing its small door will never be able to hold back the buffalo shadow. Rose dashes beside me. I feel horrible that we're leaving the caracal with Magnar's monster.

Waiting for me at the door, Jake grimaces. When I'm close, he jumps through the dark entryway. Just before the door I pause, allowing Charlie to flutter to my shoulder and clutch it. Then I hurry into the cabin.

In front of the door, Rose thumps WhipEye against the ground. *Boom!* Loudly, she calls, "Caracal."

The cat melts into a golden stream and streaks from the buffalo shadow's grasp to Rose's staff. I'm glad for that, but unable to celebrate.

The buffalo shadow stares at its empty arms and roars.

Before the door slams shut, my last image is of the buffalo shadow striding toward us, with Magnar floating at its side.

And behind them, in the darkness, something larger stirs.

TEN

Sacrifice

GUIDED BY LIGHT AHEAD OF ME, I run across the dark cabin's wood floor, through another doorway that I don't remember being there, and into bright sunshine. Squinting, I bump into Jake and grab his arm to keep from falling. Disoriented, I stare ahead.

The last time I was in the cabin, over a year ago, it was a small, one-room space. The current view freezes me. The first thing I notice is that Tom's gone. I try to comprehend the rest of it, but all I can do is gape, like Jake.

"Where are we?" he mutters.

"No clue."

"Run, children." Rose slaps my back as she rushes past us.

We follow her, Jake ahead of me and Charlie flying beside me.

Rose sprints fluidly, like a long distance runner. Another impossibility. But our surroundings are even more unbelievable.

Golden grass, high as my waist, flows nearly to the horizon in all directions, and fresh air fills my nostrils. Sunlight warms a clear blue sky. To the west is a river, to the east a high mountain range.

Only the cabin's door behind us remains visible, closed and suspended in the air. Beyond it on all sides stretches the new world we've entered. We're definitely not in Minnesota anymore.

On the plain are herds of zebra, elephants, and buffalo. The sight shocks me. I whisper the names of animals, pointing at them. "Cheetah. Brown bear. Anteater." I try to take them all in. "Honey badger. Black-tailed prairie dog. Armadillo." Some of the animals are from different continents, like elk and giraffe. Yet here they are, all in one place.

I've always dreamed of traveling to Africa and other countries, so for a minute I forget about Magnar and his monsters. A herd of water buffalo in our path parts for us, allowing us to pass through their ranks, which quickly close again as if they understand our fear.

"Did you see that, Jake?" I call to him. "Unbelievable."

"Keep running," he says over his shoulder.

Colors are more vivid here, and the air is rich in some way, making my tongue tingle with every breath I take. My worries fade and I suddenly feel light-hearted, as if anything is possible and everything will be all right.

"Do you see any kangaroos?" I huff. "I've always wanted to see them in the wild."

"Are you crazy? Run!"

But I swing my head from side to side, half-expecting to find one, wanting to in the worst way.

Boom. Boom. Boom!

Without slowing, I look back. The cabin door bulges, while darkness from the other side seeps through its edges. The pounding continues. Black tendrils curl around the edges of the door like fingers of fog.

My lungs soon ache again, my legs weary as we chase Rose up

the gradual incline of a long hill. We pass through a herd of sheep, and I murmur, "Bighorn," needing to weave around a few unconcerned grazing animals. I want to stop and touch one. They look peaceful enough.

Rose slows her pace until halfway up the hill she stops, her face red and her shoulders slumped. She suddenly appears more like the old woman she is.

In a minute, I catch up to her and Jake, gasping for air. Charlie flutters to my shoulder, his body outlined with the thin film of golden light.

An explosion shatters the cabin door into splinters. Ebony air floods through the empty frame like a river, blown forward by a howling wind that sweeps up the hill to my face, ruffling my hair.

The dark air spreads like octopus arms, and out of the darkness the buffalo shadow squeezes through the doorframe, twisting its thick body until it pops free. It stands, arches its back, and roars.

Magnar floats through the door next, and my excitement over the surrounding herds fades, replaced with worry that he'll hurt the animals or somehow ruin this beautiful place.

A hand clutches my shoulder, and I jump.

Rose's long hair is tangled around her neck by the wind. "Protect Charlie at all costs, Samantha. Find your way north. Trust that."

I stiffen, my insides cold. "What are you talking about? Aren't you coming with us?"

"What are you doing, Rose?" asks Charlie.

Rose speaks calmly. "With or without Charlie, Magnar will start his war against humans tomorrow. So you have less than a day to get his rings and free the methuselahs."

"That's crazy." My stomach drops, and I want to shout at her that I can never defeat Magnar and take his rings.

"How could she?" Jake glances from Rose to me, his eyes wide. "That's impossible."

"Take it, Samantha." Rose straightens and holds out WhipEye.

A deep urge to grasp the staff floods me again, but this time I struggle to keep my hands at my sides. "I can't fight Magnar."

Rose's eyes meet mine. "WhipEye has great power, Samantha."

Deep inside, I'm burning to have the staff in my hand, even though some rational part of me is screaming *Don't touch it!* "I don't know how to use it," I mumble.

"WhipEye is from the Great Ones who live here in KiraKu, and all the animals carved on it are Great Ones. The staff has the energy of KiraKu in it and bonds to whoever uses it. You're its master now. But you should know that WhipEye has a mind of its own."

I blink. She tricked me. "I'm its master? I only held it for a few minutes."

"Magnar wants the staff." Jake bites his lip.

Rose nods. "He'll need WhipEye to reenter KiraKu after he takes over your world, since Great Ones will close the door from the cabin when he leaves. Magnar is also afraid Great Ones will answer the staff's call. Most haven't for thousands of years. They can defeat him, but the only thing that might bring them out of KiraKu now is survival and love."

I have no idea what she means. Survival, I get. But love? "Why aren't we running?"

"Magnar won't go far into KiraKu. He's not ready to battle Great Ones and they'll fight him if he stays here."

Magnar and his monster are standing near the door, so she could be right. I swallow.

"Keep Charlie's feathers, children."

"What are you doing, Rose?" Charlie repeats.

"We've had a long journey, my friend." Rose regards the parrot with warmth in her eyes.

Gently, she lifts my right hand and places WhipEye in my palm. I can't resist any longer and clench the wood, as if urged to do so by the staff. That scares me almost as much as Magnar.

"What about Tom?" I ask.

"He's on his own," Rose says softly. "Don't count on his help."

"I knew it," says Jake.

"Make sure Magnar never gets WhipEye." Rose releases my hand. "Go, and don't look back. Find a Great One if you need help."

"Go where? Do what? What are you going to do?" Something about her eyes troubles me.

Jake looks bewildered. "You have to help us."

"You can't leave me, Rose," says Charlie.

"You picked wisely, Charlie." She gently strokes the parrot's neck. "Now trust your choice." She straightens, a single tear on her cheek.

Mom's face flashes inside me, along with a deep sadness. "Don't do this."

"I can't go any farther, children. I'm too old. I'm not afraid of Magnar, but I can only give you a little time, so use it." She looks at Charlie. "Take care of them, my friend. Safe journey." Leaving, she strides down the hill toward the buffalo shadow.

"Rosey," calls Charlie. "Rosey."

For the first time, I hear uncertainty and real worry in the parrot's voice. My knees wobble. Rose doesn't look back, and Magnar and his creature watch her, waiting.

"Come on, Sam." Jake flicks my arm.

"We can't leave without her." But I stumble up the incline after him, wheezing heavily. Every dozen steps, I glance back.

High above the door the blue sky disappears as black clouds quickly form and spread across the heavens, darkening the ground below. Animal herds stampede away from the approaching gloom as if it threatens their lives.

Something dark and enormous pulls itself through the cabin door, the shape hidden by the surrounding blackness. It has legs or arms, or both. Once through the door, it rises into the dark sky, but I can't see it clearly.

I keep watching for it, and in a few moments a dark shape bursts out of the leading curl of the black clouds. It's ghostly. A spidery figure with six long, pointy fingers. A monster claw.

I shiver.

The creature sinks lower, floating fast until it plunges into a fleeing herd of zebras, closing around one that neighs and kicks.

"No," I murmur.

Curling around the struggling animal, hiding it completely, the claw rises higher. I watch until it opens again.

Empty.

"It's killing them," I whisper.

I notice Magnar pointing in another direction, and the ghostly beast flies that way, as if following his wishes. My fist tightens on WhipEye until it aches. The claw pursues other prey, but I don't want to watch.

When I reach the top of the incline, I have to use my inhaler again.

A troop of olive baboons and a herd of llamas surround us, an odd mixture, as if aware of the approaching danger. Barks and alarm calls erupt among them. It's strange having animals trying to protect us.

Rose stops twenty paces from the destroyed cabin door, blocking Magnar as he strokes his rings. The buffalo shadow stands near its master, its shiny eyes gazing at her.

Ebony air swirls around Rose, making me queasy. Snaking tendrils of darkness circle her body, but every time the pitch air tries to grasp her, it slides off.

"Magnar can't hurt her," I say hopefully.

"You shouldn't have given her the staff, Rose." Magnar's unnaturally strong voice carries all the way up the hill. "Leave WhipEye there, girl, and I won't hurt you."

Rose remains silent.

I want to yell that I'll trade the staff for Rose, but I can't betray her.

"I'll give you one last chance to get out of my way." Magnar speaks with a hint of encouragement.

I hope wildly Rose will do it. She answers, but her words are too faint to hear.

Magnar barely pauses, speaking coldly. "So be it."

With a roar, the buffalo shadow steps forward and hunches over, wrapping its thick arms around Rose and picking her up.

Jake's hand finds mine and I grip it tightly. My legs feel weak and memories of Mom dry my mouth.

Charlie screeches, "No!"

Rose doesn't struggle, her silence bringing deep pain to my chest. The buffalo shadow crushes her, its limbs and torso completely hiding her.

"Rosey," whimpers Charlie.

A flash of gold erupts from the monster's limbs, and a solitary line of light escapes from its grasp, streaking into the sky above us before fading away.

Magnar's creature growls and opens its arms. All that's left is Rose's dress. It flutters to the ground like a blown leaf.

A tear rolls down my cheek.

Magnar floats toward us, his buffalo shadow following, and ahead of them flies the monster claw.

"Murderer," I whisper.

"Sam."

I stumble after Jake, over the top of the hill.

ELEVEN

WhipEye

AHHHHH!"

My feet and back slide down against a steep rock incline, my heels scraping stone. There's nothing to grab onto and only air beneath me.

Squawk! Charlie flutters off my shoulder.

My soles slam into a ledge, jarring my teeth. I want to let go of WhipEye so both hands are free, but my fingers are glued to it. I bring the staff close to my body to keep my balance.

Pebbles loosened from my fall bounce off boulders below, making tiny *pops!* along the way.

It takes a few breaths to get my bearings. I'm standing on a foot-wide path that drops off several hundred feet. I only slid ten feet.

I swivel my head left. A few feet away, the ledge ends in a rock wall. To the right, Jake is hurrying along the footpath away from me. Moving my head a few inches out from the cliff, I see springbok gazelle far below, grazing in a valley meadow a short distance from the base of the cliff.

My head swirls and I press back into the wall.

Heights don't bother me, but not having a guardrail or something to hang on to freaks me out. For that reason I never go on roller coasters or stand near the edge of a cliff. Even with Magnar and his monster chasing me, I can't move. However, my pulse quickens when I hear faint roars from above.

Jake stops on the path, looking at me. "Sam!"

"Enjoying the scenery," I mumble.

He hurries back, and in moments he's clenching my hand on the staff. "You won't fall, Sam. I've got you."

My feet won't move. "Yeah, right."

"Hurry up."

"Don't rush me." Slowly, I pivot my toes around inch by inch. Jake keeps his hand on me the whole time, sliding it along my arm to my shoulder, then my back until my stomach presses against the rock face and I don't have to look at the drop-off. I slide my feet sideways, allowing him to guide me along the ledge.

"Faster," he says.

"I'm not a mountain goat." I do my best, glad he's nearby. I keep my eyes on the rock in front of my face.

After a short distance, the path widens and curves, sloping down toward the meadow.

Jake pats my hand. "Now run."

Keeping my gaze on the path, so I don't have to see how high up we are, I brush my right shoulder along the cliff face and start jogging. By the time I enter the grass I'm running full tilt downhill, with WhipEye's weight yanking my hand up and down in jerky arcs.

Charlie flies near my shoulder, giving me some comfort. As I follow Jake through the tall grass, my legs swing in shaky, out of control strides. It's all I can do to keep from diving headfirst into the ground.

The antelope glance up and briefly watch us, and then continue to graze. A half-mile away to the south and west, thick jungle borders the meadow.

A loud howl fills the air.

Jake makes a sharp turn and heads west along the slope, toward the shadowed forest.

I have to make a wider turn so I don't fall. By the time I reach the jungle edge, I'm moving too fast and headed for a large tree.

A root sticking out of the ground tilts my foot and I'm able to push off and veer sideways, but I clip the trunk with my shoulder.

"Ugh!" In a few more strides my legs lurch to a stop and I fall against another tree. I'm dazed and take a puff from my inhaler. Then I rub my aching shoulder.

Jake rests behind another tree, panting and watching the cliff.

I take a quick look around. Some of the trees are massive, dozens of feet wide and hundreds of feet tall. I don't recognize the species. They have soft red bark like redwoods, but their high branches have leaves shaped like oak. Farther in, thick ferns—some waist high and some over our heads—fill in the undergrowth vegetation of vines, bushes, and saplings.

Charlie returns to my shoulder, clutching it in silence with his head lowered.

I peek around the trunk.

Growling, the buffalo shadow reaches the top of the cliff, its head moving slowly back and forth, its dark eyes probing. Magnar floats up beside it, staring down the hill.

The darker forest provides cover for us, and I motion to Jake, whispering, "We're safe. He can't spot us in here."

Jake's face remains taut.

High in the sky, above the hill, the black claw slowly scratches its way toward us, spreading shadows over the meadow. Running in wild jumps and strides, the springbok flee east.

Magnar stares up at the ebony hand and snarls, his outstretched arm swinging in our direction.

"You're wrong," breathes Jake.

"How can he know?" I murmur, my skin tingling.

The buffalo shadow hunches its shoulders and growls.

At least the beast can't follow us on the narrow ledge path. "They're going to have to find another way down," I say.

Dropping to all fours, the shadow beast leaps off the cliff and falls for several seconds until it crunches hard into the rocky bottom with a resounding *thump!* It looks uninjured. Snorting, it stomps the ground with jarring punches.

"Wrong again," whispers Jake.

Magnar floats down along the cliff face to his beast. Bellowing, the buffalo freak runs in great loping strides on all fours, headed straight for us, while Magnar floats beside it.

"Sam!" Jake flees and I run after him. Charlie flies beside me.

I'm quickly fighting through thick tangles of vines and bushes that Tom would waltz through. Worse, the bottom of WhipEye catches on plants and vines. Jake hurdles most of it, leaving me behind. I keep running and hunch my shoulders over what's coming. I'm breathing hard, my feet are pounding, and sweat runs down my face.

A loud crash makes me gasp. I look back, but trees block my view.

Magnar's strong voice hurtles after me; "You can't outrun us, girl."

Pug-face is right. Escape is impossible. Especially for me. Winded, my face scratched, I manage another hundred strides and stop, letting Jake run on. I want him to. One of us has to make it home. I hope he can find a way.

Charlie wheels and floats to my shoulder.

"Go, Charlie," I say hoarsely. "You can't stay with me."

Not moving, the parrot is silent, his body outlined with golden light.

In the distance, I see flashes of gray as the buffalo shadow smashes its way through thick jungle.

Jake notices my absence and turns, his eyes and face wild, his blond hair sticking up in places. "Come on, Sam." He motions to me with hurried sweeps.

I shake my head, one hand flopping at him. "Go."

He lopes back through the vegetation and grabs my hand. "I'm not leaving you."

"You have to," I gasp, yanking free. "I'm finished. Go on." I try to push him away, but he brushes my arm to the side with little effort and stands beside me, panting. We face Magnar's monster together.

Bits and pieces of the beast are visible now. With forceful strides, the buffalo shadow plows through plants and vines, its powerful legs tearing through everything in its way. Floating alongside it, Magnar wears an icy smile, his eyes small black orbs.

I back up with Jake. His presence gives me strength, but what if he dies here?

WhipEye hits a tree trunk and nearly falls from my jittery grasp. Shifting my grip, I jam the staff hard against the ground. *Boom!*

The buffalo shadow skids to a stop, snorting and glaring at us.

With a spark of excitement, I thump WhipEye against the ground once more, harder. It sends a louder echo into the distance.

Magnar laughs from beside his beast. "You don't have a clue about what you're holding, do you, girl?" Then softly, "You've done more than I thought possible, but you'll never defeat me. Give me WhipEye and the parrot, and I won't harm you or the boy. You have my word."

Rose's face is in my mind and a fierce resistance grows inside me. "Never."

Magnar's eyes blaze. "Get my parrot."

The buffalo shadow roars and charges.

"Call the cat," says Jake.

"It can't beat Magnar's monster." I back up with him.

Jake emphatically chops the air. "Call it."

I bang WhipEye, sending another echo off, and yell, "Caracal!" But the cat's head remains dark on the wood, the staff cold in my palm.

"Call something else," pleads Jake.

The other Great Ones refused to answer Rose, so why would they come for me? But I have to try.

My heel catches on a vine and I stumble backward. The bottom of the staff swings sideways, then back in the other direction. Steadying it vertically, I thump it again.

Boom!

But before I utter a word, trees and bushes in a path far in front of us sway first one way, then the other, pushing Magnar and the buffalo creature sideways, off balance, and slowing them down. I stare in disbelief at WhipEye.

Magnar rights himself by grabbing a low tree branch, his face darkening. "Get them."

The buffalo shadow steadies itself and howls, its thick legs driving forward.

"Move it around more." Jake grabs the staff beneath my hands and we frantically spin it in a circle, then back and forth in crisscrossing lines in a messy pattern.

I hear the buffalo shadow barreling through vegetation. "Now," I yell.

We raise the staff and slam it into the ground, sending a deeper, resounding echo into the distance.

Writhing jungle immediately thickens in front of the buffalo shadow, springing from small trees and undergrowth. Vines slither and wrap around the monster's limbs and curl around its torso, while thin tree branches circle its body and neck, all of it bringing the beast to a jarring halt, as if it ran into a pool of deep mud.

Snorting, the monster tries to take a step, slowly lifting one foot off the ground. Wobbling, it loses its balance and crashes to its knees twenty feet from us.

"Yeah!" Jake's eyes light up. "Take that you freak!" He pumps a fist.

I watch with more caution, remembering how the buffalo shadow recovered from the caracal's attack.

To the side of the monster, thick vegetation also curls around Magnar's body. But he shouts, "Keep moving!"

Rising slowly under the heavy press of vines and limbs, snapping some branches, the beast stiffens, snorts, and takes a step forward. It raises one clawed limb, then another, even though a massive press of greenery encases it. The monster appears strong enough to move the entire jungle if it has to.

"Crap." I step back.

"It can't break free," whispers Jake, moving with me. "It can't."

But Magnar's beast keeps advancing, step by step, even though more vines and plants wrap around its torso and thick neck. When the monster is five feet away, I can feel its hot breath on my face. It leans forward and lowers its bulky head as its horns push past either side of Jake and me, framing us. Its dark fiery eyes are big as fists. I'm close enough to stroke its wet nose.

The monster snorts, finally unable to move another inch as greenery continues to coil around it.

A short distance away, vines encircle Magnar until only his glaring, wrinkled face shows through. The veins on his forehead are purple. It's a relief when a last spurt of jungle growth hides him and the buffalo shadow completely.

Energy drains from my body and I lean on the staff.

After a few deep breaths, we back away from the buffalo shadow. Jake flicks a finger against the tip of a protruding horn, and then we walk away fast, side-by-side. In the park, Rose's spell froze Magnar only a few minutes. I hope WhipEye has more staying power.

I pause when the shadow's roar echoes through the jungle, followed by Magnar's fading words, "Rose died because of you, girl. You'll pay for this. You'll both pay."

I keep walking, my whole body wired. "We can stop his shadow methuselahs with WhipEye."

Not looking at me, Jake pushes up his glasses. "I don't want to see any more of his creepy monsters."

"Yeah." Stopping Magnar and his beast doesn't make me feel safe. I know it isn't permanent, and Magnar has eight more monsters. Also, Rose's death gives me a stomachache and brings up dark thoughts of Mom.

Shadows sweep over us. Above the canopy, black clouds are moving west. Magnar's ebony claw floats among them, following us.

Jake waves at it. "That's how he saw us from the top of the hill."

He's right.

It's hard work walking through the thick jungle, and mosquitoes and flies swarm us. My flannel shirt is soaked with sweat, but I decide not to roll up my sleeves. At least they give some protection from plants and insects.

Jake looks miserable, swatting his legs and arms continually. Twice he pulls out his cell phone, but each time after trying it, he jams it back into his pocket.

Finally, he stops. "Rose said to head north." His words have an edge as he brushes mosquitoes away. "Where's north, Sam?"

Glad for an excuse to rest, I wipe sweat from my face and level the compass. North points in the direction of Rose's cabin, and this time the needle remains on north.

It confuses me until I focus on the word inscribed on the compass. *Love.* "In the park, Rose told me to find north." I look at Jake. "She said to follow love." But how do you follow something you haven't felt for a year?

"Rose didn't tell us much of anything, did she?" Jake shakes his head. "So what direction?"

As if in answer to his question, the needle does its strange thing again, slowly moving off north until it points west for a few moments, before popping back to north. I signal the way and Jake stomps ahead.

It's comforting that something is guiding us. Hopefully to safety. I'd like to believe Mom is controlling the compass needle, though I doubt it's true.

Charlie is sitting on my shoulder, his head hanging. I gently stroke the bird. "I'm sorry, Charlie." I want to cradle the parrot like a baby. He's never been like this before, even when shackled in the Endless Pet Store.

The grieving parrot reminds me of what he said about Dad having a broken heart. Maybe Dad doesn't mean to ignore me. Maybe he's lost too. I want to race home to ask him if he misses Mom as much as I do.

The parrot whimpers, and then talks quietly. "Rose was my only friend for most of a thousand years, kid. She came to me whenever she could over the centuries, sometimes just for a few minutes. And she fought Magnar many times, trying to free me."

I know what it's like to lose someone close to you. It makes me care about the parrot even more. "Why did Magnar do it, Charlie? Start trapping the methuselahs?"

Jake stops to listen.

Charlie settles on my shoulder. "A long time ago, when Magnar talked about taking over your world, the Great Ones gave Whip-Eye to Rose, so she could call them for help. Magnar became jealous of the staff's power, so he figured out a way to trap a methuselah's energy in a ring."

"Where do methuselahs come from?" Jake slaps his legs.

"We're created by the energy source of KiraKu. One born every thousand years to gather wisdom and energy, and bless the earth. The usual. The Great Ones kept hoping Magnar wouldn't find and imprison us."

"Anything else?" Jake breaks a stem off a bush, nervously bending it in his hands.

Charlie continues. "Rose and Magnar are from KiraKu. The Great Ones promised that the released methuselah energy would keep them young in your world. Magnar ended that by trapping the methuselahs in his rings, so he and Rose aged. If Magnar loses the rings, he's finished. Rose returned to KiraKu a few times to slow her aging, even though the Great Ones told her to keep the door shut." He hangs his head. "She took a risk today and opened the door into KiraKu for you."

I'm barely listening. Charlie appears healthy, strong, but the golden light around his feathers is glowing brighter. Something about that disturbs me.

Jake tosses the stem away. "Why don't the Great Ones stop Magnar?

"Some tried, centuries ago, but they waited too long. Magnar was already too powerful. He had too many shadow monsters. Also, Great Ones don't like traveling to your world."

A knot forms in my stomach. "How do you release your energy, Charlie?" When the parrot doesn't answer, I say, You're going to die tomorrow, aren't you?"

"What?" Jake stares wide-eyed at me, then the parrot.

"It's how a methuselah's energy is released to the world, kids. Anyway, I've lived a full life. A thousand years is more than most. I wish I could have flown in a jungle for one day, though, without some monster chasing me." He pauses. "By the way, *Avatar* is my favorite movie. The jungle scenes did it for me."

Jake's face softens. "You'll die tomorrow, no matter what we do?"

"It's already started," he says. "That's why I'm glowing. And this time it has to happen. You can't let Magnar get me. If he just *touches* me now, he'll be a hundred times more powerful."

I swallow. "So what's the plan?"

The parrot rubs his head against my cheek. "If anyone can find a way to get Magnar's rings and rescue the methuselahs, it's you, Sam. The methuselah energy needs to be freed. Otherwise, Magnar will use that energy to start his war for power, with or without me."

The same idea that fills Jake's blue eyes bothers me. *How can we defeat Magnar when we can't even escape him?* I grip my compass. I wish Mom were here. She always knew what to do.

If we ever get back, I'm going to ask Dad about my eleventh birthday, the day she died. I'm tired of secrets and want to know everything, even if it scares me. I miss Mom so much it hurts.

Magnar's ghostly claw is directly above us.

"We're toast." Jake walks on ahead.

"Crispy," I say.

TWELVE

Strange Things

WHY ISN'T IT ATTACKING?" Jake chews his lip.

"Maybe the trees are protecting us," I say. "Or it's just tracking us."

We soon learn that no matter what, we can't escape the claw.

When we run, we pull farther away from Magnar's monster, but when we walk, the hand gains on us. If the jungle canopy hides us, the monster pauses, as if uncertain which way to go. But when a break appears in the treetops, no matter how small, and we become visible even for an instant, the claw floats in our direction again. It spooks me every time.

I hear birds and other animal calls in the distance. Then a roar sounds.

Jake stops, peering into the jungle. "What's that?"

"Not a methuselah," says Charlie.

I'm glad the parrot sounds a little recovered from losing Rose. "It's a big cat," I say. "Maybe it's the caracal."

"A cat, huh?" Jakes twirls a hand at me. "You were sure the buffalo shadow wouldn't jump down the cliff too."

"That was different. I've listened to hundreds of cat roars."

"In case it's not the caracal, we have to get out of the jungle." Jake hustles away.

Meanwhile, I have the strange sensation of being followed. However, each time I look, nothing's there.

A bit later, in the middle of a clump of ferns, I stop. Without turning, I slide the end of WhipEye near my heel and move it in crisscrossing patterns. Then with one hand I punch it into the ground near my foot, sending a deep echo into the forest.

I whirl, leaning on the staff for support. My legs are rubbery with fatigue.

A dozen feet away, a five-foot green iguana with golden eyes is lying on a tree limb. Branches and leaves wind around its body, engulfing it quietly in a prison that quickly hides it.

Jake rushes to my side. "What is it?"

I motion weakly. "I think it's a Great One. A.k.a. *Iguana iguana*. It's beautiful. Iguanas grow new tails if they lose one and can swim underwater for a half-hour."

Jake looks at me like I'm crazy, but I want to talk about something normal. Anything besides monsters and Magnar. "Green iguanas have a third eye in the center of their forehead, which protects them from being attacked from above by predators."

"Well, it wasn't too smart getting caught, was it?" Jake steps closer.

Charlie clucks from my shoulder. "Not a good idea trapping a Great One."

"It's just a lizard, Charlie." Jake slices the air with a hand. "We need answers." He frowns. "Do Great Ones talk?"

I walk closer to the tree. One of the iguana's eyes peeks through the branches. "Hey, are you all right?" I ask. Jake looks annoyed, so I add, "Why are you following us?"

"Humans aren't allowed into KiraKu." The iguana has a gentle, female voice. "I'm surprised you're here. I watched you stop Magnar's buffalo shadow. Impressive."

"It was, wasn't it?" Charlie eyes the lizard. "Tell that to your friends."

It gives me a boost of confidence that we impressed a Great One. "Can you help us?"

"Yeah, can you take us home?" asks Jake.

"We're not supposed to help humans. And Great Ones never go to your world. It's too risky to be away from the energy of KiraKu."

My arm flops. "There must be something you can do for us."

The iguana swivels her eye to me. "WhipEye can take you home."

Jake glances at me crossly, as if he's blaming me for not thinking of that sooner.

"I don't know how to use the stupid staff," I mutter. I inspect WhipEye until I find the lizard's face. The carving is an exact match to this reptile. "Why won't you answer its call?"

"There aren't enough Great Ones willing to fight Magnar anymore. They don't want to go to your world and think they're safe here."

I shrug at Jake. "The little girl couldn't fight her way out of a pile of bananas, anyway."

Jake crosses his arms, his eyebrows hunched. "Maybe we'll keep the little girl prisoner until she helps us."

"We don't want to hurt you," I say quickly, ignoring Jake's glare. "We should let her out, Jake."

"No, we shouldn't. How would you do that, anyway? We don't have a knife, and you don't know how to use WhipEye to free her."

He's right, but I don't want to leave the Great One trapped.

The lizard's eyes glow brighter until golden light fills her prison. The tree branches and vines slowly slither away and resume their normal shapes. Simultaneously, the iguana grows a few feet in length, her snout and torso rapidly expanding.

We back up as the lizard's weight bends the branch until she slides off it, plopping on the ground. She steps into the ferns, and in a flash expands to thirty feet, her large eyes staring down at us. I note the long spines on her back and tail—which she could whip at us.

"Nice trap, kids."

The Great One takes a step forward. I back up, unsure how angry she is. In a burst of speed she runs a few steps, barely touching each of our upper chests with her snout.

Jake and I cry out and fall back into the ferns. Charlie squawks and flutters off my shoulder.

The lizard straddles our bodies.

I'm looking up at Godzilla. "We were kidding about the prisoner stuff. And the little girl cracks."

"Yeah, totally," gasps Jake.

Charlie lands on my shoulder, cocking his head up at the iguana. "Be nice. They're kids. You know how they are."

I'm grateful the parrot is brave and loyal. I'm also glad he doesn't make one of his sarcastic comments.

Lowering her head close to our faces, the iguana flicks her tongue between our heads. "You shouldn't use WhipEye's power irresponsibly, even with trees and bushes. Or by trapping Great Ones." The lizard pauses. "Remember, some Great Ones won't be this nice."

"Good to know," I squeak.

"Sorry," mutters Jake.

Very softly, she says, "Beware. Our eldest knows you're here. You're being tracked. Leave while you can."

Just the way the iguana says it sends shivers through me.

She steps away, shrinking to her previous size and crawling through the ferns. Scaling a tree, the lizard runs along a low branch to its end, leaping twenty feet to another tree. She keeps jumping until she disappears into the jungle growth.

"That went great." Charlie fluffs his feathers.

I stand up, helping the parrot to my shoulder.

"Great?" Jake pushes to his feet, brushing dirt off his shorts. "She wouldn't even help us."

"She didn't eat us, kiddo."

Jake frowns at me. "The cat we heard can't be the caracal."

I'm as disappointed as he sounds. "Charlie, do you know who the eldest is?"

"No idea, Sam."

"We need to find a Great One that will help us," mumbles Jake. "Or show us how to use the staff." He looks at me as we continue walking, but I ignore him.

Soon monkeys appear, chattering and leaping through the branches on either side of us. Other animals arrive with them. I stare in wonder.

Glad for the distraction, I say, "Squirrel monkeys, Jake. And there's an Indian muntjac deer, and an emerald boa!"

"Wonderful." Jake grimaces and gives the snake crawling along a tree branch a wide berth.

A small rhino walks out of the jungle ahead of us, and Jake quickly drops back to my side.

"Sumatran rhino," I whisper. "Hairy. Very rare."

"Yeah, super." He looks at me and shrugs. "Okay, kind of cute."

I look at the two horns on its head, and when I pass by I run a palm lightly over its back. It doesn't even flinch, only making an *eep* sound. "Unbelievable."

Warblers sing in nearby trees. I'm stunned when a crimson finch lands on my free shoulder. A bright yellow canary lands on Jake's, and he grins at me. Something loosens inside and I smile back. I'm in love with KiraKu.

"It's better than the Galapagos," I whisper. "Animals have never been hunted there, either."

After a short walk, the animals slowly melt back into the vegetation. I hate to see them go.

Jake's arms make big whirls. "Okay. Even I have to say that was awesome. And the air is different here. Sweet."

My tongue and throat tingle too, and a light breeze carries the scent of orchids. Also, the sensation I had when we first entered KiraKu—that anything is possible, burns stronger now. I somehow *know* I'll see a kangaroo, but none appear. "What does it mean, Charlie?"

The parrot clucks. "Rose said KiraKu has old energy in the air and water that affects all life here. The Great Ones get their power from it. Your world started losing it when it was cut off from KiraKu, especially when humans introduced more technology over the last ten thousand years. It's one reason why Magnar wants to turn back the clock."

"That's why Magnar wasn't tired chasing us," I murmur. "KiraKu's air must have energized him."

A roar fills the jungle. It sounds closer, and this time it's a little nerve-wracking.

Branches snap above us. I stop to look. Dark blotches are pushing though the canopy. It takes a few moments to understand what I'm seeing. It's the claw, aggressively squeezing its way through tree branches pointy fingers first, like a dive-bombing raptor.

I freeze. "Jake."

"I see it."

I shriek and dart past him, but he quickly passes me. Looking back, I see the monster scurrying down through the trees like a giant spider at the end of a web line.

"Find a place to hide!" I shout, waving frantically.

"No kidding, Sherlock," yells Jake.

When it's fifty feet above the ground, the claw rights itself and floats after us, twisting sideways to slip between trees growing close together, so it can follow us in a direct line. It lowers until it's only ten feet off the soil.

We race into a tight clump of six large trees, and I stop in the middle of them. "Jake!" I shout.

"It can get in there," he yells, stopping ahead of me. "Keep going!"

A thick assortment of bushes, vines, and smaller trees surround the big tree trunks. I hope the ringing vegetation is enough for what I'm thinking. Charlie circles to my shoulder.

Jake runs back to me, his gaze on the approaching claw. "Sam, are you nuts? We're not protected here."

"That's the idea," I say softly. I don't know if I'm right, but I'm too tired to run.

Pausing outside the trees, the monster rotates sideways until its palm faces us. Slowly, it floats around the trunks, its fingertips tapping along the trees as it scurries along. My throat turns dry.

Jakes hunts until he finds a good-sized rock, and throws it hard at the monster. It bounces off its skin. The beast doesn't even pause.

"Dang." He tries another rock with the same results.

Shapes are pushing up inside the claw, against its outer skin, as if trying to escape. The figures remind me of the zebra and other animals the creature captured when it arrived. Sickening.

Charlie shakes himself. "Creepy, like Magnar."

We slowly pivot in a three-sixty, while the creature crawls around us.

"It can't get in." Jake sounds hopeful.

But after one complete circle, the monster stops between two trees and slips its pointy fingers between them, slowly pulling itself through. I remember how it forced itself through the small cabin door into KiraKu.

"Sam." Jake inches back.

"Not yet." I back up slowly toward the opposite side of the tree ring, waiting. The creature's oily skin throbs with pulsing shapes.

"I trust you have a plan, kid." Charlie fluffs his wings.

"Kind of." When the claw heaves half its bulk through the trees, I hit Jake's arm. "Come on."

Stepping just outside the ring of trees, I stop and move WhipEye in a small circle in front of my feet. After several rounds, I run the staff across the imaginary circle's diameter in a number of places.

The monster manages to squirm all the way through the trees, and then floats toward us.

"Sam!" yells Jake.

"Grab the staff." I raise it, and he grips it firmly. We slam it into the dirt.

Boom! The echo blasts into the distance and the creature pauses in the center of the trees, its fingers jerking half-clenched.

Vines, bushes, smaller trees, and other vegetation snake around the outside of the larger trees, wrapping tightly around the trunks from the ground up, creating a tight cage. When the wall reaches twenty-feet high, vines whip through the circle of trees above the claw.

I hold my breath when the monster floats up, bumping into the crisscrossing vegetation. The vines don't break.

"Yeah!" Jake raises a fist. "All right. Take that you stupid freak!"

Charlie clucks. "You're a born monster trapper, kid. That's three in a row."

"True." I feel good about that, but say, "Let's get out of here, Jake. We don't know how long it will last."

"That was great." Jake walks away with me, checking back often like myself as the vegetation continues to thicken on the outside and top of the cage. In minutes we can't see the monster anymore.

"Way to go, Sam!" Jake pumps an arm. Flicking my shoulder softly, he asks, "So how'd you figure that out, genius?"

My cheeks warm. "Before we stopped the buffalo shadow, I was thinking about how I'd like the vines and plants to stop it. At first I thought it was just the way we moved WhipEye, but later I wondered if visualizing was part of what made WhipEye work. So I tried it with the iguana, imagining the animal following us wrapped up by plants. With the claw, I visualized the cage and then tried to draw it with the tip of the staff."

"Awesome."

"Let's hope it's permanent." Although even as I say it, I don't believe it.

THIRTEEN

Parrots

AFTER FIGHTING THROUGH VEGETATION for another hour, a wide plain of tall grass appears through the trees ahead. Far across the grassland, KiraKu's large trees rise into the sky.

Exhausted and thirsty, I walk to the edge of the tree line. My hands and face have dozens of scratches on them and my hair is a tangled mess. I'm sweaty and dirty, but at least my flannel shirt and jeans have only a few small tears in them.

Scratches cover Jake's bare legs and arms, and several large rips mar his red shirt. His hair looks like it got sucked up by a vacuum.

Giraffes and lumbering tortoises are grazing in the grass, and vultures wheel in the sky over the plain. A mob of kangaroos is grazing, leisurely hopping south, their reddish-brown fur shining.

"Look," I say excitedly. "Red kangaroos can leap eighteen feet and hop thirty-five miles an hour." Jake turns away, but I watch them jump south, marveling that I've finally seen them in the wild.

"Sam." Jake points north beyond the trees.

A blue butterfly with a thirty-foot wingspan faces us, its massive wings slowly beating. Its underwings are a mixture of soft brown, bronze, and white, and its multifaceted eyes shine gold. Another Great One. A score of smaller butterflies of all sizes and colors, all with golden eyes, flutter around it.

"A blue morpho, a.k.a. *Morpho peleides*," I whisper. "And coppers, monarchs, and Tiger swallowtails." Their large sizes and bright colors mesmerize me.

Jake steps forward and holds his arms straight up. "Hey, we need your help."

"You shouldn't have brought an Original here." The large butterfly's voice is male and stern. "Nor that monster." He flutters closer. "You don't belong here."

Jake drops his hands, frowning.

"What's an Original?" I ask.

"Special humans. They were sent out of KiraKu long ago, and were forbidden to return."

The gold in Tom's eyes, and the way he talks and moves, seems to fit.

"So Tom's an Original." Jake eyes me. "Which means he's very old."

Movement draws my attention up. Magnar's claw is floating directly overhead, black clouds filling in around it.

Jake peers at it. "Your trap didn't hold it very long."

He sounds as disappointed as I am. We'll never be rid of it. However, this time it remains high above the canopy. Maybe it's scared of the Great Ones. However, I can't see how butterflies, even Great Ones, could fight it.

The large butterfly flaps his wings, flying south over the grassland, his iridescent blue sparkling in the waning sunlight. Creating a weaving trail of color, the smaller butterflies follow him. I'm bummed to see them go.

"Hey, wait." Jake runs after them, never leaving the safety of the trees, yelling and waving his arms wildly.

A two-foot Tiger swallowtail leaves the stream of butterflies and flutters to him, hovering at the edge of the forest. Trees mostly block my view. In moments, the yellow and black butterfly chases after the others. All of them are soon distant specks.

It doesn't inspire me that so many Great Ones have refused to help us.

Shoulders drooping, Jake tramps back.

When he rejoins me, he holds out a palm. "The butterfly gave me this. It fell off its wing."

On his hand is a thin, flat oval object, with bright iridescent colors of yellow, orange, and red. An inch long, it's slightly tapered at one end, its other end flat with four short, rounded prongs.

"It's a wing scale from the swallowtail." I bend over to look at it, tapping it with a fingernail. "It's strong. Made from chitin. Beautiful. Wow, that's so cool."

"Yeah. Super. Wonderful." He says it like he could care less.

"Well, did the swallowtail say anything?"

Jake scoffs. "'Here's a gift. Good luck.' Then it flew away. It sounded like a child. They're idiots." He shoves the scale in his pocket and gestures west. "It'll be easier to run here. We can put the claw farther behind us. And the big cat."

"Are you kidding? That monster will get us for sure out in the open."

Another roar comes from the jungle, sounding even closer.

Charlie shakes himself. "Magnar's claw is chasing *me*, kids."

"Why didn't you say so?" Jake's hands do back flips. "We could have hidden you."

The parrot stretches a wing. "Magnar knows I'm with you. I'll lead it south. You two keep going west."

I shake my head. "I'm not leaving you alone, Charlie, no matter what."

"Sam, don't be stupid." Jake glares at me. "Charlie flies faster than we run. At least he can escape. Let him go."

I stroke the parrot. "Can you fly faster than that thing, Charlie?"

The parrot ducks his head and doesn't reply.

"He stays with us, Jake."

He whirls a finger in the air. "Then run."

Just looking at the grassland numbs me. "We'll be easy targets out there."

"The claw might just be tracking us now. Look how high it is. Rose said Magnar wasn't ready to fight Great Ones." Jake gestures into the jungle. "Besides, we can't stay here. You heard those roars. The iguana warned us about the cat."

Charlie clucks. "He's right, Sam."

I shrug. "I'd rather go south or north, so we can stay inside the jungle."

As if arguing with me, my strange compass needle swings west. This time I ignore it.

"You're the one who said we should go west." Jake points across the grass. "That's west, isn't it?"

"Yeah, but we'd be protected in the jungle and could eventually loop around to west."

"What's your problem?" He crosses his arms, giving me his intense gaze.

"You're not making sense, kid."

"Arachnophobia. Big spiders freak me out."

"What spiders?" asks Jake.

I point a finger up.

"Oh. I guess it kind of looks like one." He moves his fingertips across his arm like a spider. "I let a tarantula walk on my hand once. I thought you loved animals."

"Spiders aren't animals," I snap. I take a deep breath. "I think it's because I can't look them in the eye."

His face softens. "No worries. Keep your eyes on my back. I'll watch it for you, so you don't have to look."

"Great. At least I won't see it grabbing me, huh?" I dig out my inhaler and take a puff. After exhaling, I say, "Let's do it."

He lopes into the waist-high grass in his flowing stride. I follow with weary steps. Even WhipEye is heavy. Charlie flies beside me, barely flapping his wings.

"Don't look back, you're doing fine." Jake runs sideways, watching me and still moving faster than I am. I'm jealous. He glances past me and his forehead creases. That makes me nervous and I can't resist looking back. I gasp.

Like a spider darting forward, the claw spurts over the grassland, scattering the grazing animals. Hoofbeats and snorts fill the air, leaving a dust trail several feet off the ground.

I run harder.

"Don't look, Sam," yells Jake. "We're pulling away from it."

"Really?" I huff.

"Yes."

"You're not saying that just to make me feel better, are you?" I imagine the monster swooping down at my back.

"I'm not lying to you."

"Cross your heart and hope to die?"

"Totally. We're ahead of it now."

If that's true it should be safe to sneak a peek again. He wasn't lying. I'm farther ahead of the claw, which remains high in the sky. Maybe it is just tracking us.

"Not much farther," Jake calls back. "You're doing great. Way, way ahead of the thing."

"Whoopee."

"Don't stop, Sam." Charlie is flying circles around me. "Pretend your life depends on it."

"Thanks, Charlie."

I can't help it, and look back. My foot stubs a clump of grass and I tumble. Twisting, I land hard on my side and grunt, grass and dirt in my mouth. Pushing to my knees, spitting out grass, I glance up.

Magnar's creature soars closer, erasing all doubt. The monster was just waiting for the best time to attack.

Using WhipEye, I pull myself to my feet and stagger forward.

As the claw draws nearer, the eerie figures push out from inside, stretching the surface outline of the ebony fingers. It's as if they're half-dead prisoners of the monster. The thought of ending up like that makes me cringe.

"Move faster." Jake waves me on like a running coach.

"Charlie," I gasp. "Fly ahead to Jake."

"No way." He circles me. "I like the view from here."

Jake sprints toward me, his strong legs fluid. "Don't look!"

I don't, but I'm jittery over who will grab me first. Stumbling ahead, I extend my arm toward Jake, the hairs on the back of my neck on end.

His hand finds mine, his feet skidding to a stop as he changes direction. Then he's dragging me along. Charlie flies beside us.

"I told you not to look," he grumbles.

Gulping air, I say, "Hey, you try not looking at a monster spider chasing you." Guilt fills me for not encouraging him to go on without me, but I don't want to die alone.

It's all I can do to keep my balance as I wait for Magnar's monster to pluck us off the ground. When it doesn't happen right away, I look back and gasp.

The fingers are floating twenty feet off the grass, arched like a monster tarantula ready to pounce. Pulsing. Black. Gross. I want to scream.

An explosion of flaps and feathers erupts from the grass in front of us.

Jake lets go of me and we both shout, raising our arms protectively. Wind buffets our bodies as a collection of wings and white-ringed eyes rise around us. Hundreds of Congo African gray parrots noisily circle us, squawking loudly.

Stunned, I slow down, but Jake says, "They're helping us, Sam. Run."

The cloud of flapping parrots keeps pace with us as we flee, forming an expanding circle. Magnar's claw strikes down into the band of birds, the throbbing black skin a few yards from me, blocking the horizon.

The monster's pointy fingers close on the parrots. Feathers fall from wings amidst terrified squawks. The ebony claw drifts up a short distance and opens. Empty. It darts forward again, this time a little farther away from us, following the widening circle of parrots.

I pause. "Charlie." He lands on my shoulder, and I grab and cradle him against my body, hiding him.

Squawks fill the air. I want to cover my ears as I chase Jake. I'm aware of the birds slowly leading the monster away from us, flying south. Abandoning the parrots to Magnar's beast wrenches my stomach.

We draw farther and farther away from the ravenous claw until the parrot calls fade in the distance.

By the time we cross the grassland, Magnar's creature has shrunk to a black dot near the horizon. It quickly disappears. We stop near the edge of the forest, and I put Charlie on my shoulder again. Then I slump against WhipEye.

"That was a nightmare." The parrot moves back and forth. "Those birds could have been me."

My chest feels hollow as I stare south. "They'll all be killed."

"And then that thing will hunt us again." Jake's eyes are dull.

I take out my inhaler for another puff. My watch reads six-thirty p.m. Only four hours since I helped Charlie escape from the pet store. It feels like a lifetime.

"Why were all those African gray parrots here?" Jake sweeps a hand. "Where'd they come from?"

I want to change the subject, and ask, "Why were the Originals kicked out of KiraKu, Charlie?"

"The first humans." The parrot sounds tired as he speaks. "Rose said Originals lived with Great Ones long ago in the First Time. Rose and Magnar were enhanced Originals."

"What happened?"

"When some Originals showed interest in technology, the Great Ones feared it would change KiraKu, so they separated KiraKu from your world and kicked out all the Originals. Not all the Great Ones agreed with this, and many decided to go with them. Originals formed many of the early societies and cultures of your human history."

"Is that why Tom's able to see Magnar's shadow monsters?" I ask.

"Originals and Great Ones don't need my feathers to see shadow methuselahs."

"Why did Tom want to come back here?" Jake takes off his glasses, using his shirt to clean them. "He must need something from KiraKu."

I recall the three canteens Tom carried. "He was after KiraKu's water."

"So Tom used us." Jake flaps an impatient hand. "How do we get home, Charlie?"

The parrot flutters to a low tree branch, the glow around his body extending an inch from his feathers now. "Sam's the expert."

I'm instantly gritting my teeth. "What are you talking about?"

Jake points at me. "Rose said you're the master of WhipEye."

"Yeah. I studied it for years in WhipEye School." His eyes narrow, and I roll mine. "I've only had it a few hours and it didn't come with instructions."

"Great. So we'll walk west until Magnar's claw catches us or we die." His face turns sour. "I want to go home."

"Give it a try, kid."

Sighing, I swish WhipEye back and forth, while imagining home, then thump it. An echo flows into the distance and the grass in front of me sways first one way, then the other.

A few animals lift their heads, then continue to graze.

Lame. Worse, I bend over, more tired than before. WhipEye drains my energy every time I use it, but the desire to hold the staff increases. I'm becoming its slave.

Jake's eyebrows hunch. "Let me try." Without waiting, he steps closer and yanks it from me.

Annoyed, I waver, unsteady on my feet.

Moving the staff as if he's stirring soup, he says, "I want to go home. I want to go home." He thumps it hard into the ground, sending an echo across the grassland.

Grass swirls across the meadow. Impalas to the south raise their heads and some giraffes walk farther away. A few warthogs grunt and scamper a short distance.

It surprises me Jake can use WhipEye alone. He must have bonded to it when he helped me use it against the buffalo shadow, as I did when I helped Rose. That grates on me, but I control the impulse to grab it from him.

He hangs his head.

"It tires you when you use it," I say.

"Super." He throws it down and whirls on me, poking my shoulder for every sentence he utters. "It's your fault. If you hadn't stolen Charlie, none of this would have happened. Rose would be alive. We'd be home."

Magnar's accusation, blaming me for Rose's death, echoes inside. "No one twisted your arm. You wanted to be part of this. You said everything was so cool."

His hands fly in rapid-fire gestures. "I didn't think anyone would die, and you never told me we'd be chased by monsters."

"I didn't expect that, either." I force the next word. "Sorry."

He sits hard, knees up, burying his head in his crossed arms. "What if we never get home?"

"We will." I stare at WhipEye as if I'm drowning and it's my life raft. "Look, it's okay, we'll—"

"It's not okay." He lifts his head and glares at me. I don't have an answer and he turns to Charlie. "You must have watched Rose use the staff."

The parrot shakes his wings. "I've been Magnar's prisoner all my life, Jake. The few times I saw Rose didn't involve WhipEye class."

Jake grimaces. "We need to find a Great One that will help us."

"A rule breaker." Trying to act nonchalant, I pick up the staff, my fingers curling tightly around the wood. I'm almost giddy that it's in my hand again.

Jake stands, eyeing WhipEye, his fingers opening and closing. "I should carry it. I can figure out how to use it."

"No," I say hoarsely. "Rose gave it to me." For a moment it looks like he might take it from me. I form a loose fist with my other hand, though I wouldn't have a chance of stopping him.

He pivots and stalks ahead. "And if we ever get home, I'm done, Charlie. I'm . . . I'm sorry you're going to die tomorrow, but I'm through with this crazy journey."

I check my compass and yell after him, "You're not heading west."

He waves dismissively and keeps going.

I hurry after him, another thought occurring to me. What if Dad goes to Rose's cabin to look for me, and runs into Magnar? Magnar said he'd make us pay. If he hurts Dad, I'll never forgive myself.

Charlie flutters to my shoulder. "Listen to your inner compass, Sam. Your gut. Intuition. Sometimes when we lose confidence, we have to look inside to get it back."

I hardly hear the parrot. What choice have I had since the beginning? Charlie intended I steal him from Magnar and take him to Rose's cabin, knowing all along how dangerous it would be. He and Rose probably planned it together. Jake has a right to be angry.

A big cat roars from somewhere on the plain, and the sun's lower in the sky.

FOURTEEN

Great Ones

AN HOUR LATER, near dusk, we stumble out of the jungle into a swath of tall grass bordering a wide river. The air smells sweeter here, and animals graze on the far side of the water.

"Kudu," I say tiredly, pointing across the river.

Jake ignores me.

In the middle of the slow moving river, crocodiles and harbor seals sun themselves on opposite ends of a long sandbar. Galapagos penguins waddle among the seals. Bullfrogs croak, soft-shell turtles rest on stones, and terns peck for food along the shoreline. Crayfish burrows dot the muck. If we weren't running for our lives, I'd love to sit and watch animals.

I haven't traded a single word with Jake over the last hour. Maybe quitting the journey means he's also ending our friendship. I even miss his weird hand movements, taps, pokes, and flicks.

The idea of losing Charlie *and* Jake sinks my thoughts into dark places.

We have a clear view south along the river. A dark spot floats in the sky near the horizon.

"Dang." I stare at it, trying to estimate how fast Magnar's claw is moving. "It's about three miles away."

Jake motions north. "Let's follow the river."

I'm glad he's finally talking. Even so, my throat thickens. Magnar's creature detected Charlie's location again, which means it captured the other parrots.

Facing the river, I imagine jagged teeth ripping flesh. "The compass needle is pointing west, across the river." Scarier, my gut is telling me to follow it.

Jake comes close to me, squinting at the compass. "So what? It's broken."

"It did this on the way to Rose's cabin and after we stopped the buffalo shadow. It's telling us we need to cross here."

He stares at the needle and rolls his eyes. "So a broken compass is deciding what direction we should take?"

"My gut says it's the right direction." I'm exhausted. Just saying those words is overwhelming. I walk through the grass toward the river, grasshoppers flying from my path.

"It's safer to go north." Jake trails behind me.

We both stop where the tall grass ends. A hundred feet of stinky mud leads to an old stump a dozen feet tall. Beyond the stump, ten more feet of goo leads to the water.

Sunlight glints off Jake's blond hair. He flicks a hand out. "Why do you get to decide what happens? Who made you boss?"

"You did. You said you didn't want to be part of the journey anymore, so you're free to do whatever you want." I ignore his hurt look and walk out of the grass a few steps to eye the water.

The mud sucks at my tennis shoes, which sink several inches. I hope I don't lose them.

Remaining in the grass, Jake walks a few steps north and sweeps a hand in front of him. "What's so important about crossing here?"

Charlie stretches his wings. "When Sam discovers how to use the staff, we want to be as close to home as possible."

"Thanks for reminding me," I say.

"Are you blind?" says Jake. "Look at those monsters."

I avoid his eyes. "They're just trying to earn a living."

Some of the crocs are twenty feet long. The record in our world is close to twenty-two, measured from sand impressions on an African beach. But even five feet would be too long if I have to swim near them. "Crocs are territorial. They'll attack even when they aren't hungry."

"Well then, genius, how are we going to get across? What if west isn't the same here? You have no idea where you're going."

"Stop talking like Laurel and Hardy, kids." When we look at Charlie with blank stares, he says, "You know, the comedians." He cocks his head. "Listen."

Glad for the diversion from Jake, I watch Charlie crane his neck. Except for the flowing water and a few birdcalls, it's quiet. "What do you hear, Charlie?"

"Wait here." The parrot flies to the stump and perches there. He bends his neck again, but no animals are visible on the mud or in the water near shore.

I half expect a beast to spring up from the goo. We don't know anything about this world, nor what all the Great Ones look like. Those carved into the staff appear normal, but others might not be.

I call softly, "What is it, Charlie?"

The water near the shore erupts in a wild spray as a gigantic shape lunges out of it.

"Charlie!" My grip tightens on WhipEye.

The parrot flutters away just before wide jaws close around the stump.

With one jerk of its head, the saltwater crocodile rips the stump out of the ground, thick roots and all, and tosses it to the side where it bangs and rolls.

Charlie wheels in the air and lands thirty feet beyond the crocodile's snout.

I tense, ready to bolt. Jake's rigid beside me.

The beast opens its mouth and bellows.

Everything in me screams *Run!*, but I can't because Charlie isn't flying away. When the monster's green eyes shift to bright gold, I understand why. A Great One.

From the gray bumpy projections on its back to the yellowish scales of its belly, everything about this croc is oversized. Especially the dagger-sized teeth pushing out of its mouth. The beast looks fifty feet long and must weigh ten tons. Big enough to devour us whole.

Charlie stares down the croc. "Throwing a temper tantrum won't help."

The Great One gives a throaty growl. "You gave the humans your feathers and Rose gave them WhipEye. Along with KiraKu's energy, the girl and boy have power here. They change things. They have no right. Rose should never have allowed humans into KiraKu."

I cringe in the face of his fury. He has to be the Great One the iguana warned us about. The eldest.

As if unconcerned over the monster's anger, the parrot lifts a foot from the muck, shaking it. "Rosey said Great Ones would help us."

"Rose saved our lives," I say.

Jake cuts the air with a hand. "It's not our fault we're here."

The massive crocodile lowers his head, his eyes boring into mine. "Surrender your feathers and WhipEye." His words project enough power that it seems like he could chew his way through the jungle.

Loudly, with some of my own anger, I say, "Forget it. The staff is our only chance to return home and we need Charlie's feathers to see Magnar's shadow monsters."

"You put penguins and seals on the river," snaps the crocodile. "Humans ruin everything. You upset the balance with your desires. Always wanting something different. The Originals did this and were sent away. Human desires won't be allowed again in KiraKu."

He lumbers forward several steps. "Leave. Now."

"We would, but we don't know how," I say.

"Help us," says Jake. "We want to leave."

Charlie doesn't move. "These kids are the best chance we have to defeat Magnar, you big piece of leather. And Magnar's your responsibility. You gave him power, so quit complaining and help. If you want us gone, show us the way."

The crocodile hisses. "I'll never leave KiraKu to help humans in their world."

The parrot cackles like a ringing telephone. "Hello. Your face is on WhipEye, you big lunk."

With narrowed eyes, the croc says, "Long ago, when Rose could be trusted, I pledged to answer WhipEye's call. But when she broke our rules, I ended my loyalty to the staff and forbade all Great Ones from answering it."

Charlie tilts his head. "Then we need time. How about until dark?"

Lowering his head, the crocodile gives a low grumble.

Maybe I could trap the monster in the grass with WhipEye, but this Great One is more powerful than the iguana. Besides, I'm so tired I'm not sure I can use the staff again.

Hissing, the crocodile thrashes his tail in the water, splashing the beach. A deep-throated growl tumbles from his mouth as he rushes forward.

I stumble back, the goo tugging at my feet, and catch Jake's shoulder to keep my balance. Charlie takes off and flies toward us. Too tired to outrun the charging monster, I stop, bracing myself with the staff.

Ending his charge in a spray of mud a few feet from us, the crocodile's raised snout is level with our heads, his belly high enough to crawl under. White teeth glint like swords in a jagged pattern around his lips.

Charlie flies up from behind and lands on my shoulder. His presence gives me courage.

"Give me your feathers and WhipEye," rumbles the croc.

"Just do it, Sam," I murmur, knowing I can't give up either.

"Don't give it to him, Sam," says Jake.

Slowly the crocodile opens his mouth, his eyes forming slits.

"Do you really want to be the first Great One to hurt a methuselah?" asks Charlie.

The golden eyes of the crocodile keep me in a trance, much like the cobra did. I struggle to fight it, but it's like trying to swim through the mud at our feet.

The crocodile takes another half step forward, the tip of his snout a foot from my head.

Sweat runs down my face. The mucky scent of the river covers the reptile and I'm close enough to grab one of his teeth. "Go, Charlie."

"Not a chance, kid."

"Give me WhipEye," whispers Jake.

The crocodile inches closer. It's crazy, but even with my life on the line, I don't want to part with the staff. I loosen my fingers on the wood and Jake takes it. In one smooth motion he rams the staff upward into the croc's lower jaw. I'm awed by his bravery, but shocked when golden light flashes down WhipEye to its end, nearly simultaneously running over the monster's head in jagged, crackling lines.

Jake gapes.

Giving a throaty roar, the croc jerks his head away from us.

I shuffle back. Jake's eyes look bleary from his effort, and I seize his elbow and pull him with me.

A hiss comes from behind us. Crap. The cat must be working with the croc.

Before I can look, a large shape sails over me at an angle, blocking the sky. I gasp and jerk up my arm for protection.

But the massive feline lands to the side of the croc. The black markings on its face are recognizable. It *is* the caracal Rose called. Relief sweeps through me. It must have tracked us to ensure we remained safe.

The crocodile twists to face the cat, his rear claw sweeping toward us.

I clumsily yank Jake out of the way of the crocodile's thrashing tail. Off balance, we fall. Charlie floats to the ground.

"Umph." Jake drops the staff and rolls in the grass.

I quickly grab WhipEye and wearily push to my feet, covered with reeking muck. Jake gets up, eyeing the staff and shaking his head at me.

The caracal crouches and springs over the crocodile's snapping jaws, landing past the reptile's tail.

My stomach clenches when I recall the caracal's fight with the buffalo shadow. I don't want it hurt again.

The crocodile runs forward in a half circle on the mud. Twisting until he's completely around, he faces the caracal again, poised a foot above the goo. His mouth opens slightly and his eyes narrow.

The cat keeps its head lowered and stares back. As fast as the cat is, I fear the crocodile will catch it.

Charging again, the croc runs hard.

The caracal responds by sprinting at the monster. However, this time when the cat leaps, the croc stops and lifts his head vertical, his front legs stiff.

"No," I murmur.

Jake whispers, "Higher."

The croc's teeth snap shut, like spikes pounding into metal, but just miss the caracal's feet. The cat lands and pivots.

Whirling around much faster this time, in a one-eighty-degree spin no reptile in our world is capable of, the crocodile glares at the cat. The caracal bares its fangs.

I get it. Instead of actually fighting, they're testing each other's resolve, like wild animals often do in our world. I'm not sure who'll back down. They hiss and growl at each other for several moments, not moving. Then they grow quiet.

The reptile tilts his head at us, his voice grating like churning gravel. "Healing water heals everything, but it will destroy Magnar's shadow monsters. You have two hours." He crawls toward the water.

Silently, I cheer for the cat. Finally, a Great One willing to help us.

From the ground, Charlie gives a sharp whistle. "Hey, leather face. What happens then?"

I bend and lift the bird to my shoulder, grateful for his courage but wishing he wouldn't taunt the croc.

At the river's edge the crocodile opens his jaws, closing them with a loud snap. "What's born of the land will return to it." He digs deep gouges in the mud as he pushes himself into the river, water bubbling around him as he sinks.

A hiss snaps my attention away from the disappearing crocodile.

The cat's head is lowered—the towering feline is stalking me. Its paws are wide as my torso. My hand goes to my compass.

"Where's Rose?" The caracal is female and sounds angry.

I wince. "Magnar killed her."

The caracal throws back her head and howls, leaving my ears ringing. She continues approaching. "How did you get WhipEye, girl?"

"Rosey gave her the staff." Charlie sounds annoyed.

The caracal hisses. "What gives you the right to wield WhipEye?"

I don't have an answer and I'm glad when Charlie keeps talking.

"Are you deaf, big ears? Rose chose her. So be a nice kitty and either help us leave KiraKu or run along."

Ignoring Charlie, the caracal steps forward. "Speak, girl. You called me earlier and you're not a guardian."

"Rose said to find a Great One," says Jake. "And so far none of you have been great."

"We needed help to fight Magnar," I say quickly. "Thanks for helping with the croc."

Growling, the caracal takes measured steps toward me, her mouth open, revealing four large white canines. Sunlight glints off her reddish hair, her tail tucked as the wind blows her ear tuffs.

Words tumble from my mouth with ferocity. "I didn't ask for any of this. I just wanted Charlie to be free. I want every animal free to live its life." My face is hot and sweat runs down my back.

The caracal pauses a few feet in front of me, her warm breath caressing my face. "You speak from the heart, girl. Most elders of your world have lost theirs and are blind to the pain they inflict on others."

A great pride and sadness fills me. "Dad always helps animals and so did Mom." I fight back tears.

The caracal hisses softly. "So your parents taught you well. The strong must take care of the weak." She leans closer. "But that's not enough. Whoever holds WhipEye must pledge to protect methuselahs."

I'm silent, unsure I can do it. But when I think of Rose and Charlie, there's no choice.

Straightening, I meet the cat's eyes. "My name is Samantha Green, daughter of Bryon Green and Faith Sommers, and I promise to do my best to save Charlie and defeat Magnar."

For the first time in a year, I said Mom's name around others. It gives me strength. By using it, I also know I'll never be able break this pledge, no matter what happens.

Looking satisfied, the caracal raises her head. "You've spoken your given name, so I'll give you my true name. If you strike the ground once with WhipEye, Samantha Green, and call Tarath, I must and will come."

I'm awed the Great One trusts me. "Thank you, Tarath."

"The crocodile said no Great Ones are allowed to come to our world," says Jake.

The cat hisses sharply, her eyes narrowing. "The crocodile doesn't rule this Great One." She lowers her head to within inches of my face. "Remember, never show your true strength until it matters." I wait for her to say more, but she gazes at Charlie. "It's an honor to meet a methuselah."

"A friendly Great One's not bad, either."

Tarath glances at Jake's tattoos. "Nice markings."

He shrugs. "Thanks."

I purse my lips. "Can you take us home?"

"Rose mastered the staff, not Great Ones. If you can't solve WhipEye, you'll fail anyway." Softly, she says to Jake, "The girl needs you."

She rears back and leaps over us to the grass beyond, leisurely walking south, gradually shrinking until she's a medium-sized cat.

My chest heaves, but I'm comforted when Jake rests a hand on my shoulder.

"You're no longer a girl, Sam." Charlie shakes himself. "Your parents would be proud."

I sit down, the crocodile's accusations inside my head. Mom wouldn't be proud of what I've done.

FIFTEEN

Crocodiles

I STUDY MY COMPASS.

Jake's muddy black tennis shoes are in front of me, but I don't look up.

"So why did the croc blame us for changing things here?" he asks.

Charlie clucks. "With KiraKu's energy, WhipEye, and my feathers, your desires become real here. You're able to move animals around just by focusing on them."

"Really?" Jake looks at the river.

My voice is dull. "When we first entered KiraKu, I wanted to see kangaroos, and later we did. I also wanted a flock of Congo African gray parrots to confuse Magnar's claw." I whisper, "I wanted to save you, Charlie. I couldn't bear to lose you, so I sent those parrots to their death."

"Who knew your wishes could change things here, kid? I didn't. Besides, the parrots helped willingly. They sensed your need and they had a choice."

That doesn't make me feel any better. "The crocodile is right. We don't belong here."

"There's a reason for coming here," says Charlie. "There's always a reason. Or at least there's a bright side. You learned how to use the staff and Tarath is behind you now."

I must look glum, because Charlie whistles sharply. "The parrots gave us a chance, Sam. If Magnar wins, their deaths are meaningless. Magnar is the other reason Toothy wants you gone. The croc figures if you leave, Magnar's monster will too. Trouble is, Magnar wants it all, so he'll be back no matter what."

Jake motions to the river. "I put the Galapagos penguins and harbor seals out there. I wanted to see them."

His face scrunches, but it doesn't strike me as dorky now, just worried. And he knows more about wildlife than I thought.

"We have no idea what else this place is doing to us. The air . . ." He wipes mud off an arm, smearing it. "You have to remember how to use the staff, Sam."

I glare at him. "How many times do I have to say it? Rose never showed me how to use it."

"I hate to break up the excitement, kids."

I follow the parrot's gaze to the south. Magnar's claw is floating two miles from us, ahead of black clouds.

Jake swings his hand half-heartedly out from his leg. "Call Tarath."

I shake my head. "No." He turns away, his jaw stiff, but I don't care. "No more animals are going to die because of me."

I also have no idea what it will take for other Great Ones on the staff to answer my call. Tarath should have explained it to me. Everyone has kept things from me ever since I stole Charlie, and I'm sick of it.

Jake lifts a hand. "I'm not swimming across the river with that monster in the water and crocodiles waiting for us."

I can't blame him. I don't want to, either.

Chatter drifts to us from near the shore. Large, multicolored shapes in white, black, and gray arc through the current.

"Pacific white-sided dolphins," I murmur. "They're beautiful."

"Who did that, kiddos?"

Jake pokes my shoulder. "It wasn't me."

I don't meet his eyes. "Before . . . I thought dolphins might be nice to carry us across. I . . . I love dolphins. I've always dreamed of riding one."

Jake jabs a finger at the river. "Why couldn't you pick something big?" He screws his eyes shut, then opens them. "No elephants."

Charlie clicks. "I'm guessing it's more from your heart than your head, kid."

"Great," mumbles Jake, throwing up his hands.

I trudge toward the water. Mud tugs at my shoes, smelling of earthworms and decayed plants.

Jake trails behind, his feet squishing on every step. "This is gross."

"It's nature." I scan the shoreline as I near the river, but the Great One doesn't reappear. "Hey, that was cool when you hit the croc."

Jake's eyes brighten. "Yeah, who knew WhipEye could do that."

The dolphins swim toward shore. One eyes me, then floats closer. Images of teeth slicing flesh fill my head and I almost stop, but another quick glance shows the crocs haven't moved.

"Careful," says Jake. "It might not be safe."

"Dolphins would know if it wasn't." At least I hope so. Squinting against my fear, I wade out, my feet sinking into the river bottom. I try to concentrate on the eight-foot cetaceans. As I walk deeper my arms float, but I don't smell salt in the water. Whatever is causing the buoyancy will make it easier for the dolphins to carry us.

Squatting at the shoreline, Jake scoops water, lifting his hand to his lips.

"I wouldn't," I say. "It might have parasites." I'm thirsty too, but Dad taught me safety in the woods.

"It looks clean."

"You can't see microscopic eggs and bugs."

"Yuck." Sounding disappointed, he empties his palm into the river.

I slide a sopping leg over the dolphin's back. Gripping the dorsal fin with my free hand, I lift WhipEye out of the water with my other. My soaked jeans cling to my legs.

The smooth skin of the dolphin ripples beneath me as the animal pushes a short distance from shore. Warm water splashes over my thighs, taking off some of the mud, and the marshy scent of the river fills the air. Despite my fear of the crocs, excitement runs through me. The dolphins' chatter sounds eager.

When I look, Jake is standing on the shore, staring at the dolphin floating in front of him.

"You can do it," I call.

"No, I can't."

"The dolphins will keep us safe." I try to sound encouraging. Crocodiles and dolphins usually don't swim in the same areas in our world, but dolphins attack sharks.

"I'm not a good swimmer." Jake waves at the river. "Water scares me, all right?"

"Why didn't you tell me?"

He shrugs.

I'm a great swimmer, and I'm amazed I'm better than him at something. "Trust your neighborhood dolphin."

"Easy for you to say." He wrings his hands, then hurriedly splashes out and mounts the dolphin, his eyes wide as he grasps the dorsal fin.

"Hey!" A tall figure runs from the jungle to the water. Tom's white T-shirt and jeans are torn, his muddy feet bare, his spiked red hair messy. But his eyes shine.

The young man quickly removes the stoppers on his canteens, crouches, and extends one hand—as if he's afraid of what's in the river, plunging all three containers under the water. "Take me with you, Samantha, please."

Jake dismisses him with a gesture. "Leave him. I don't trust him."

A few dolphins click signals, slowly swimming near shore, but eyeing me. I have the power to leave Tom here, but I don't want it. However, I don't trust him, either.

"Sorry for pushing Jake." Tom raises a tired hand. "Afraid what might come through the cabin door. Didn't want him hurt."

It sounds plausible, but I don't believe that's the whole story. I think he wanted to be first through the door if it opened.

Jake glares at him.

Tom lifts the full canteens and stoppers them. "Water's for someone dying." He plunges a cupped hand under the surface, brings it out, and drinks from it.

I lick my dry lips. But his body might be able to handle things in the water we can't. "Where have you been?"

Tom stands, his arms hanging with the canteens. His face sours as he lowers his head, and I hear sadness in his words. "Great Ones despise Originals. Would have been a burden, not an asset. Wanted to see if they'd help you."

Jake looks away. "I *still* don't trust him."

I study Tom, uncertain.

He lifts his head, his face drawn. "If I stay, my friend dies. I die."

His words make it an easy decision. I don't want responsibility for any more deaths. "All right, join the party."

Jake doesn't look happy, but I eye a nearby dolphin, one of the largest, and point to shore. I'm not surprised when the cetacean swims closer to Tom, stopping in front of him.

"Closer," says Tom. "Can't it come closer?"

"We have to go, Sam." Jake stares at me. "We're losing light."

Tom paces back and forth along the water's edge, his face taut. Extending one foot out over the lapping waves, he takes it back, giving an agonized cry. "What if the Great One is here, waiting?" His fists press the canteen straps to his chest.

Jake thumbs at the crocodiles on the sandbar. "Now, Sam."

I motion to Tom. "Close your eyes and walk out. You'll be fine." It bothers me that Originals fear Great Ones. After all, according to Charlie, Originals were some of our ancestors.

Looping the canteen straps over his head, Tom walks stiff-legged into the water, his eyes closed. His cheeks puff out as if he's holding his breath.

When he bumps into the dolphin, his eyes snap open and he hurriedly climbs atop it. Somehow he manages to stand barefoot, perfectly balanced, as if remaining upright on a slippery dolphin back is as easy as standing on dry land. But his face pales as he eyes the water.

My dolphin swims out into the river, chuffing through its blowhole.

The last of the sunlight sparkles on the water and warm air massages my face. On the sandbar, the big reptiles eye us without moving. I'm beginning to think we'll make it.

Several dolphins swim beside mine, their sleek bodies slicing effortlessly through the river. Their white striping and black beaks give them a bright appearance. Three escorts playfully leap out of the water. The river cools my legs, calming me, and the sweet scent is stronger here, as if coming from the water itself.

The crocodiles don't move.

Heaving a breath, my arms relax. Jake gives a small wave, his face drawn, while Tom stands clutching the canteens, his shoulders hunched.

When we're a third of the way across, crocodiles on the sandbar run and slide into the water. All of them.

I flinch and try not to picture my legs trailing below the surface as crocs swim toward us, their tails working hard.

"Faster." Tom eyes the water, inching his feet back and forth along the dolphin's back.

I pat my dolphin gently. "You can beat them." But the crocodiles gain on us. Our friends can't outrace the reptiles while carrying us.

"Hurry up." Jake tries to lift his legs out of the water. "They're going to catch us."

"Swim harder," I urge, stroking the cetacean. But the water doesn't move by any faster.

Tom wails.

Dolphins peel off from the pod, ramming the crocodiles' torsos with their snouts. Crocs thrash their tails wildly in response.

Some crocodiles submerge. Squeaking dolphins dive after them. Water churns below the surface as more dolphins dive.

Dolphins repeatedly ram crocodiles on the surface. Some reptiles keep coming, but after continued butting they all retreat. I look into the water near my legs, imagining a gaping mouth rising from below.

Glancing back, I cry, "Keep your legs up." The idea of losing Jake sickens me. I'd never be able to live with it, especially since I insisted on crossing here.

"I'm trying." He leans back, lifting both of his legs inches above the surface.

I've watched videos of crocs rising six feet out of the water when fed from river tour boats, their tails keeping them impossibly vertical. *No, please, no.*

Tom peers into the water, his lips clenched.

One crocodile surfaces nearby, leaving a small wake as it surges toward my leg. I try to lift my foot out of the water, but I don't have the leverage or strength to do it.

Jake shouts, "Sam!"

"Incoming, kid."

I lift WhipEye with both hands. When the croc is three feet away, I slam the staff into the tip of the reptile's upper gums, where they're most sensitive. A faint line of gold outlines the croc's skull, but the reptile opens its mouth anyway.

When the beast reaches for my leg, I jerk my limb forward. A gray shape slams into the croc from the side, but the reptile's teeth rake along my calf. I shriek.

Another dolphin hits the reptile from the other side, and my dolphin swims past the croc.

Slumping on the cetacean, I barely hang on. My head starts to spin from the burning in my leg and I close my eyes.

"Wake up, Sam." Jake's voice is far away. "Sam!"

A stab of pain on my cheek stirs me, but I'm exhausted and don't move.

Another sharp prick hits my neck.

"Okay," I mumble.

A third peck hits my jaw.

"Ouch. Stop already." I sit up, woozy. My lungs heave and I wipe sweat from my face.

"You're welcome, kid. How's your leg?"

"Are you all right, Sam?" Jake calls.

My jeans are torn near the calf. I can't see the skin, but my leg aches horribly. A red tint in the water trails from my limb. "I'm fine," I lie. I hope I can walk on it.

In minutes, large crocodiles float to the surface a short distance away, their eyes above the water. Smaller crocs swim back to the sandbar, but I'm not sure we're safe yet.

"What happened to the dolphins?" asks Jake.

Bleak images flood my mind. Dolphin deaths can't be added to those of the parrots.

Shadowy figures approach from below, near my leg. A fearful shout is stuck in my throat until curved dorsal fins slice the surface.

I lift the staff a foot. "Yeah." I say it tiredly, but mean it.

"That will make it easier to sleep tonight, kid."

"All right!" yells Jake. "Woohoo!"

Tom remains quiet, watching the water.

While we complete the crossing, no threats appear. I struggle to hang on, fatigue making me drowsy.

When we reach shallow water, Charlie flies from my shoulder. Jake and I slip off our dolphins, images of lunging, toothy jaws driving our legs.

But I fall immediately, my right leg burning fiercely.

"Jake." Water splashes over my chin as my hand sinks into mud.

Jake grabs my arm and puts it over his shoulders. We stumble on, water splashing our waists and mud sucking at our feet. Several times my feet sink into the river bottom and I teeter, but Jake keeps me upright.

Something splashes ahead of us in a foot of water, bringing us to a halt. It's Tom. He jumped over us, and with one more leap he covers thirty feet to the top of the short riverbank.

"Safe!" He jumps up, his arms spread wide. "Safe." He jumps in a complete circle and then kneels to kiss the soil.

We scramble ashore, pulling ourselves up the bank by grasping clumps of grass. It's painful, but I don't relax until I'm lying on my back on dry land, exhausted and gasping. Charlie lands nearby.

After a few minutes, when I catch my breath, I sit up. Cautiously, I peel back my ripped jeans, expecting deep, bloody cuts. I'm stunned when I see jagged white lines on my skin, indicating teeth marks. Maybe the croc never punctured the skin, but I remember the pink water. I gently press a finger against the leg. It's very sore.

"Are you all right, Sam?" Jake sits up, his eyes worried.

"Yeah, I am."

The dolphins that carried the three of us chatter calmly, swimming along the shoreline. Herds of wildebeest and zebras farther west show little interest over our arrival.

Charlie hops on my good leg. "That went well."

"Easy for you to say," I reply.

"We did it!" Jake raises both hands. "We rode dolphins!"

I grin foolishly. It's getting easier to smile. "By the way, did you know every zebra has a unique striping pattern and they sleep standing up?"

Jake wraps his strong arms around me, his chin on my shoulder. At first it's awkward, but then I hug him back. I view him differently then, as a friend, an ally, and someone I can trust. Yet he's deserting the journey and that hurts.

Lifting a fist into the air, Tom shouts, "Yes!"

Jake ignores him, but I grin back and give him a thumbs up. Hope sweeps through me. Hope that I can return home, stop Magnar, save Charlie, and talk to Dad. Have a real family again.

Sending a few clicks, the three dolphins that carried us swim away, joining the rest of the pod as they move downstream in the waning light.

"Thank you." Tom swirls his hands above his head at the dolphins. "Thank you."

Jake smiles. "Dolphins a.k.a. crocodile beaters."

I beam at him.

When he stands, my mouth drops. "Wow. Your legs."

"What?" All the scratches and cuts from fighting through the jungle are gone, his skin smooth and unblemished. He pats his legs gingerly, murmuring, "The river."

I look at my leg wound again, the truth dawning on me. "It has to be the healing water the croc talked about."

I rest, while Jake walks to the water's edge on sopping but clean black shoes, kneeling to flip more water onto his arms. His remaining cuts close, then fade away. He takes off his glasses and splashes water on his face and neck with the same results. The tattoos on his forearms even fade a little. "You have to try it, Sam."

I'm nervous about standing on my leg, but say, "Why not?"

I lift Charlie to my shoulder and slowly get up, testing my weight on the injured limb. It hurts, but not as much as I expected. I limp back down the bank to the river. Unwilling to release WhipEye, I use one hand to rub water on scratches covering my arms and face. The cuts heal. I trade smiles with Jake.

He cups clear water in his palm and sips from it. His eyes shine. "It's great." He scoops up more.

I can't resist and follow his lead. Cool, sweet water runs down my throat and refreshes me. I take a few more drinks and my fatigue vanishes. My leg even feels better. And I have energy again. Lots of it. "Wow."

Jake's face lights up.

I wipe my mouth. "Would it help you, Charlie?"

"It won't extend my life, kid, but I'm thirsty, so give me some."

Disappointed, I cup water in a hand and bring it close to the parrot.

Between sips, Charlie bobs. "That's good stuff. If we could bottle it we'd make a fortune."

"The ultimate power drink," I say.

"We have to take some." Jake glances at Tom's canteens.

"No." Tom's lips clamp shut and he shakes his head. He clutches the canteens and steps back, his eyes flashing gold. "Lewella."

I wonder whose name he utters. If Tom's an Original, I really don't know anything about him.

"You better hurry, kids. This isn't a shopping trip."

Jake quickly tears big leaves from a nearby bush and forms a large cone, giving it to me to hold. Finding small vines, he wraps them around the curled leaves.

I'm impressed. "Clever."

He glances at me, his eyes bright. Squatting by the river, he dips the cone in, filling it with water. "At least we'll have a way to protect ourselves if we can't leave."

Unable to be upset with him, I say, "Always good to have a Plan B."

With a hint of a smile, he shakes his head.

Charlie trills like an alarm clock. "I hate to spoil the party, but it's time to quit the happy stuff."

I look across the river, my good humor vanishing. The ebony claw floats less than a hundred yards away.

SIXTEEN

Magnar's Claw

I'M NOT RUNNING ANYMORE." I'm scared even as I say it.

"Good choice." Charlie nudges my cheek.

Jake bites his lip. "The forest?"

"WhipEye will be strongest there," I say.

We hurriedly climb the bank. Tom's staring across the river at the claw, wide-eyed and stiff.

I motion to him. "We're leaving."

His arms relax slightly. "Good."

Pressing one hand over the cone of healing water and keeping it close to his stomach, Jake leads us in a sprint toward the jungle.

I focus on his smooth flying legs, my sopping shoes squishing on every step. My injured leg barely aches. This time Tom follows me, moving effortlessly, silently. Charlie flies nearby.

Deep shadows stretch from the trees ahead. We're losing light fast now.

Hippos, with yellow-billed oxpeckers sitting on their backs, slowly meander out of our way and nearby kudu watch us. The calm doesn't last.

An east wind billows my shirt as the grass around us bends over and the blackening sky races west. Water buffalo and other animals neigh and snort, then stampede away from the approaching darkness. When we near the jungle, I look back and stop.

"Impossible." Tom is staring up.

The giant claw stretches wider above us. As I watch, the six fingers split along the middle like tearing fabric, forming two disfigured bodies that reform into ghostly monsters. Both quickly grow to the size of the first, each with six pointy appendages, but faded as if stretched too thin.

One claw moves south of us, one north. Magnar doesn't intend to give us any chance of slipping away. I hustle after Jake.

When we enter the darkening jungle, animal calls erupt all around us. Parakeets and macaws screech and fly away, while colobus monkeys chatter and swing through the trees. A whipsnake slithers away on a branch. Every living thing flees the two claws above. Soon the only sounds in my ears are my heavy footfalls snapping brush.

The monsters fly over us, meeting above the canopy to the west.

In a small patch of ferns among the trees, Jake stops and I quickly join him. Black clouds create walls behind and to the sides of us, stretching from the sky to the ground.

"What now?" Tom backs up beside me, his eyes wild with the same fright he had on the river.

"Time to see what WhipEye can do." My grip hardens on it. "We're fighting."

"What?" Tom's eyes grow round. "Crazy. Can't win."

"We have to try."

"No no no." He stares all around, looking ready to bolt.

"If you run into the black fog, I don't think you'll escape Magnar."

"Lewella," he murmurs.

Ahead, the shadow claws descend through the canopy, tearing through trees, sending smaller trunks and branches crashing to the jungle floor. It allows more light to reach us from the setting sun.

"Sam." Jake grasps the cone of water with one hand, cocking his arm.

Facing the monsters, I step forward and swirl WhipEye in a crisscross pattern, weaving it back and forth in front of my legs, visualizing what I want. My body feels strong and energy is building inside me as the river's healing water works its magic.

Raising the staff, I slam it into the ground.

Boom!

The strong echo carries into the distance, and I feel tired, but not exhausted like previous times.

Branches and vines spring out of the undergrowth and from trees, wrapping around the two monsters plowing through the woods like giant scoops. This time even medium-sized trees bend over, their two-foot-thick trunks curling around the giant claws.

WhipEye's power is stronger than I expected, making me hopeful. Either the user's energy determines the staff's ability or else WhipEye matches the user's need. Possibly both. The largest trees don't budge, but I don't expect them to.

All around us pitch fog rolls along the ground, cutting off any retreat, and the sky is layered in black.

Two hundred feet from us, the two monsters rip through the jungle. Beneath their oily black skin different shapes rise, vaguely lifelike before they sink again. The number of animals that died to create these freaks tumbles my stomach.

More and more vegetation whips around the black claws, covering their surfaces in green and brown, finally slowing them. But they continue to churn toward us.

"Stop!" Tom rocks from one foot to the other.

Charlie clutches my shoulder tighter.

"Come on," I whisper.

Jake stands beside me, his hands fists.

Thirty yards away, the claws slow further. More plants wrap around their black surfaces, nearly hiding them.

They still creep along until six feet from us they shudder to a halt, encased in a thick cocoon of branches, vines, and small tree trunks. Branches strain when the monsters surge another inch.

Silence.

We wait, watching. The creatures don't move again. I'd love to believe the massive claws will be trapped here forever.

A few leaves tremble.

A small branch breaks.

Rustling.

The claws keep moving, inch by inch.

"No." Tom steps back.

Jake offers his cone of water to Tom, which he takes with questioning eyes.

Turning to me, Jake says, "Give me WhipEye, Sam."

Charlie bobs his head. "Do it, kid."

A strong desire inside me says *Don't*. But the smaller voice of reason says if the strength of the staff matches the strength of the bearer, we're better off with Jake holding it. Still, it's getting harder every time I part with it.

"Remember what it did to the croc." Jake extends his hand.

Hesitantly, I offer WhipEye and he grips it. Unable to release it right away, my fingers slowly slide off the chestnut wood.

Raising the staff with both hands, Jake looks ready to charge one of the claws. He pauses when a roar comes from the south.

Out of the black fog leaps Tarath, her eyes blazing. She barely touches the ground when she jumps again, landing close to us. Tom backs away, his face drawn, but Jake and I eagerly step forward.

Relief sweeps me. The caracal has come to fight Magnar's monster for us.

But Tarath steps closer to Jake. "I can make you stronger if you want my help."

He doesn't hesitate. "Heck, yeah. Load me up."

Tarath's eyes brighten until a stream of golden light shines from them, bathing Jake's entire body for a few seconds. When the light stops, the Great One sinks to the ground, panting.

"Now we're talking." Jake's eyes are bright as he lifts WhipEye. "This is a Plan B!"

My hopes rise, along with a hint of jealousy. Actually, more than a hint. I want that energy, and WhipEye in my hands.

Charlie bobs excitedly. "Go get it, kiddo."

One pointy finger of the claw bursts through its green prison. It's dark and blotchy, and I can see shapes writhing beneath its surface.

Jake strides forward, dwarfed by the monster, and stabs Whip-Eye into the exposed fingertip.

Golden energy crackles along the staff to its end, shooting over the entire surface of the finger in a web of lines. Both claws go rigid. After a pause, fine cracks appear where Jake struck the creature, running back along the finger's surface in a pattern like a spider web.

"Yeah." Jake slashes a hand.

I wait, my mouth dry.

Tom raises a hesitant fist.

But the cracks stop before the palm, as if out of energy.

There's a moment of silence, and then both claws continue to inch ahead.

I step forward. "Hit it again, Jake."

"Again," Tom pleads beside me.

Jake slumps against WhipEye and shakes his head. "I can't."

Whatever the caracal did for him, it was a one shot deal and he doesn't have anything left.

"Tarath!" I swing around, shocked to see she's gone.

Jake stumbles back to us, holding the staff out to me. I wonder if it's as hard for him to give it up as it is for me. Eagerly I wrap my fingers around the wood. For a moment I don't care about anything except that WhipEye's in my hand again.

"You have to remember, Sam." Jake retrieves the cone of water from Tom and watches the approaching claws. I doubt healing water will stop the monsters.

Charlie taps my cheek. "Rose must have shown you something, kid."

"She didn't. Haven't you been listening?"

The parrot eyes me. "Think back to every time you saw the staff, Sam. Rose was careful with everything she did."

"You don't know how to go home?" Tom looks aghast as he clutches the canteens. "Lewella," he whispers, swaying side to side.

My shoulders droop. Lewella. Another person I might fail.

"Hurry up." Jake flicks my shoulder.

"Quit hitting me, I can't concentrate." I close my eyes. For the hundredth time I replay in my mind everything Rose did when she called Tarath. I only saw her use the staff that once.

Once. No. Not quite true.

An image comes to me from far away, a vague recollection crystallizing in a flash in my mind. There was another time. In the park. Rose moved WhipEye in front of her legs, whispering . . .

"Do something," yells Jake.

"Anything," murmurs Tom.

"It's now or never, kid."

Crashing and shouts surround me as the claws move farther, shredding my nerves. But I keep my eyes closed and try to picture the pattern Rose traced in the park. Like a racecar track. A sideways figure eight.

I get it. The infinity symbol in math.

No limits.

My eyes snap open as roots tear from the soil and branches snap off trees. Four feet from us, the freaks are breaking free of the vegetation, about to fly forward, and the black walls of fog are closing in.

In front of my legs I rapidly trace the infinity symbol three times.

Tom's whispering, "Lewella Lewella Lewella."

"Sam!" shouts Jake.

Charlie shrieks.

Closing my eyes again, I focus on the word Rose murmured. It hangs at the edge of my consciousness before it topples to my tongue, and then I can't get it out fast enough. "Home. Home. Home."

My eyes fly open. "Jake, grab the staff. Tom, hang on to me."

Tom clasps my free shoulder.

Jake grips WhipEye with one hand, and we lift it together and bang it into the ground. But the destruction caused by the ebony claws drowns out the staff's echo.

"Three times," I shout.

Tom wails. Charlie holds my shoulder so hard it hurts.

Jake and I lift and thump the staff twice more against the soil before the shadow hands surround us like a great, dark tent. I close my eyes, bracing for impact, expecting capture like the parrots. *Please, not like this.* Trapped forever in Magnar's monster.

The sound of tearing vegetation is deafening. I cringe, waiting for the claws to crush my body.

The sounds fade away.

Quiet.

We must be floating inside Magnar's creature. I've failed Rose and Charlie. I don't want to open my eyes. But I do.

SEVENTEEN

Home

A SMALL MEADOW.

No black pointy fingers. No black walls. A dusky sky with a few moving clouds. My back is to a tree. Jack pine and spruce surround us in all directions, their tops bent over in a strong, scented breeze.

I slowly slide down against the trunk to the soil, resting my forehead against the staff. Jake sits beside me, holding the cone of water.

"That gave me a few more gray feathers." Charlie preens a wing. "But nice job, Sam."

"With time to spare." I stroke the parrot's back.

My wheezing lungs force me to use my inhaler. I look at my watch. Eight-thirty. We've only been gone six hours. An eternity.

Jake smiles. "You did it."

"We did it." I grin back. "You were right. Rose did show me." It registers then. We escaped Magnar. Energy surges through me, and soon I'm beaming.

Jake's brow knits as he regards WhipEye. "If you're tired, I'll carry the staff for you."

"I'm good." My lips press tight. "Besides, you have the water to carry."

He winces. "Tom used us again." He motions in disgust. "He just needed a way out of KiraKu."

Tom silently disappeared, probably running into the forest. But he's more a mystery than a problem.

A dash of red, barely noticeable in the wan light, scores a nearby tree trunk. I roll to my knees and get up. Shuffling to the tree, I run my fingers along the bark. I spot another red slash on another tree farther ahead. Lining the compass along the two marks, the direction reads northwest.

Jake comes to my side and I point. "It's the south trail I used to walk with Mom. She took me here in spring to show me wildflowers." I ignore the memories popping into my mind.

As this sinks in, Jake and I lock eyes. Then we're running as best we can on our tired legs, northwest through the woods, between *Trust* and *Love*.

Jake keeps a hand over the cone of leaves to minimize water loss, and Charlie flies beside us. I have WhipEye in one palm, the compass in the other. This time the compass needle points north, as it should.

Worries about Dad fill my mind, along with Magnar's threats. The creep might have already hurt my father, or worse.

The compass has always glowed in the dark, and I use it to guide us until I see the rear gate of the fenced acres. I stop there to catch my breath.

Lights are on in the house, muted yellow in the windows. It's a good sign. A bulb above the back door casts a dull glow over the patio and nearby grass.

Charlie lands on my shoulder.

The yard is dark, reminding me of the king cobra. Fearing the worst, I search for warning signs. Shadow monsters will be nearly invisible now.

A light breeze rustles nearby leaves and branches, tensing my neck, but the lynx and bobcat are lying in their cages, watching us intently. They're relaxed. My shoulders sag.

I look at the parrot.

Charlie stretches his wings. "No methuselahs."

"What's the plan?" asks Jake.

"What do you care?" I instantly regret my words.

"Just curious." He shrugs.

I don't have a plan and try to think of something. "All right. Charlie, fly to my bedroom window. If it's closed, sit on the sill and wait for me."

The parrot walks back and forth on my shoulder. "That's it? Fly to a window? Humph. Well, hurry up, Sam. I'm scared of the dark. And bring me some food. Nuts, sprouted seeds, or how about some broccoli and carrots? And a small piece of cheese."

"I'm hungry too." Jake yawns and stretches his arms. "I hope Bryon and Mom cooked a big meal."

I'm starving, but say, "We have more important things to worry about than stuffing our faces. Come on."

Charlie leaves my shoulder, flapping hard toward the upper window, the golden light around his body making him shine like a beacon. Any nearby raptors will see him, but maybe the parrot's glow will scare them away.

I quietly open the gate. The lynx and bobcat stand up, eyeing us.

Closing the fence, I scramble to the greenhouse, slowly sidling around it. Wind rattles the plastic, making me jumpy.

At the far corner, I peer into the yard. Jake presses into my shoulder, but this time I don't mind. Deer huddle near the north fence, but look calm.

I want to run inside the house, to make certain Dad's safe, but I swallow my impatience. Relieved when Charlie climbs inside my bedroom window, I run across the grass to the patio, pausing to peek through the dining room window.

Dad's sitting at the table, his back to me, and Cynthia is sitting next to him. Magnar must have been overconfident he'd capture us in KiraKu.

Although he's safe for now, Dad will be angry. He won't believe a story about giant shadow creatures or Great Ones. I wonder if Charlie would talk to him.

I also notice that the desire to see certain animals—to change things—which ate at me so strongly in KiraKu, has faded away. Glad about that, I wonder if it's the same for Jake.

A shadow moves in the windowpane and I whirl. It's a tree branch swaying in the wind.

I hustle up the deck steps to the back door.

"Sam." Jake points to an empty coffee can we use to water the animals. I hold it while he pours the healing water into it. Finished, he says, "I'll carry it."

His face shows the same weariness I feel in every muscle and bone of my body. As if we've been running from Magnar for days. I want to say something to him, but can't find any words.

When I open the door and walk in, chairs scrape the floor in the other room.

Dad comes out of the dining room first, his face drawn, disapproval in his eyes. "Sam, we've been looking all over for you."

Cynthia appears beside my father, frowning, wearing a T-shirt and jeans, like Dad. I notice Dad is clean shaven too. Only half-zombie.

Jake sets the can down and flies through the hallway, wrapping his arms around his mother. "Mom."

"Is everything all right, Jake?" Cynthia hugs him, glancing at me. "We were about to call the police."

"I'm all right, Mom," he says.

Dad's eyebrows arch with his usual disappointment. "Where did you get the staff, Sam?"

"Rose." I walk toward him, setting WhipEye against the wall.

In one step I'm in front of him, trembling, but not out of fear. He doesn't appear imposing anymore, as if I've grown taller in the few hours I've been away.

"Why didn't you tell me where you were going?" He lifts a limp hand. "I was worried."

"I'm sorry, Dad."

His face softens and so does his tone. "I thought you might be hurt."

"I'm all right."

He doesn't respond with words, but his strong arms wrap around me. The whole world begins to right itself. The sensation of being lost that I've had for so long melts away.

Words spill over my lips. "I want to talk, Dad. About Mom. About everything."

"Okay." It's barely a whisper.

Confidence in him, and in the way things were before Mom died, seeps back into my thoughts. Dad will help us, and Cynthia might too, if we tell her about Magnar. And she has a gun and can convince the police.

Someone bangs on the front door.

EIGHTEEN

Magnar's Revenge

MAGNAR. IT HAS TO BE.

He must have left KiraKu long before we did and controlled his claw from this world. And now he's here. This time he'll order his shadow monsters to kill our parents and capture us. My hands clench.

I know Dad and Cynthia won't run, even if I scream at them.

Jake pales.

"Who could that be?" asks Dad.

"I'll get the door, Dad." My head fills with ideas, but there's only one option.

I grab WhipEye and hold it a few inches off the floor. No matter what the odds, I have to call Tarath. I can't lose Dad, and I can't let Magnar have Charlie.

A loud snap comes from the dining room and I jerk around. It's wind rattling a tree branch against the bay window.

The pounding on the door continues, and I hurry to it. Steadying myself, I flick on the outer light, glad when Jake comes to my side. I open the door a crack and peek out.

Bright lights sweep across the door, making me blink. Police cars are parked in the street and four officers stand on the front stoop, along with two officers wearing brown U.S. Fish and Wildlife Service jackets. A few neighbors are gathered outside the fence.

Relief and disbelief hit me simultaneously.

The police are here to arrest me for stealing Charlie. Magnar set this up. I realize how horribly simple it will be. They'll find Charlie and return him to Magnar. End of story.

The door pushes in and we step aside.

"Dad." My mind races as I set WhipEye in the corner behind the door, wanting to hide it from the officers striding past me. Maybe Magnar told them I stole the staff too.

Dad takes the warrant the police hand to him as they sweep into the house. After reading it, he looks at one of the officers. "This is ridiculous."

"Then we'll be out of here in minutes," says the man.

I hate that I lied to Dad, but I can't tell him I stole Charlie. Not yet. Backing toward the staircase, I glance at Jake. He twitches his head, telling me to go upstairs.

Cynthia moves beside him, her eyebrows hunched and arms crossed. It's easy to see where Jake gets his intense gaze from.

A female Fish and Wildlife officer opens the basement door in the hallway and goes downstairs, while other officers hurry into the kitchen and dining room.

One officer remains with us in the entryway. The police pull open closet doors and cupboards, inspecting any space large enough to hide a parrot.

My fingers find the banister and I move slowly, but the stairs creak under my weight.

The officer beside my father motions to me. "Stay here, miss."

"It's okay, Sam."

Dad sounds calm, and when our eyes meet something changes between us. Like we're in this together, the two of us, for the first time since Mom died. It gives me strength.

I consider yelling to Charlie, but the officers might capture the parrot before he escapes. *Please hear them.*

He can get out the window, but outside might not be safe for him, either. Officers could be waiting. Worse, Magnar might be waiting for him with his snake. Maybe that's the plan.

A hinge creaks.

The basement door, neglected like everything else in the house, swings open and the female officer appears with a birdcage in her arms. In the cage sits a small, yellowish-brown furry animal with a long thick tail and large brown eyes. Its small paws, round ears, and small head give it an innocent, gentle appearance.

I recognize the species immediately and gape. "That's impossible."

"It's here." The officer lifts the cage. "And it's a kinkajou."

Dad's jaw drops. "That's not my animal."

"He's telling the truth." I want to protest more, but my thoughts jumble. How did an animal from Central America get here?

An agent turns Dad around and cuffs him. "Bryon Green, you're under arrest for trafficking illegal exotic animals."

"He didn't do it!" I step off the stairs. "Dad."

My father looks over his shoulder. "I'll be fine, Sam. Stay calm, and remember to feed and water the animals tomorrow if I'm not back. I'm depending on you, honey."

The last words he says gently, and he hasn't called me *honey* in a long time.

He focuses on Cynthia. "Will you watch Sam while I'm gone?"

She steps forward, her face taut. "Of course."

Flashes of Mom sweep through me. I shuffle to the front door, silent as several officers escort my father to a car, place him inside, and drive away. Jake stands beside me.

Cynthia talks to one of the officers, then walks over and rests her hands on our shoulders. "Sam, Jake, let's talk."

Gently, she steers us into the dining room, while the remaining officers search the rest of the house. I wait for them to shout they've found Charlie.

Walking into the dining room is like traveling back a year, when Mom was here. The room is clean from top to bottom, the old papers and musty odor erased. Daisies rest in a vase on the shining buffet.

Salad, veggies, fresh bread, and brats fill bowls and plates on the waxed table, and four place settings lie on placemats. The food smells great. A pan of pumpkin bars—my favorite, sits in the middle of the table, holding twelve unlit birthday candles. Two gifts rest beside it.

My intended celebration makes my feet heavy. It's the kind of birthday party Mom would have given me. I'm stunned Dad did this. One package is neatly gift-wrapped, one in newspaper; Cynthia and Dad.

I imagine what it might have been like to enjoy a meal, then unwrap gifts. To talk to Dad. I don't want to disturb anything, not with Dad gone. My stomach sinks as I sit across from Jake.

"What happened to you two?" Cynthia sits at the end of the table, pushing blond bangs out of her eyes.

Jake lifts a finger. "It's my fault. I wanted to visit Rose's cabin and didn't listen to Sam." His hair is a mess and mud streaks his torn shirt, but his face and voice are calm.

How does he find it so easy to lie for me? I sit quietly, thoughts swirling in my head.

"Well, I'm glad you're both all right." Cynthia pats our hands.

"Mom," blurts Jake. "I want to know the truth. Why did Dad leave us? Was it because of me?" His hands are flat on the table.

Her eyes widen. "We'll talk about it later, all right, hon?"

My fingers curl into fists. "You turned my dad in."

Cynthia leans back, her face calm. "Sam, I've never been in your basement."

"Mom wouldn't do that." Jake's hands are flying.

My accusation sounds stupid, even to me, but my hands remain clenched. Something about Dad asking her to watch me burns inside. Why did he do that?

Cynthia rests a palm on my wrist. It's almost like gazing into Mom's eyes and I can't pull away. Her face is thinner, her nose sharper, but the warmth of her slender hand on my forearm helps steady me.

"The police received an anonymous tip that your father had a kinkajou," she says.

I shake my head vigorously. "Dad would never trade illegal wildlife. He hates people having wild animals as pets."

Jake rolls his eyes. "Mom, anyone can see it's a frame-up."

"I agree, it's suspicious." Cynthia covers his hand with hers. "I'll see if Bryon needs a lawyer." She leans toward me. "I'm so sorry, Samantha."

The truth of what happened comes to me at the same time Jake mouths one word: *Magnar*. It has to be. He won't rest until he has Charlie.

"When can I see Dad?"

"There's a good chance he'll be home tonight." Cynthia's face is anything but certain. "I'll help you pack some things for an over-night, Sam. We have an extra guest room in our house."

The front door closes and quiet replaces stomping footsteps. The officers didn't find Charlie, but where did the parrot go?

"I can pack my stuff." My limbs are stiff when I rise and leave the dining room. I hear Jake talking to Cynthia.

"I'll help her, Mom. Is Bryon in big trouble? What'll happen to the kinka-thing?"

In the hallway, I grasp WhipEye and pause. The piles of maga-zines and other collections that lined the walls and staircase for the last year are gone. I'm not the only one who went through changes today. But it doesn't take away the gloom.

I hurry up the stairs to my room, but Charlie isn't there.

All the laundry on the floor is missing, the layers of dust gone, and the room has a fresh scent. Cynthia must have helped Dad. In another way, everything feels different here too. This was my prison for a year, a place to hide. But now it's just a bedroom. I'm finished with hiding from Dad, from Mom's death, from anything.

I let my gaze wander over the animal mosaic on the walls, but that's too much.

There's a glow outside the window, which is closed. I hustle over and open it, pushing out the piece of torn screen. Charlie climbs through and I heave a breath, glad the parrot is safe.

"It's creepy out there." He flies to the bed mattress, wobbling a little. "Did you bring me some food?"

"I'm sorry, Charlie, I forgot."

The aura around the bird glows brightly, a few inches from his body now, and his head hangs a little. "I went out when they tossed the room. Then someone closed the window and I was stuck outside."

"I'm glad you're safe, Charlie." I shut the door and sit near the parrot, resting WhipEye beside me against the mattress.

"I heard enough, Sam, and I'm sorry."

For one moment I wish I had never helped Charlie, but I can't bring myself to say it. It's because of the parrot I have the courage to talk to Dad. The thought of him sitting in prison for years is too dark, and I push it away.

"It's my fault Dad's in jail."

"It's Magnar's fault."

I want to help Dad, but I can't think of anything to do. "I still think about the parrots that died, Charlie."

"I'd be worried about you if you didn't, kid."

In a few minutes, Jake comes in, opening and closing the door softly. He has the coffee can in one hand, a bag of mixed nuts in the other, with a glass of water squeezed between a strong forearm and his torso.

He puts the can down, gives me the glass, and pours some nuts into his palm. "I told Mom I wanted a snack."

"You're my hero, kiddo." Charlie jabs at the nuts with his beak, bits of food flying everywhere.

I drink most of the water, the liquid cool against my parched throat. I pour the last of it into my cupped hand, and Charlie sips it in-between attacking the nuts.

Jake studies me. "I brought the healing water so you can put it someplace safe."

"Thanks."

When Charlie's done eating, Jake sits beside me. "Your whole house is clean." Then softer, "Mom's waiting." Even softer, "I'm sorry about your dad, Sam."

"It's been a heck of a birthday." I dry my wet hand on my jeans and walk to the closet. Dad didn't clean everything. From the pile of equipment inside, I dig out a small daypack. Opening a dresser drawer, I begin stuffing the bag with clothes.

Jake pulls the butterfly scale from his pocket, rubbing it between his thumb and forefinger. It shines in the light. "It's pretty. Do you want it?"

Grateful that he's trying to make me feel better, I shake my head. "The Great One gave it to you. You should keep it."

"Yeah." He pockets the scale and watches me. "I felt the pull to cross the river too."

"You could have told me." I wonder why we both felt the same thing.

He continues. "The desire to change things is gone."

"Same here."

"How did Magnar get the kinka-thing into your house?"

"Kinkajou."

"Whatever." He sounds hurt.

"Magnar can do little tricks over short distances, with small objects that don't have a will of their own." Charlie cocks his head. "Humans, large things, and methuselahs are beyond his ability to move. Even with the small stuff, he tires after one effort. Magnar and Rose lost most of their power when Magnar enslaved the methuselahs."

That fits. I remember how tired Magnar was after chasing me through the park, and how weary Rose was after freezing him. Magnar's ability also kind of matches Jake and I moving animals around in KiraKu with our desires.

"Where would Magnar get a kinka-thing?" asks Jake.

I stop packing, looking at him. "That's it! He probably already had one. He has to be importing illegal exotic animals. I have to prove it, so I can show he framed Dad."

"How?" Jake stands. "Magnar wouldn't keep a kinka-thing at the pet store."

"No, he'd keep it hidden somewhere." A surge of energy floods me.

Dropping the pack, I hurry to the bed and start pulling the sheets off my mattress, waiting for Charlie to flutter to a bedpost. One of the parrot's feet slips on the perch and he drags it back.

It reminds me that he's dying, which hurts, but I pretend not to notice.

Jake frowns. "What are you doing?"

"Plan B. I'm going to talk to Tom." I strip the sheets from my mattress and throw them on the floor. "I saw him pay Magnar rent once. He lives above the pet store with his mother and might have an idea where Magnar would keep illegal animals." A thought hits me. "Maybe Lewella is his mother."

"I love it, kid."

"Are you crazy?" His hands revving, Jake kicks the sheets. "You could be walking right into Magnar's hands. It's probably a trap. Also, Tom doesn't care about us, only himself. He's an Original and probably doesn't even have a mother. You're too trusting."

"I trust you." I stare into his blue eyes, and his hands drop.

"And I trust Sam." Charlie looks at Jake. "You'll never have a friend if you can't trust someone. At least trust yourself. Not everyone leaves, kiddo."

Jake's lips twist as he glances from the parrot to me. "Mom's responsible for you. She won't let you go anywhere."

"Jail break. I'm going to hang sheets out my window." I go to my dresser and pull out a few more.

"You should wait." Jake crosses his arms. "Your dad will probably be home tonight."

"I'm sick of letting Magnar decide what I do, and I want to find out what his plans are."

Charlie trills. "So do I."

Jake gapes, his hands whirring again. "But you'll have to go through the park. Magnar could be waiting with the buffalo shadow or the cobra."

"Then I'll fight them."

"It's stupid."

"When did that ever stop me? Stall your mom."

"You can't fight all of Magnar's monsters."

I look at him. "You can't talk me out of it. End of story."

Charlie sounds excited. "Let's give Magnar some of his own medicine. He won't expect it."

I look at the parrot. "It's not safe, Charlie."

"Yeah, Mission Impossible, kid. But I've been waiting a thousand years to stop the creep."

Clutching sheets, my hands drop to my sides. "I thought so."

"What do you mean?" Jake glances at each of us.

I move closer to the parrot. "You planned all of this from the beginning, didn't you Charlie? Taking us to Rose, getting us into KiraKu, and meeting Great Ones. You wanted all of it to happen."

"Guilty as charged, Sam. Rose and I had to find a way to get Great Ones onboard. Convince them there was a chance to defeat Magnar, that he poses a risk to them, and that they should care about humans. Magnar's claw should worry them plenty."

He tilts his head at Jake. "And Tarath was experimenting when she gave you energy, Jake, to find out what you kids are capable of. She'll tell others, and so will the iguana. They broke the crocodile's rules when they talked to you. So did the swallowtail butterfly."

The parrot pauses, his voice lowering. "We never thought it

would get this dangerous for you. And Rose sacrificing herself wasn't part of the plan, but Magnar's claw surprised us." Then softly, "It was her choice, not mine."

Charlie looks at me. "We needed someone who cared about animals, who might be able to wake up the Great Ones. Someone with a good heart. Then one year ago, you showed up, Sam." He cocks his head at Jake. "We lucked out when we got two for one."

Jake blushes.

"A plotting parrot." I'm in awe of Charlie. He was always more concerned with stopping Magnar than saving himself. "Does Magnar know how smart you are?"

"Magnar thinks he can outsmart everyone. That's his biggest weakness."

Jake regards Charlie. "You think we can beat him?"

"You just have to listen to your heart, trust it, and act." The parrot fluffs his feathers. "Whatever happens, happens. It's the journey that counts."

Jake puts his hands on his hips. "I'm going with you, Sam. You can't do this alone."

"But you said—"

He cuts me off with a stiff hand. "We have WhipEye, Tarath said she'll help, and we have the compass and healing water." He adjusts his glasses. "Magnar said we'd both pay. He could go after Mom next." His eyes focus on mine. "Besides, Tarath said you need me."

I desperately need him. And the resolve in his eyes gives me strength. "So we're partners?"

"Look, I was scared after Rose died and Magnar's claw chased us, and then we met the stupid crocodile. I'm not always brave like you."

"Like me? I'm a chicken when it comes to Magnar's monsters." I lift a hand. "I'm brave when I'm with you. You're strong, you're fast, you have good ideas, and I don't want to face Magnar alone." I pause. "I wouldn't have made it this far without you."

He eyes me. "So we're a good team?"

"Five-star."

"Well, quit staring at me and tell me what you want me to do."

"Tie sheets." I have to work to keep from smiling.

"Do you have something to put the water in?" He walks over to the closet, eyeing the mess inside.

I find a canteen in the pile of camping equipment. While I hold it, he crimps the edge of the coffee can and carefully pours the healing water into it.

After I screw the top on, he reaches for it and I give it to him. He slings the strap over his head, carrying the canteen on his hip.

The warmth I felt for him after crossing the river in KiraKu returns. I know he won't leave again. I remember how annoying I found him just a few hours ago, and now all I want is to have him with me. My lips stretch into a grin.

He rolls his eyes and turns away, but he's smiling.

I study the parrot. Maybe nothing will happen tomorrow and we can save Charlie. Perhaps like learning how to end The Silence with my father, there's a way to stop the parrot's death too. I've always wondered if I could have saved Mom, however she died.

Jake says, "I didn't mean what I said before, Charlie. I want to help you and I'm sad you're going to . . ." He doesn't say it and his eyes are downcast.

"It's all right, kid. All for one and one for all."

I'm beginning to like those words.

A square purple envelope appears out of nowhere on my stripped mattress.

I stare at it, dumbfounded, not sure I should touch it.

"Weird," says Jake. "Has to be from Magnar."

"You've got mail, kid."

Carefully, with two fingers, I pick up the envelope.

"I want to read it too," says Charlie. "I never get mail."

I lift the parrot to my shoulder, then open the envelope and pull a cream-colored card from it. Jake peeks over my other arm as I read out-loud the sloppy handwriting in purple crayon.

BRING PAROT TO OLD RIVER BRIGE AT ELEVEN IF YA WANT TO GET YORE DADDY OUT OF JAIL. COME ALONE. (NO ADULTS, BUT FRENDS OK.) BE CARE FULL. IF YA DON'T COME, SOMETHIN BAD WILL HAPPEN.

The card and envelope disappear from my hands the instant I finish reading it.

Squawk. "Blackmail."

NINETEEN

Rattling Chains

"THAT CAN'T BE MAGNAR'S HANDWRITING." I hurry through the park, looking ahead.

Spaced lamps break the darkness on the tree-lined path, but deep shadows fill the woods. Crickets chirp a steady rhythm and my skin chills in the warm air. Everything spooks me.

Jake checks over his shoulder. "How do you know?"

"Magnar's been alive for ten thousand years, so he probably speaks dozens of languages. I bet he'd win an international spelling bee. In fact, he must be a genius after living that long."

"Sam's right," says Charlie. "Magnar has great penmanship."

I recall the large computer monitor in the pet store. Magnar wasn't wasting time on it. More likely he was plotting his takeover of the world.

Jake's hands do cartwheels. "It didn't even look like an adult wrote the note."

There's a soft hum behind us.

I jump through bushes at the side of the pavement and stumble. Jake trips over me.

"Klutz," he mutters, picking himself up.

"It's genetic."

A police car creeps along the park path toward us. Charlie flies to a higher branch to hide his glow. A spotlight on the car shines ahead and to the sides into the woods, forcing us to duck.

Jake's cell phone plays a few bars of some rock song and he hurries to answer it.

"Geez." I press into the tree trunk, keeping my face and Whip-Eye hidden.

Jake squeezes the phone to his ear as the police car stops on the path. "It's okay, Mom," he whispers. "I'm helping Sam. We'll be fine. I . . . I . . . I gotta go." He ends the call and shrugs.

The police car drives on.

When its lights disappear around a corner, I step back onto the path. "Set it on vibrate. That's the third time she's called."

Jake glances over his shoulder. "I did. And she's worried. And a little upset. Actually, a lot upset. She said we're making things worse, so we should go home."

"I'm not going back. You can if you want to."

"I didn't say that." His hand splits the air.

"I guess you didn't. Sorry." Shadows and Magnar are putting me on edge. I look up. "Charlie."

The parrot flutters to my shoulder and clutches it, but one foot slips off and he has to grip it twice. The white patches around his eyes are visible in the night and the golden light shines even brighter around his body. I tell myself the parrot just glows more in the dark.

Before the next curve in the path, Jake slows. "Magnar could ambush us anywhere."

"Hello." Charlie trills a few notes. "Remember, I can sense if methuselahs and Magnar are nearby."

Jake sighs. "Thanks, Charlie. I forgot."

Clanking metal and eerie singsong words break the night's quiet.

Around the last turn, a hundred feet back, a large figure shuffles along the side of the path, staying in the shadows. When the giant reaches a park lamp, I see chains swinging out over the pavement.

"Not a methuselah, kids."

I hurry along with Jake. "Magnar might know that you can detect methuselahs, Charlie, and sent something else to grab us." Jake was right. Magnar anticipated we'd come, and the note was a setup.

"How many monsters does Magnar have, Charlie?" I ask.

"Heck if I know."

"At least it's not the snake." Jake runs along the pavement.

"Or the monster spider," I huff, following him. Charlie looks like a light bulb flying down the path.

Even though the parrot is confident, every time we round a corner I expect Magnar's monsters to be waiting.

Soon I'm wheezing. Jake slows to a fast walk to let me catch my breath. Charlie lands on my shoulder, and the way he droops I'm sure it's to rest.

The chinking chain is closer, the singsong words a little louder.

Something about the voice is familiar, and it's high-pitched, as if from a child. I imagine the monster whipping us with a handful of chains as it sings. Ugh.

Jake taps my shoulder. "We have to run. Keep up."

"Do you think I like running behind you every time monsters chase us?"

His brow knits and he jogs on. Charlie takes off again.

The chain rattles louder, gaining on us. I run faster. The giant's voice dips in and out of humming, mostly with garbled words. But two words are clear: *wittle* and *children*. Very creepy.

At the next crossroad in the path, Charlie lands on the pavement and stops us with soft words. "Hide in the trees, kids. I'll fly down this side path and lure the brute away, then I'll cut through the woods to find you."

I can't outrun the monster, but the parrot is too weak to fly. "Let's fight it with WhipEye."

"We don't understand what the game is, Sam," says Charlie. "Let's play it safe. We'll have a better chance of surprising Magnar."

"And we should save the staff for when we need it." Jake motions to it. "It's stronger when we're not tired."

I shake my head. "I don't want to split up. We can drink the healing water if we're tired."

Jake looks back along the path. "We might need it for something else."

"I don't care. It's too dangerous for Charlie."

"This isn't Magnar's claw chasing us in KiraKu, kid. I can fly higher than this lunk can jump." Without waiting, the parrot flaps into the air, glowing like a lantern.

I stare after him until he disappears around a corner. Jake yanks my wrist, pulling me into the trees.

Words float through the night to us; "Hey wittle children, where are you?" Then humming.

The singsong giant rounds the last curve, accompanied by chain clinking. I duck. Sweat runs into my eyes. When the chain and voice go quiet, I freeze.

From down the path Charlie squawks, and the chain clanks after him. The large figure disappears in the shadows, the noisy chain fading away too.

"No footsteps," whispers Jake.

"An Original," I murmur. "Helping Magnar." That's disappointing and worrisome. "Why would any Original help the creep?"

"Who knows? Let's go." Jake runs in the opposite direction.

I follow, glancing over my shoulder repeatedly, hoping the parrot is all right.

At the park bridge, lights illuminate everything within a small radius, but Charlie isn't there.

My coat rests on the bench exactly where I left it when I first met Rose. I grab it on the run, glad it's too dark to see the dead frog.

Jake stops several times to let me catch my breath, and as soon as I'm not doubled over, we keep moving.

At the end of the park we wait inside the tree line, next to the street. I put on my coat, peering into shadows. Terrible images of raptors attacking Charlie float through my mind.

Jake stands close to me. It helps steady my nerves.

Something occurs to me. "I've heard that giant's voice before."

"When?" asks Jake.

"Today. In the pet store when I stole Charlie."

A small whistle comes from above. High up, a glow seeps around the edge of a tree branch, dropping toward us in a slow spiral. My back relaxes, but only for a second.

Near the treetops, a large bird is flying toward Charlie.

Straining, I recognize the silhouette of a great horned owl.

Fear for Charlie builds inside me, along with anger at the owl. Strangely, I want to plead with the raptor, but I can't get the words out of my mouth. I almost slam WhipEye, but Magnar's monster would hear the echo. Silently, I wave off the bird, as if it will understand.

"What is it?" Jake peers up, but in the wrong direction.

The predator keeps flying at Charlie. Concern for the parrot explodes inside me as I jump up and down and motion wildly. "Don't!"

At the last moment, the owl veers away.

Jake stares at me and I shrug, unsure what happened.

When the parrot lands on my shoulder, I heave a sigh. "I was going crazy, Charlie." I gently stroke his neck.

"Good job with the owl, Sam."

"What happened?" I ask.

Charlie sneezes. "Hard to say. It's probably a side effect from KiraKu."

I'm unsure if the owl understood me, or if it was put off by Charlie's glow and my yelling. Either way, my friend's safe.

"What took you so long, Charlie?" Jake asks gently.

"I wanted to take the big lunk as far away as possible." The parrot leans against my face. "That wasn't a methuselah, but he's big and ugly. And when he learns what happened he won't be smiling."

"Thanks, Charlie." Jake strokes him once with a finger.

"Don't mention it, kiddo."

There's no traffic, so we cross the street mid-block. On the shadowed sidewalk, I transfer the parrot to Jake's shoulder. "Wait here with Charlie."

Jake's eyebrows arch. "Why?"

"Back in a minute."

His face tightens, but I run to the front corner of the building, and peek around it. The sidewalk is empty, so I jog to the Endless Pet Store. My hand tightens on WhipEye.

The store is dark inside. It's hard to believe I spent so many hours talking to Charlie in the small place, afraid of Magnar. I still hate seeing animals in cages. I run back to the corner.

Jake's waiting, arms crossed. "Don't ever do that again. Leave without telling me what you're doing."

"I had to check out the pet store. No one's there." He's frowning, so I add, "I didn't want Charlie with me in case Magnar was waiting."

"Thanks, kid."

"Oh." Jake flicks my shoulder. "You could have said that, goofball."

"Yeah. Sorry."

I transfer Charlie to my shoulder, then hurry along the sidewalk to an alley behind the buildings. A faint light bulb in the middle of the narrow lane reveals a few broken bottles lying at the sides of cracked cement.

"This doesn't look good." Jake bites his lip.

"It's where Tom lives. He's our last hope." But I don't want to go in, either.

From the park we hear faint rattling chains.

"The big ugly figured it out, kids."

TWENTY

Lessers and Originals

W E HURRY INTO THE DARK ALLEY. I'm glad when the sound of the chains fades away, blocked by stone and brick. I hope I'm not leading one of Magnar's monsters to Tom.

The back of the Endless Pet Store is the second building in from the street, with a wooden staircase running up the outside of it. While climbing the steps, I'm wondering what to say if Tom's mother answers the door.

At the first landing I pause, listening. Jake bumps into me, grumbling, and I keep going.

At the second story landing, the weathered wood door swings open before I can knock.

Tom.

He's wearing a red T-shirt and fresh jeans, and his red spiked hair is as clean as his bare feet. His seven ear studs shine.

"Not smart to return to the scene of the crime." He regards us coolly, running a hand through his hair. "You need to go."

His aloofness annoys me. "After all we did for you? Remember the river and our escape from Magnar's claw? Where we saved your life?"

His gaze slides to WhipEye.

I clench the staff and back up.

Jake slashes the air with his hands, talking loudly. "I told you he didn't care about anyone except himself."

"Shh." Tom's forehead wrinkles and he puts a finger to his lips.

"Jake." I nod to the alley, in case the big ugly is close by.

Jake quiets, but scowls.

A soft voice calls from inside. "Who's there, Tom?"

A short, slender woman in her late forties appears beside him, barefoot and wearing a black silk robe. Golden hair flows to her waist, surrounding a small face with deep wrinkles. Her green eyes dazzle me.

"You," she cries. She pushes past Tom and wraps her gentle arms around me, which feels a little awkward. She hugs Jake next, and his face reddens.

"Thank you." Beaming at us, she rests a hand on each of our shoulders. "Tom told me everything you did for him, and us."

She extends a hand to me more formally. "Lewella."

"Samantha." Her grip is warm and her eyes warmer.

"And you must be Jake." Lewella takes his hand next. "A lovely name."

Jake brightens, and I'm suddenly glad we helped Tom get healing water and escape KiraKu. Everything about Lewella appears kind, like Mom.

Gently, she touches the parrot's neck. "And of course, the lovely methuselah parrot, Charlie."

"Compliments will get you everywhere, dear."

"Are you Tom's mother?" I glance at the shadowed alley.

Lewella covers her mouth with a palm and giggles.

Tom looks annoyed.

A stocky young man in his twenties appears beside Tom. He has a dark crew cut and wears a sleeveless green T-shirt and jeans. He's also barefoot. He smiles mischievously. "Name's Brandon. Thanks for the water."

Jake nudges my shoulder.

I take a deep breath. "We need help."

"Don't want to get involved. Leave." Tom begins to close the door, but Lewella blocks it with her foot.

"We're helping them, Tom." Her tone leaves no room for disagreement.

Tom's frown deepens, but he disappears inside.

Lewella cocks her head, facing the direction of the park.

I look too, my hands sweaty. She steps farther onto the landing. My shoulders tense, but there's only silence.

Jake bends over the railing to peer into the darkness.

Lewella doesn't move for several moments. I feel guilty about putting her into danger and decide to tell her about the big ugly, when she says, "Inside, children."

Whirling, she ushers us through the door with strong hands on our backs. She's not as frail as I thought.

Brandon closes the door behind us.

Once inside, Lewella moves in front of us impossibly fast.

The light is dim, but Jake's wide eyes show he noticed it too.

We're led through a shadowed living room, which is empty except for a sofa and a big bookshelf crammed with books.

Brandon turns off a table lamp so the room goes dark.

We pass through a hanging cloth curtain into the kitchen,

where a soft overhead bulb leaves the room more shadowed than lit. Baskets of fruit and vegetables hang from hooks on the walls and ceiling. The room is cozy.

"Sit." Lewella motions us into chairs surrounding a round table.

Brandon takes a chair next to Jake, glancing at the parrot and WhipEye. For some reason his attention doesn't bother me. Tom sits sullenly across from me, arms crossed, while Lewella and Jake sandwich me, the staff in the crook of my elbow near Jake.

Tom continues to eye WhipEye, and I grip it beneath the table.

In the center of the table, the three silver canteens rest on their sides, open and empty. Two half-filled glasses of water sit in front of Tom and Brandon, a full glass in front of Lewella. Apparently, they don't plan on saving any of the healing water from KiraKu.

A bowl of homemade bread is on the counter, its scent filling the room. Odors of onions and other food swirl through the kitchen. My stomach grumbles. Lewella notices when I eye the bread.

With movements faster than normal again, she leaves her chair and flits about the kitchen. In moments, she sets down a plate of whole wheat bread rolls covered with butter and honey.

I grab one, its sweet, buttery flavor reminding me of times when Mom baked bread. "Yummy."

"Mph." Jake chews a mouthful. "Love whole wheat bread."

"Give me a taste, Sam."

I break off a piece and put it in my palm. Charlie chomps on it eagerly, crumbs flying everywhere.

After sipping water, Lewella touches my hand. "Please, honor me with your story, Samantha. All of it, from when you helped Charlie escape, to KiraKu, to now." Her eyes show sadness. "I haven't lived in KiraKu for a long time."

Tom turns to her. "You're a Great One."

I wipe my lips and lean forward, excited. "You are?"

She shakes her head. "A Lesser. There's no going back, Tom."

"What's a Lesser?" I ask.

Lewella pats my wrist. "Great Ones that chose to leave Kir-aKu with the Originals are called Lessers. They're not allowed to return."

I wonder what kind of Great One she was in KiraKu, and what it means to be a Lesser. She looks weak compared to the crocodile or Tarath. Regardless, I hope she'll help us.

Jake's face wrinkles when he asks the same question I have. "Are some Great Ones human?"

Lewella shakes her head. "Some Lessers took on human shape to blend into your society, but others kept their Great One form and remained in hiding. Without the energy of KiraKu, all Lessers' bodies altered over time and they became the creatures of your human mythologies."

She pauses, her eyes lowering slightly. "All Lessers have lost some of their power, and eventually require healing water to replenish their energy. Otherwise, after several centuries they weaken and die."

I consider all the mythologies I've ever read involving weird creatures, a.k.a. Lessers. My head spins, and I'm curious how many Lessers are alive in the world today.

Jake peers at Brandon, who grins back.

"I'm an Original." Brandon's skin is smooth and youthful.

"How come you haven't aged?" asks Jake.

"Originals and Lessers remain as youthful adults, unless they're away from the water and air of KiraKu for long periods." Brandon winks at us. "We've had help getting the water."

"I'm glad," I say.

Silence surrounds us. Lewella gives me an inviting nod and I tell our story. Jake fills in details.

Lewella listens intently, sometimes with excitement on her face, sometimes sadness. Brandon hunches forward, his eyes screwed shut, while Tom sits back, his face hidden in shadows. All of them sip water.

When I come to Rose's death, I choke up.

Lewella says softly, "How could Magnar kill her? He once loved her."

"Rose of the Staff." Brandon shakes his head. "The true guardian."

"My best friend for a thousand years." The parrot sounds sad.

"It was horrible," Jake says softly.

Even the corners of Tom's mouth turn down. I wonder if it bothers him that he abandoned us at the cabin.

I explain the caracal's offer to help us. But Lewella and the others don't respond, sinking my enthusiasm. I add, "I pledged to Tarath to do my best to defeat Magnar."

"Tarath." Lewella's eyes shine. "One of the oldest Great Ones gave her true name to a modern human. To my knowledge this has never been done before."

"Wow, really?" asks Jake. His round eyes mirror my own wonder.

Tarath's pledge to me suddenly feels more important.

Brandon smiles. "She must have high hopes for you."

"We all do." Charlie rubs his head against my cheek.

Tom remains mute, his face dark.

After I describe our escape from KiraKu, Lewella sits back. "I understand the crocodile's wish for you to leave. He's the eldest of the Great Ones and it's his duty to ensure KiraKu survives without change."

I remember the croc's teeth in my face. "He needs an upgrade in manners."

"He almost ate us." Jake's hand flies off the table.

"Always excusing the Great Ones for forcing out Originals," says Tom. "And refusing to allow us and Lessers to return."

Lewella pats his arm. "No, Tom. I don't excuse them, but the Great Ones who left KiraKu understood the risks. And I agree with the crocodile's fear. If KiraKu becomes contaminated like this world, what's left?"

"Nothing," says Tom.

Lewella regards WhipEye. "The door at Rose's cabin will be closed now. The staff will be the only way into KiraKu. That's why the crocodile wanted it. It's a legend, even among Great Ones. Few of us saw how it was created, along with the methuselahs, and only a few Great Ones pledged to it."

I study the chestnut staff, abruptly aware I've taken it for granted ever since Rose gave it to me. I also notice Jake looking at it.

Lewella continues. "The WhipEye tree in KiraKu is small, rare, and very hardy." Her eyes light up. "The bearer of the staff also appears to be very durable."

My cheeks warm with the compliment.

"Why is the tree called WhipEye?" asks Jake.

"In a strong wind the tree's thin branches move like whips, and the trunk has knots on it that look like eyes." Brandon winks at me. "We don't know who first named it, but its roots are almost unbreakable—the strongest wood in KiraKu, and the staff was forged from them."

I'm even more in awe of WhipEye. I also think Brandon is comparing me with the roots of the WhipEye tree. Embarrassed, I don't know what to say to that.

"What about this?" Jake brings out his swallowtail scale. "A Great One gave it to me." Even in the dim light, its yellow, orange, and red hues shine.

"Amazing," says Brandon, leaning forward.

Lewella extends a hand. Jake hesitates, but hands it to her. She strokes it in her palm for several moments, then gives it back to him. "It has great strength, but I'm not sure how it can help you."

Jake looks disappointed as he puts it away.

Tom taps the table. "Great Ones are scared. Need Magnar defeated."

"By two children." Lewella pats my hand. "How can we help?"

"Magnar brought a kinkajou to my house, so my father was arrested for trafficking in exotic animals."

Tom scoffs. "Originals and Lessers avoid human affairs. Not keen on helping Great Ones, either. Magnar's going to win. Great Ones have no idea how strong he is."

Lewella sits back. Her silence surprises and disappoints me.

"Jail isn't that hard to break in or out of." Brandon crosses his arms over his thick chest.

Tom's eyes widen.

Breaking Dad out of prison won't help anyone, but I remain quiet.

"Why do you want our help, Samantha?" Lewella covers my hand with hers, her green eyes on mine. "Speak from your heart."

"I gave my word to Tarath I'd try to stop Magnar, and I want to free the methuselahs in his rings." I pause. "I don't want Charlie to die. I love him and Dad."

"I do too," says Jake.

Charlie nuzzles my cheek. "Thanks, kids. The feeling's mutual."

Saying those words reminds me how deeply I care for the parrot, and the fact that Charlie loves me warms me inside. For the whole last year I wanted Dad to say those words to me. Mom said them every day.

Lewella gently strokes Charlie's back. "The methuselahs were an attempt by the Great Ones to guide the use of technology in your world, Samantha. But the effort created a bigger problem with Magnar. No one knows what would have happened if the methuselah energy had been released as planned."

She stares at the table. "I left KiraKu to help Originals, but it's been hard. This world keeps changing, often for the worse."

"It's not all bad." Brandon winks at his brother. "But some Originals never joined human society, and some that have still refuse to talk like humans."

I think of Tom and his odd way of speaking.

Tom runs a hand through his hair. "You two love the parrot." He shrugs. "Life of methuselahs. Live a thousand years, then kick off. Nothing anyone can do about it."

His words make me glum.

"Let's not forget what a positive influence Magnar had on my life." Charlie clucks like he's choking. "But I can't complain. I'd make a good movie critic."

Tom continues. "Our family lost KiraKu. Brandon and I lost our parents in your stupid wars."

Brandon speaks softly. "They died as they lived. With valor and honor."

"For nothing." Tom studies the table.

Brothers. I wouldn't have guessed it, but there's a slight resemblance in their cheekbones and eyes.

Tom lifts his head. "Not the only one who's lost things, Samantha. Listened to your chats with Charlie every day. Hoping for a way into KiraKu. But just your sob story. Over and over. Miss Mom. Dad won't talk to me. Want my life back."

While Tom talks I stare at the table. The image of Mom's face floats into my thoughts, and the darkness comes, but I push it away.

When he's finished, I find the courage to look at him. "At least I was honest."

Lewella and Brandon give Tom sharp looks and he sits back, his face in shadows.

"Everyone loses things in life," says Charlie. "What matters is how you handle it."

Jake glares at Tom. "You use everyone, don't you?"

Tom was never the friend I imagined, but I understand what it might be like to lose your home and parents. I did when Mom died. "Do you want Magnar to win?"

Tom snorts. "Might not be bad. World was beautiful before humans ruined it. Took your breath away. Now pollution does that."

"We have to help them, Tom." Lewella's eyes flash gold. "Rose was an Original, like you, and she risked bringing us healing water for a long time."

"So?" Tom's eyes narrow. "Stopped bringing us water when Great Ones said to."

"So this is our world now." Lewella clasps her hands together on the table. "It has been for thousands of years."

Tom grips the edge of the table, his face hard. "Fighting Magnar takes power. Waited forever to get back into KiraKu to drink its water, breathe its air." He shakes his head. "Not risking becoming weak and sickly for centuries, dying slowly. Besides, no way to stop Magnar, with or without us."

"A suicide mission." Brandon has a sparkle in his eyes. "Might be fun."

"Excellent." Charlie whistles. "I like the way you think, buddy."

Brandon smiles at the parrot.

His words surprise me. Maybe he's sick of sitting around and doing nothing, like I was after the last year.

Tom regards his brother. "No."

"Why not?" Brandon speaks calmly.

"Need each other to survive here."

"Tom." Lewella briefly rests a palm on his shoulder.

"You're only half-recovered, Lewella."

I clutch the staff. "You owe us at least one favor, Tom."

His eyes flash gold, his face nearly as red as his hair, his knuckles white. "Don't owe anyone anything. Everyone for themselves, way I see it."

Jake sweeps a level hand. "That's very human of you."

"There must be some way we can help," Lewella says firmly.

"Three of us have to agree. Way it's always been." Tom locks eyes with me. "Tarath's one Great One. No other Great Ones will risk coming here to help you. No Lessers care."

"We're helping," says Lewella.

A loud crack makes me jump. Jake's shoulder twitches against mine.

Tom slowly lifts the piece of the table he broke off, staring at it. He tosses the scrap aside, where it clatters on the floor. "Magnar has another building."

He reaches to a nearby stool, grabs a pen and pad of paper, and writes the address. Ripping off the sheet, he holds it out. "Go."

Lewella takes the paper, quickly reading it before passing it to me. I wait, hoping for more from her, but she remains quiet.

"Thanks for your concern, Tom." Jake says it with sarcasm.

Brandon regards Tom, then leans forward. "Tom said the pet store doesn't make enough money to pay expenses, either."

Tom scowls at his brother.

"That's another reason Magnar would sell illegal exotic animals." I look at Jake. "The pet store's a front."

"We have to go, Sam." Jake rises.

I stand. "I'm glad the water helped all of you." I force myself to include Tom with my next words. "Thanks for helping us."

"Good luck, children." Lewella hugs Jake, then gently brushes my tangled hair from my face and hugs me. This time I hug her back.

When I pull away, the overhead light shows her more clearly. During our short visit the wrinkles on her face have partially faded and she appears about thirty now.

She smiles. "Lessers need more water than Originals to maintain their youth. I looked ninety in human years when Tom returned with the water. They've given most of it to me."

Tom motions to her. "Deserve it."

"She's saved our lives many times." Brandon looks warmly at Lewella.

She shrugs. "It's what I'm here for."

"Better than a doctor," Tom says earnestly.

If a few small handfuls of healing water filled my tired body with energy, it doesn't surprise me that several canteens of it could reverse Lewella's aging.

Tom rises and moves fluidly to the curtain, blocking our way. "Need WhipEye more than they do."

"No." My foot slides back and I clench the staff. The way my foot moved into the stance felt automatic. As if WhipEye moved me. Also, I suddenly want Tom to charge. To fight. To hurt him.

Jake raises his hands in a martial arts pose.

"No, Tom." With one smooth movement, Lewella steps beside me.

"Only way to get water now," insists Tom. "Only way into KiraKu."

"They're guests and friends, brother." Brandon moves beside Jake with the same speed and grace of his brother. "We're not hurting them."

Tom looks from Brandon to Lewella. "They can't win. Magnar gets the staff, we'll never get back to KiraKu."

A flash of gold fills Lewella's eyes, making me ponder again what kind of Great One she was.

Softly, she says, "Tom."

He steps aside, head lowered. "Leave."

I take a deep breath and relax, my anger disappearing. What caused that? WhipEye? I don't want to hurt anyone. I sheepishly glance at the others, glad everyone is looking at Tom.

Everyone except Lewella. Her green eyes find mine, and I think she knows. But she doesn't say anything. Instead, she slowly reaches to WhipEye, her eyes brightening. For some reason this tenses me.

"Some of these faces are old friends." Closing her eyes, her fingertips barely touch the wood. "So much power, and it wants more."

Opening her eyes, her hand falls to her side. "Safe journey."

"Thanks." I don't understand her words about WhipEye, but I'm relieved she didn't grab it.

Brandon pats our shoulders. "Best of luck." He glances at Tom several times, as if he wants to come with us. He points to Jake's forearm. "Nice tattoos."

"Thanks." Jake's fidgeting, ready to leave.

We walk past the curtain, into the darkened living room, and I stop. "We were followed through the park by an Original that's helping Magnar. Or maybe it's a Lesser."

Lewella looks surprised. "I wonder why." She moves from the curtain to the door so fast it's as if she took one giant step. Pressing a finger to her lips, she opens the door and steps out.

In moments she returns, her face relaxed. "It's safe, but don't dawdle. Go through the alley." Moving aside to let us by, her green eyes meet mine as I pass her. She knows I want her to come with us.

I follow Jake, but when I step onto the landing I'm stopped by a hand on my shoulder. Tom. Stiffening, I swing WhipEye away from him.

Lewella and Brandon watch from the doorway.

Tom meets my eyes. "You have guts, Samantha. Stood up to Magnar."

I choke back a rude reply. "It took guts to return to KiraKu, Tom."

His eyes widen, then he nods.

Charlie clucks. "When I allowed you to join us, Tom, I knew you weren't being honest."

He frowns. "Why'd you do it?"

"Everyone deserves to go home. Even Originals and Lessers."

Tom's eyes flash gold at the parrot.

I hurry down the steps after Jake, the door closing quietly behind me.

TWENTY-ONE

Running from the Big Ugly

MAGNAR'S PLACE IS NORTH, outside of town." I study the address Tom gave us. "Not far from the Old River Bridge."

We're on the main street again, north of the Endless Pet Store, and the compass reads north, as it should.

"They could have helped us more." Jake brushes back his blond hair. "Stupid Tom."

I'm just as disappointed, but I think I understand Tom. "In a way, he's blaming us for his parents dying in our world."

"Idiot. It's not our fault."

"I trust Lewella and Brandon."

"Overall, a good meeting, kids. Lewella cares. And the bread was great." Charlie glows brightly in the dark.

"At least we lost the big ugly," I chime in. I'm happy about that until chain rattles from the direction of the park, two blocks away. "Or maybe we didn't."

Jake walks faster. I hustle to keep up.

"The big ugly is smart," says Charlie. "I bet he was waiting for us quietly, so Lewella wouldn't hear him."

That raises the hairs on my neck. Jake wipes his forehead and starts jogging, making me work harder. Charlie flies ahead of us.

"Dad always wondered how Magnar could have a successful pet store in a small town," I mutter. A lump forms in my throat, which grows when my thoughts turn to Mom.

What's wrong?" asks Jake.

"Nothing."

"Partners don't lie to each other. Neither do friends."

For once, I'm glad he's pushy. And I like it that he says we're friends. "I'm thinking of Dad. And Mom."

"Oh. Well, don't worry about Bryon. We'll send Magnar to prison for a long time. As for your mom, sometimes if I miss my father, I remember the good times I had with him."

"Thinking about the good times with Mom just makes me sad."

"Well, you have your dad."

"Yeah, and I want him back."

At the end of the line of stores older houses appear, and after a few more blocks newer houses take their place. The streets have fewer lights with deeper shadows along the sides.

A car approaches and we huddle behind a tree. Charlie flies up into the branches until the vehicle passes by.

Chains rattle somewhere in the background and creepy sounding words echo along the street.

"How can it track us at night?" Glancing over his shoulder, Jake runs faster.

My lungs labor. "Maybe it can see in the dark."

Jake flips a hand. "Or the big ugly knows where we're going."

"Ugh."

In a few blocks, dirt replaces the paved street and the houses disappear. A little farther along we come to a dead end.

Ahead, in the center of a stony lot rests a large cement warehouse that stretches east, back into the night, its size hidden by the dark. A dim bulb casts a faint glow over a faded sign hanging above the metal door.

Endless Warehouse
Private
KEEP OUT

A deep urge to go inside prods me forward. Walking across hard-packed dirt, I stop in front of the door, breathing hard. It takes a few moments bent over, palms on my knees, to catch my breath.

The clanking chain and singsong voice grow louder.

"Now what?" Jake's panting, his hands whirring.

I straighten and inspect the building.

A thick chain loops through the metal door handle to a U-bolt on the cement wall, held in place by a bulky padlock. The chain and padlock look new and unbreakable. The roof is too high to climb and the building has no windows.

"We can't get chain cutters anywhere this time of night," I whisper. "And getting Dad's isn't an option."

"Let's hide and see if the big ugly goes in," says Jake.

"Use WhipEye, kid."

I glance at the parrot. "The staff?"

"We don't have a hammer, so improvise."

Striking wood against chain might damage WhipEye, and I can't bring myself to do it. "Wood isn't stronger than metal," I mumble, and hunt for a large rock.

Charlie clacks. "Do you need a hearing aid, Sam? Use the staff. And hurry."

"It might work." Jake looks back down the street. "Remember what it did to the croc."

"All right, already." I hold WhipEye vertical with both hands and tap it against the padlock.

A trickle of light leaves the end of the staff and surrounds the padlock, but nothing happens.

"Smash it," says Jake.

"Use some muscle, kid."

I lift it again, hesitating, hoping the WhipEye tree root is as strong as Brandon and Lewella say it is. I slam the padlock hard.

The impact jolts my shoulders, making me wince, but golden light flows down the chestnut wood beneath my grip, outlining the lock, which breaks apart and falls, thudding on the ground. The chain slithers after it.

I quickly examine the end of WhipEye, and relax. It's not cracked or chipped. I'm also not drained after using the staff this time. It makes sense. Smaller tasks shouldn't require as much energy.

Chains rattle louder with singsong humming. A block away, beneath a street lamp, a large figure shuffles toward us, a shadow stretching out in front of it.

"Time to move, kids."

I open the door and we slip inside.

TWENTY-TWO

The Endless Warehouse

T HE INSIDE OF THE WAREHOUSE immediately reminds
me of entering Rose's cabin, but unlike KiraKu, nothing
in this place is beautiful. I stop and stare.

There's no ceiling.

Instead, lightning crackles above in a solid mass of clouds, pro-
viding regular but intermittent flashes of light. Like a weird strobe
light going off in a darkened room, it gives everything a kaleido-
scope appearance. Thunder echoes.

I swallow. "Bizarre."

"Weird," says Jake.

Charlie clucks. "Like Magnar."

In front of us, rows of cages separated by large aisles stretch into
the darkness. Some enclosures are as big as a small garage, some
tiny as a birdcage. Smaller ones are stacked on top of larger ones,
with a metal framework of posts and shelves supporting cages
above ground level.

Behind us, the wall with the door stretches to both sides into shadows, and upward, disappearing into the stormy sky above. Ammonia and manure odors fill the air, but the urge to keep going overpowers everything else.

I hurry with Jake across the cement floor toward the closest aisle.

"Do you sense methuselahs, Charlie?" I ask.

"Vaguely. Magnar's here somewhere."

"He is?" My surprise matches Jake's face. We stop and look at each other.

Slashing a hand, Jake says, "Okay, we find out what he's up to and we end it here."

"Maybe we can sabotage whatever he's doing, without having to fight him."

"I like it, kids."

We continue on. The first cage we pass has a koala bear sitting in it. During flashes of light, the koala's ash-colored fur appears matted, its big ears ragged.

The bear blinks, its black eyes staring at me, and then lowers its head.

Quickly, I look for a latch or some way to open the pen, but the cage is seamless. It has to be electronic. Other than a water bowl and a food dish, the pen is empty.

"Sam," pleads Jake. "There's nothing we can do."

I jog beside him, glancing back at the bear. It reminds me of the days I spent alone in my bedroom over the last year. "I've always wanted to see a koala bear, but not like this."

"Yeah, I hate it too," says Jake.

We speed down the aisle, Charlie flying beside us. Jake often looks back. Cement gutters run alongside the cages with coiled water hoses spaced in intervals of fifty yards.

The animals take all my attention. I murmur their names as we pass by; "Panda, chimpanzee, anaconda, goanna lizard, stork." There are even larger animals, like a leopard, wild boar, and tapir, staring out from dark cages, only their eyes moving.

The next aisle over has aquariums of different sizes, some with saltwater creatures such as octopi, coral sea snakes, and a large ocean sunfish, all floating in silence.

Lightning illuminates the glass containers, and the eye of a solitary bottlenose dolphin follows me, reminding me of the dolphins in KiraKu. The hopelessness of the animals seeps out of their eyes. I want to set them all free.

"It's like a graveyard," says Charlie.

"Magnar can't have permits for these animals." Jake covers his nose and mouth with his hand. "Many are illegal to trade. We have to call the police. This proves he's using the pet store as a front to order their food."

I scurry past the cages, my fingers trailing over the bars while vacant eyes peer back at me. "Why does he want them?"

Jake sweeps an arm. "To make money."

"Magnar doesn't wear expensive clothing or drive nice cars. And he doesn't need to fund an army."

Jake gestures to the cages. "He'd need lots of money to get all these animals here."

"Yeah, but I bet he's made millions over the centuries. And these animals were probably gathered over years."

Jake digs out his phone.

"It won't work," I say. "And even if it does, no one else can get in here."

Phone in hand, he regards me.

I lift my chin. "I went into our cabin for years before Rose lived there, but I never saw KiraKu."

"That's because you weren't with Rose. Or Rose changed something."

I shake my head. "You ran in before Rose."

He gestures impatiently. "Then what?"

"We both had Charlie's feathers. They allow us to see Magnar's shadow monsters and cross over to KiraKu, and now they're allowing us to view this place. Like a key in a lock. Originals and Lessers don't need them, but humans do."

"You're smart, kid."

"Sometimes." But Charlie's comment makes me feel good.

Jake's hand drops. "So if we call the police, you're saying all they'll find is an old empty warehouse?"

"Yeah, and your phone won't work here."

He dials 911, his taut face flashing in and out of the dim light. "Nothing."

An urge pulls my feet forward.

"We're on our own then." He puts the phone away. "And where's the big ugly?"

A flash of lightning shows a black door in a wall a hundred paces ahead of us. My stride quickens. I level my compass and the needle swings east for a few moments, toward *Trust* and the door, giving me confidence.

Jake's fingers twitch. "This place creeps me out."

Charlie slowly inches back and forth across my shoulder, the layer of gold light around his feathers stronger. The parrot says, "Magnar wants to return nature to its pristine state, but he doesn't care who or what he hurts in the process."

When we arrive at the black door my throat tightens. I pause with my hand on the cold doorknob. It isn't a choice about whether or not I should open the door. I have to. But all I want to do is run.

Jake grips my wrist.

"You too?" I ask.

"It's the staff. It has to be. Like at the river. As if it's encouraging us to do what we already know we should." He pauses. "So it's probably the right thing to do, and it's probably going to be scary again."

"Wonderful." Gulping, I push the door open and step through.

It's another room with another cloud-covered sky spattered with lightning, illuminating rows of cages again. But this time they're all empty. Occasional thunder crashes.

Bang.

I jump as the door slams shut. The closest aisle is to my right and we hustle into it. A putrid odor fills the air, making me gag.

"What's that smell?" I pinch my nose. "Like rotting meat."

"Ugh." Jake shivers. "Gross."

"Shh." Charlie tilts his head.

Our shoes make soft scrapes as we walk between two rows of dark, empty cages. Lightning crackles overhead. I hum until Jake elbows my arm, a finger pressed to his lips.

During a lightning flash, another wall appears ahead, with another identical black door. I wonder if it'll lead to another room, and another and another, endlessly.

In minutes we're at the end of the aisle, five yards from the wall. The stench is unbearable.

To the left of the black door, against the wall, two large cages sit side-by-side, hidden in shadows. Each pen has a large piece of cardboard in front of it, one with LYON scribbled on it, the other with CROCADIAL. Both are written in crayon.

I move closer. "It's the same handwriting as the blackmail note."

Jake grunts. "And he still can't spell."

Lightning flashes reveal the cages are empty. But in the shadows farther left of the enclosures are hints of paws, tails, and heads, some higher than myself. Chills run through me. I clench Whip-Eye and shuffle forward.

Lightning flashes and I stop.

A large number of dead animals—crocodiles, lions, and other things that aren't clear, form a heap twenty feet high. The carcasses give off a horrible stench. I've seen road kill, but never this many animals piled like garbage, as if they don't matter. Fierce words choke my throat.

Light strikes the pile again. Everything's all wrong and my eyes have to work to understand the patterns. An orangutan's head on an anteater's body, the head of an emu on the body of a sloth, and other bizarre combinations.

"How's he doing this?" I murmur. "And why?"

"Magnar's sick," mutters Jake.

A deep growl makes me yell and whirl.

"Ah!" Jake's hands fly up.

I can't see anything until lightning flashes. "No way."

"Momma mia!" says Charlie.

Wedged between the outer aisle cages is a big enclosure, and in the pen stands an animal. At first my brain doesn't believe what I'm seeing. A crocodile head is attached to the neck of an unusually large female lion's body.

The creature's bright eyes, catlike in shape, shift from me to Jake, then back to me. The live chimera takes all the air out of me.

The crocodile-headed lion bangs into the bars.

Darkness.

Lightning flashes. I gasp. The creature bent two of the bars three inches wider with its snout. Its reptilian mouth opens, as if in anticipation, its large eyes finding mine again.

It bangs into the bars twice more, pushing them apart another six inches. With a savage hiss, it shoves its toothy snout through.

The animal is stronger than any crocodile or lion could ever be. The whole sight is so strange I can't move.

With two more charges, the beast widens the bars farther. It squeezes its head through, growling wildly.

"Time to exit, kids." Charlie flies to the next aisle over.

Jake races after the parrot. I follow, staring at his back, hating that I'm last again. I look over my shoulder whenever lightning flares overhead.

Running past cages, I gape at more bizarre live animals. Bird wings on a Komodo dragon, the head of a polar bear on a Siberian musk deer, and the body of a rhino with an elephant head. Other things appear and my stomach lurches.

Bang! Bang!

When there's another flash of lightning, I check back.

The crocodile-headed lion is at the end of the aisle, charging after me in big, bounding leaps that make my legs pump faster.

Jake's already at the door, propping it open and motioning frantically. Charlie flies through.

"Is it gaining?" I yell.

Jake's scrunched face says yes. "Run! Don't look back."

That doesn't give me confidence, but I make it to the door and jump through.

Jake slams the door shut in the face of the leaping beast.

Bang. Growl. Bang. Growl. Bang!

Breathing hard, I watch the door while Charlie flaps back to my shoulder. We're quiet as the door bulges a few inches in three different places as the chimera pounds into it from the other side.

"Spooky," says Charlie. "And I hate horror movies."

"Now what?" asks Jake.

"We have to find out what Magnar is doing." My gaze travels along the wall, past the last aisle, where lightning reveals another wall with another black door. My gut tugs me in that direction. I trust my instincts, but check my compass anyway. It points south, toward the door.

Jake views the compass, then looks at me. "I feel it too." But he grabs my arm, stopping me from going forward.

I'm not sure why until I follow his gaze toward the last aisle before the door. Something is moving behind the cages, accompanied with the singsong voice.

"Where are you, wittle children?"

TWENTY-THREE

Trapped

I RUN AFTER JAKE into the aisle opposite the door, looking for a place to hide.

"Here." Jake squeezes sideways between cages into a space only a few feet wide, alongside posts supporting the upper shelves. I'm right behind him. The odors are stronger and animal dander is clogging my lungs.

"Take Charlie," I whisper. I transfer the parrot to Jake's hands.

Charlie's head droops.

Resting WhipEye against the cages, I take off my coat. Jake places the glowing parrot in it, and I gently wrap the cloth around him to hide his aura, leaving a small opening for him to see out of. Grasping the staff and cradling Charlie in my other arm, I stand sideways to hide him.

Jake whispers in my ear, "Hold your breath."

I suck in air and clamp my lips.

Bang. Growl. Bang. Growl. Bang!

"Hey, wittle crocle-lion, let's be good now. All's okay."

I peek out as thunder booms overhead. A massive man walks past the end of the aisle, humming. I only get a glimpse.

He must be over eight feet tall, his shoulders half as wide as the aisle, his big feet bare. The man speaks like a child, his words sing-song and high-pitched. As he walks in and out of shadowed light, loops of leather cord are visible—hanging over his shoulder, with a few yards of chain attached to the ends.

The giant swings the lengths of silver chain in one hand, clinking them together rhythmically. That freaks me out.

He stops in front of the door the crocle-lion is banging into. I hope he'll go through it.

"Wittle crocle-lion is a wittle upset, is he? All's gonna be okay, wittle crocle-lion. Uncle Biggie is here now."

Bang. Bang. Bang.

Lightning flashes illuminate a man with shaggy hair, a thick neck, and lumpy shoulders. The man's legs are shorter than his arms, his waist small, though his head reaches the second row of cages. His oversized bib overalls, crudely cut and sewn together from several different pieces of cloth, reach his calves. Beneath the bibs he wears a patchwork shirt.

He could crush me in his grip as easily as I might squeeze a paper cup.

Uncle Biggie twists our way and I duck out of sight. I don't move until a door opens and slams shut.

The banging stops immediately.

My lungs are burning and I exhale loudly.

"That man's a block of muscle, kids."

"I bet he wrote the note," says Jake. "It was a trap. That's why he chased us in the park."

"Yeah, you're right." I set WhipEye against a cage, bend over, and dig out my inhaler.

"Let's go." Jake pushes my shoulder, trying to move me into the aisle.

"Wait," I say hoarsely.

"Someone's here, is they? Not supposed to be, is they? Uncle Biggie hears ya, though."

I stick my head out. A dark figure is moving toward us. Uncle Biggie never went through the door.

I scoot back several steps, bumping into Jake, who grunts. My lungs have no air and I clumsily use my inhaler while bent over, then hold my breath.

"Come out, wittle children."

Pocketing the inhaler, I straighten and reach for the staff, but Jake hooks two of my belt loops and tugs me backward.

I exhale and whisper, "Let go, Jake." My fingertips graze Whip-Eye. I try to step forward, but instead stumble back as Jake keeps dragging me. My legs have the strength of cooked noodles and I barely struggle. "Hey, let go!"

"Listen," he hisses.

Silence.

Squashed by cage bars on either side, my lungs labor. Something rustles nearby.

During a flash of lightning a red and blue snout with big teeth appears inches from my face. "Geez. A mandrill." If its canines weren't so close I'd be curious.

Jake shouts and I snap my head around. He's staring at a large fruit-eating bat hanging upside down in a cage next to him.

Charlie sees it and shrieks.

"Uncle Biggie hears ya in there, he does. He saw ya break the chain on the door outside. Better come out now."

An eye with a hint of gold peers in at us, confirming Uncle Biggie is either an Original or a Lesser. The eye disappears and a loose fist pushes through the crack between the enclosures, sliding past WhipEye, just missing it. It reminds me of the large hand pushing through the back room curtain in the Endless Pet Store when I stole Charlie.

Backing up, my attention darts between the staff and the fist.

I step on Jake's toes and he mutters, "Watch out."

During lightning flashes, large fingers float toward me. I crane my head back as a finger wiggles back and forth an inch from my nose.

Charlie pokes his head out of my jacket and jabs it with his beak.

"Owwie!" Uncle Biggie slowly withdraws his hand. "That's not nice. Ya don't want to hurt Uncle Biggie, do ya?" His arm brushes against WhipEye and I panic.

The staff wobbles against the cage, then slowly rolls toward me. I reach for it.

The baboon barks and I jerk my hand back. All the animals wake up with roars, trumpets, and chirps, filling my ears with a deafening chorus.

Uncle Biggie reaches in again.

Jake pulls me backward through the pens.

"Stop, Jake!" But the animal chatter drowns out my words.

WhipEye falls and bounces on the floor.

In moments, Jake yanks me into the next aisle, and I stumble a few yards.

Across from us in a cage, a lowland gorilla appears in a flash of light, drumming its chest. In another pen a coyote howls.

"This way, Sam." Jake motions toward the outer door of the warehouse, hustling away from me.

"I have to go back."

"Are you crazy?" He turns, his hands mini-tornadoes. "Uncle Biggie's there."

"I don't care." WhipEye is calling to me and I step toward the space between the cages. Jake's right. I *am* crazy. But something like pain fills my stomach over separation from the staff.

He leaps in front of me, his hands pleading. "We'll come back for it."

"I can't leave it."

"Then let's hide somewhere until Uncle Biggie's gone."

"The big ugly's here, kids."

Lightning flashes at the far end of the aisle, and the massive shape of Uncle Biggie rounds the corner.

Darkness.

Jake wheels and runs. I race after him. Uncle Biggie doesn't make a sound, but I'm sure he's chasing us.

Thunder booms overhead.

Past laughing hyenas, yipping red foxes, and chirping parakeets we race until we reach the end of the aisle. Jake turns right, heading toward the door pulling at my gut. Next to it is an oversized garage door.

Jake runs to the smaller door. I worry it might be locked, but he snatches it open and we slip through.

Magnar stands fifty feet away.

TWENTY-FOUR

Creating Monsters

MAGNAR HAS HIS BACK TO US.

I close the door quietly, hoping the crashing thunder and lightning above us will drown out the burst of animal cries from the other room. Panic digs fingers into my throat.

Cringing, I expect the creep to turn around.

Flashes of lightning show him standing in front of a waist-high, metal computer workstation, while the large monitor he used in the pet store displays bright swirling images. To the side of the screen, a control panel on the workstation has a large, brass-handle switch.

I sidle along the wall beside Jake, past the large door, wrapping my coat tightly around Charlie to hide his glow. But the parrot pushes his beak to create a tiny opening.

Darkness hides Magnar, leaving only the bright monitor visible.

My legs are rubbery. I've brought Charlie to Magnar and I don't even have WhipEye to protect us. But the urge to understand what Magnar is doing keeps me alert.

Jake stands shoulder to shoulder with me, his face hidden in the dark.

In front of Magnar, in the center of the room, I see two large cages during lightning flashes. A square glass pen glints between them. Several more flashes reveal glass tubes, several feet in diameter, arcing from the top of the glass pen to the top of each cage. A twenty-foot wire antenna sticks out the top of the glass enclosure.

It's confusing until I glimpse an enormous glass sphere, probably a hundred feet in diameter, behind the glass cage and connected to it by a tube. Barely detectable in the light, curled up and floating in the middle of the globe, is Magnar's claw. Shivers run down my spine.

Vague shapes from inside the monster push against its surface, as if trying to remember what they were, before collapsing again into the whole. One of the fingers has fine cracks running along its surface where Jake struck it. It's satisfying to see it's still injured.

The small door slams open, and the racket from the animals in the warehouse pours into the room. Uncle Biggie ducks through the doorway head first, then squeezes through sideways, bending his knees, fragments of him appearing in the flashing light. He barely forces his chest through.

Though he's facing away from us, he has us trapped. He has to know we're in here. We're so dead.

My knees wobble when Magnar turns.

His leathery face is hard to see in the light, but his gold pupils shine. "Where have you been, you incompetent fool? I'm waiting for the specimens. And quiet those blasted animals."

I swing Charlie behind me. The parrot's glow will be easy for

Magnar to spot. *Please don't see us.*

The door closes, silencing the animal calls.

In a flash of light, Uncle Biggie appears facing Magnar, his hands fumbling together in front of his waist. The huge man's face has a childlike quality, making his age hard to guess.

"I sorry, Magnar. Chain broke. Uncle Biggie fixing it."

I'm stunned. Uncle Biggie's lying for us. Why?

Magnar speaks softly, as he did when he talked to Rose. But he killed Rose, so his kindness is creepy. "It's all right, Uncle Biggie. And I'm sorry I lost my temper, but that chain was brand new and thick chains don't just break, do they?"

He poses it like a friendly question, but my jaw clenches.

Uncle Biggie's singsong words slide to a higher pitch. "Uncle Biggie pulled it too hard."

"But what made the animals scream?" Magnar sounds kind. "You're good at keeping them quiet."

"The chain making too much noise."

Lightning reveals Magnar taking a step forward, mostly in shadows, rubbing his thumb ring. I want to run before he unleashes his snake, but there's nowhere to go.

"So you broke the chain and disturbed the animals?" Magnar's voice is scary calm.

I press my back hard against the wall. Lightning strikes show flashes of the creep's hands.

"We've been together for a long time, haven't we, Uncle Biggie?" Uncle Biggie makes a gesture and Magnar sighs, his tone sweet. "You're a dolt sometimes, but I'm fond of you and good help is hard to come by. Now, do I have to spell out what I want?"

I hope Uncle Biggie is shaking his head.

"Just get them." Magnar talks to Uncle Biggie as if he's a child. "You can do that, can't you?"

I want to melt into the wall.

"Yes, Magnar."

"Good."

Lightning flashes show Uncle Biggie backing, twisting sideways, and again contorting through the door.

Magnar returns to his workstation, muttering as equations and symbols appear on the bright monitor.

Jake nudges me toward the door, but I shake my head. I can't leave until I know what's going on.

In minutes the large door slowly rises, grating like chain dragged over broken cement. Uncle Biggie somehow quieted the animals in the other room. Another mystery.

The big man's feet come into view, along with animal legs. As the door rises it reveals an ostrich and domestic water buffalo.

"It's okay wittle buffalo and ostrich. Ya can trust Uncle Biggie." His large hands rest gently on their necks as he stands between them.

The ostrich flaps its wings and hoots deeply, but Uncle Biggie murmurs words I can't make out until it calms. With soft pats, he gently encourages the animals toward the cages.

Hooves clatter on cement.

I want to shout at Magnar to stop. Shame sweeps over me as I keep silent.

After he pushes the cage doors shut, Uncle Biggie steps back and rubs his palms together, mostly in shadows. "We needs to do this, don't we, Magnar?"

"No," I whisper.

Magnar doesn't turn around. "That's right, Uncle Biggie." Lightning crackles and he pulls the brass switch. "These two are sacrificing themselves for the good of the species."

White-hot light in the sky arcs down, streaking into the antenna and changing to a bright stream that flies through the glass tubes into the cages, bathing the ostrich and water buffalo in a glow. The animals remain motionless and the air carries a burnt odor.

Magnar steps away from the controls, toward the cages, his back to us. A soft sound. Metal against metal? Magnar's rings?

Lightning flashes. Magnar's arms are extended, his fingers spread wide, palms down. One hand faces the ostrich, the other the water buffalo. A tiny ray of golden light shines from each of his nine rings, joining into two single bands, one for each animal, spreading a film of gold over them.

After several seconds, Magnar lowers his limbs and his whole body droops.

Gradually the ostrich and water buffalo turn gray. Both animals melt away, fading into shadows that remind me of the captured methuselahs. I want to scream at Magnar. Jake's eyes are wide.

Magnar steps back to the control panel. Both animal shadows, looking like streams of fog, fly through the tubes leading to the glass pen, where flashes of light show the two shadows swirling and mixing into one single mass.

Magnar throws the brass switch in the opposite direction and a loud vacuum roar fills the room.

The shadow rips in half.

Jake turns rigid beside me. My stomach heaves and Charlie whimpers.

"No." Magnar braces his hands heavily on the computer station.

The two pieces of shadow move in reverse through the glass tubing, one blown to the ostrich cage, the other sucked to the glass sphere where it sinks into the massive claw. Soon a new shape pushes from beneath its skin.

In fragmented views, the swirling gray in the ostrich pen takes shape. Too quickly, lightning reveals a water buffalo body with an ostrich neck and head.

Jake gasps and I freeze.

The animal stands motionless, blinking.

Uncle Biggie claps once.

Lightning flashes.

The chimera collapses to the cage floor. My knees buckle.

Uncle Biggie cups his face with both hands. Wailing loudly, he rocks from side-to-side. "Oh, nooo." Lightning reveals tears or sweat glistening on the man's face.

Silently, I wail too. Jake clutches my arm.

Magnar's eyes shine. "Do you think this is any easier on me? The chimeras are accidents, the price we pay for not having ten rings. But we're doing this to save all ostriches and all buffalo, to return nature to its rightful throne. I'm using technology to destroy all machines. Now quit acting like a blubbering idiot and get rid of that thing. And get two more specimens."

"But maybe machine not ready for this." Uncle Biggie sniffles. "Maybe ya should do one animal."

I want to charge Magnar and smash his computer monitor, but I'll never get there before his snake appears. If I had WhipEye, it might be possible. The idea of getting it and coming back to fight Magnar gives me strength. I'll destroy his computer and permanently ruin his experiments.

Magnar's eyes glint with gold as he glares at Uncle Biggie. "One animal at a time would take forever, you dolt. I want to be able to do a hundred at a time. A thousand. The process just needs tweaking, and we have plenty of subjects to experiment on. It's how you conduct science if you want results. Now get more specimens."

"But . . ."

When lightning flashes again, the cobra is staring down at Uncle Biggie. "Doesss Uncle Biggie need sssome help?" The snake's heads sway side to side.

I panic the cobra will see the aura surrounding Charlie, and I twist farther to keep the parrot hidden.

"We're through talking," snaps Magnar.

Uncle Biggie has fists at his sides.

In the dark, metal rubs against metal again.

A flash of lightning reveals Magnar extending one hand. A small stream of golden light from his five rings strikes Uncle Biggie's face, and the big man's fists relax and he lowers his head.

"Now do as you're told." Magnar drops his arm and faces the control panel.

The cobra floats in the air near the creep. "That'sss right, little man, follow directionsss."

In fractured images, Uncle Biggie shuffles to the cage and lifts the dead animal, cradling it. When he walks out the large door, the cobra slithers back into Magnar's ring.

I shakily slip along the wall to the open garage door. Peeking around the corner, the way appears clear. Thunder echoes above as I sneak out with Jake.

When we're far enough away, we run to the aisle where we lost WhipEye. I keep Charlie wrapped in my coat, so if Uncle Biggie's nearby he won't see the parrot's glow.

My legs wobble as though I'm running on a tilted surface. Reaching the aisle, I veer left toward the front of the warehouse, determined to go back and fight Magnar.

"Where is it?" Jake wrings his hands.

Like following a trail, my gut leads me to the separation between the cages. "Here."

Sssssssss.

I pivot.

"It'sss lovely to sssee you again, girl and boy."

All fifty feet of the cobra is slithering through shadows just above the floor near the end of the aisle. The snake's two heads rear up twenty feet. "There'sss no need to run. I could ussse a little sssnack."

For a split second I glance at the cobra's shining eyes. "Don't stare at it, Jake."

But he's already stiff, his hands at his sides.

I grab his wrist and drag him into the crack between the cages. As I squeeze through, he wakes up and shouts, pushing against my back.

Bang.

"Move," yells Jake.

Off balance, stumbling forward, I look back.

Pushing cages aside with its snouts, the cobra is coming after us.

A panther in one of the cages snarls. A hawk screeches from another.

Shoving the outer cages aside with its heads, ignoring the animal cries, the snake jams itself forward with one head atop the other. Its dark eyes are level with mine. Two tongues flick at us.

Jake ducks and charges with his palms pushing my back. To keep from falling, I clutch a cage. I see WhipEye lying on the cement floor five feet in front of me.

"Go," yells Jake.

"I'm trying." I move sideways, making sure I don't hurt Charlie.

Squawk.

"You . . . can't . . . essscape." Pushing with its coiled bulk, the snake slides a whole row of cages a few feet apart, wedging its writhing body into the crack.

A howler monkey screams and a boar squeals. Metal grinds against concrete and more animals add to the din.

Jake keeps pushing me through the cages. I kick the end of the staff, sliding it along the cement floor ahead of me until I stumble into the next aisle, teetering.

Unwrapping Charlie from my coat, I say, "Fly to the door, Charlie." If we have to fight the snake, the parrot is safer away from us.

Flapping down the aisle, wavering side to side, Charlie looks like a bright ghost.

I bend over and snatch WhipEye. As soon as my fingers curl around the wood I'm whole again, as if I've regained a lost part of myself.

"You . . . will . . . regret . . . thisss." Hissing, the snake writhes wildly between the banging cages, stuck. Its thick body is unable to squeeze past the center pens, but its two heads glare at us from three feet away in the narrow space. I'm careful to focus on its neck, not its eyes.

All the animals wake up and the warehouse explodes with cries again.

"You stupid snake." Jake cocks his arm, holding the open canteen as if he's going to toss healing water at the monster.

I grab his shoulder. "We can't, Jake. You'll kill the methuselah."

Wild-eyed, he stares at me, and then he plugs the flask and we run for the front door.

"Uncle Biggie sees ya, he does."

Jake looks back and shouts.

I gasp.

Taking long, silent strides, the huge man is running toward us. Ahead of Uncle Biggie, held on the leather and chain leash, the crocle-lion is growling, showing dagger teeth.

Cages shudder against cement as the cobra squirms wildly into the aisle, ramming into Uncle Biggie. The two monsters tumble to the floor and the snake winds itself around the big man's legs.

Uncle Biggie grabs the cobra below its two heads, while the crocle-lion circles the snake with snapping jaws.

"Ssstupid dolt."

As I race past cages of imprisoned creatures, they stare at me. I hate leaving them behind.

Near the outer door, Charlie perches on top of the koala bear cage. There's no sign of Magnar. Too busy making his monster, he must have sent the cobra to check out Uncle Biggie's story.

Jake flings open the door and we fly through it. Charlie glides above me.

The door bangs shut and we run.

TWENTY-FIVE

The Old River Bridge

I RUN IN MY SLUGGISH PENGUIN GAIT for a half-mile until wheezing forces me to walk.

The night is fresh, but the odors of the Endless Warehouse cling to my clothing.

Images of the dead chimeras and all the caged animals swim through me, and the thought of the crocle-lion twists my stomach. Magnar changed two magnificent animals into a hideous freak.

"Come on," says Jake. "I don't want Uncle Biggie or the snake to get us."

I follow him down the street with weak legs. Charlie lands on my shoulder and perches quietly.

The warehouse door never opens, so no one is chasing us, but the cobra will ensure Magnar knows we were there.

"So much for a surprise attack." I can't keep the disappointment out of my words.

"You tried," says Charlie. "No one could have guessed what Magnar was doing. Rose and I had no idea."

Ahead, Jake stops beneath a tree near the curb, his fingers fumbling over the keypad of his cell phone.

Hurrying to him, I touch his forearm. "Don't call your mom."

"We have to tell somebody." He keeps pushing buttons. "They're killing animals."

"They won't find Magnar or the animals."

"So what?" But he leans against the tree, his face drawn. "We have to do something. He's creating monsters." He looks at the parrot. "Charlie, could you give the police feathers?"

"Not enough to matter." The parrot hangs his head. "Giving my feathers away takes energy, so it won't exactly perk me up to lose more now."

It's obvious Charlie is dying. Even his voice is weaker. I have to believe we can save the parrot. I can't lose this friend. Not now.

But everything is worse than I imagined, and we have no way to stop Magnar from running his experiments and eventually starting his war.

Jake gives a half-hearted gesture. "If we go to the Army, we could guide them against Magnar's shadow monsters. Or they could destroy the warehouse."

Charlie clucks softly. "We don't have time to convince anyone of that, kiddo. And Magnar will have an escape plan if tanks appear at his door. Even if he doesn't, we'd be killing all those animals in the warehouse and the methuselahs trapped in his rings."

"Then what are we going to do?" asks Jake.

Charlie is quiet, and I don't have an answer.

Bright lights of a slow-moving car sweep the street.

Charlie flies, and we jog across the sidewalk and lawn, ducking behind bushes near the side of a house.

When a spotlight sweeps over the grass, we run into the back-yard and continue cutting behind houses, always surrounded by shadows. The moon breaks through the clouds, giving us enough light to avoid running into trash cans, swing sets, and hoses. I trip once anyway.

Finally blocked by a fence, we pause at the back corner of a house and sneak around to the front so we can view the street again. Empty. I sag against the side of the house, while Charlie flutters to my shoulder.

Jake lifts a tired hand. "Those empty cages must have been filled with animals that Magnar already killed in his experiments."

"He might have been creating his claw for centuries," I say.

The parrot shivers. "We can't let Magnar win. All those poor fellows waiting to die."

I try to find something hopeful and images from KiraKu sweep through me: stopping the buffalo shadow, crossing the river, and escaping the claw. "We made it through KiraKu, so we can find a way to stop Magnar."

"That's the spirit, kid. Anything is possible, if you believe it is."

"I want to stop Magnar," says Jake. "But how?"

I look at him, glad he's with me, and that he cares. "Come on."

We cross the lawn to the street and head toward town. I want to put more distance between us and Magnar's warehouse.

"I feel sorry for Uncle Biggie," I say.

"Sorry?" Jake slashes the air with his hands. "He helped Magnar kill those animals. Turning them into freaks."

"Uncle Biggie cared when one died. And he tried to stop Magnar. Maybe Magnar's forcing him to help."

"Who cares? He's guilty. They both belong in jail."

"Uncle Biggie lied to Magnar to protect us."

"Uncle Biggie chased us with the crocle-lion." Jake shakes his head. "We were lucky to get away from him. Did it ever occur to you that he might want us for himself, for who knows what? Like Magnar said, he's half idiot."

"Maybe the chase was an act." I think of my parents. "Someone that gentle with animals can't be evil."

Jake waves off that idea. "The blackmail note about meeting at the Old River Bridge is another trap."

"We have to go. The note said he'd hurt my father if we don't."

"He's probably lying."

An idea jolts me and I stop. "Wait a minute. Uncle Biggie wrote the note. It has to be his writing, so it's him we're meeting at the bridge."

Jake stops, hands on his hips. "Magnar will probably be there too."

"But if Uncle Biggie planned to give us to Magnar, he would have already done it. Think about it. Why did he take so long to go into the warehouse after us? He was hoping we'd come out right away. Then he lied for us. He wants something from us and might be willing to help us fight Magnar."

"What could we have that he wants?" Jake sounds doubtful.

"What if he wants to stop Magnar and needs our help? What if Magnar's controlling Uncle Biggie with the rings, with the gold light he sent into his eyes?"

"Or trying to." Charlie clicks. "Maybe Uncle Biggie's faking that he's under Magnar's control."

Jake motions excitedly. "What if that's how Magnar plans to control humans? He could use his rings to force them to do whatever he wants. Leaders, generals, presidents."

"He could go to the United Nations and hypnotize everyone there in one sitting." I glance sideways. "Would he have enough power to do that, Charlie?"

"If he gets me, he could do it." The parrot cocks his head. "And I'm guessing that trick will work much better on humans than on Originals or Lessers. Magnar can't use it on you, as long as you have my feathers. You make good detectives, kids."

"All right," says Jake. "If Magnar is at the bridge, Charlie will sense the methuselahs and we figure out a Plan B."

"Great plan," I say. He gives a flicker of a smile, and I add, "If Magnar isn't there, we talk to Uncle Biggie."

His brow furrows. "Tarath should be able to take care of the big lunk. So should WhipEye." He checks his phone. "All right, we have enough time to get to the bridge early."

"The blackmail note said eleven. Why be early? "

"To avoid a trap."

He heads north and I hustle after him. Images of Magnar's experiments run through my mind. How did Magnar start out like Rose, protecting methuselahs, yet end up heartless?

With every shadow I pass, I imagine Uncle Biggie and the cro-cle-lion jumping out at me, or worse, the cobra.

After a few blocks we head west, toward *Trust* again, to another deserted dirt road. Two miles later the Old River Bridge appears in the moonlight.

The small bridge has metal arches and a wooden base. The sight of it pulls at me, like the river in KiraKu and the black door in the Endless Warehouse.

We slip among a clump of trees on the side of the road.

"Charlie?" I ask.

"No methuselahs anywhere near here, kids. No Magnar."

Jake looks at me. "What does the compass say?"

I already know what it will say, but I show it to him. The needle moves from north to northwest, aimed at the bridge. We exchange glances.

Slowly, we move through trees until we run out of cover and have to step onto the road. Uncle Biggie could be hiding anywhere, but I'm hoping he isn't here yet. That hope is immediately dashed.

A piece of cardboard taped to one of the arches has a big arrow drawn on it, pointing across the bridge. Beneath the arrow are large sloppy letters in crayon:

THIS A WAY. FALL O AIR O.

"Uncle Biggie's already here." I stare across the bridge, which is only ten feet wide. A sign on one of the supports reads:

NO MOTORIZED TRAFFIC.
Pedestrians and bicycles only.

Jake turns in a slow three-sixty, whispering, "Uncle Biggie could be watching us now."

"Lucky us. Look, if we go halfway across, he can't block both ends of the bridge." I spin WhipEye in the moonlight until I find Tarath's face, which gives me reassurance. The pull to go onto the bridge is growing inside me.

Jake's hands make small arcs. "It's too easy."

"What if I go to the center of the bridge with Charlie? If Uncle Biggie won't talk or join us, Charlie can fly away and I can jump. I did it once with Mom and Dad during the summer. The water's not deep and I'm a good swimmer."

But the last time I jumped, Dad was in the warm water and Mom stood beside me, the sun bright and hot. Now the black water sends a chill into my limbs. This time of year it has to be cold.

"I've heard worse plans," says Charlie. "Let's do it."

Jake says, "I'm coming with you, Sam."

"You should wait here. If there's trouble, call your mom or the police. They can handle Uncle Biggie."

Jake bites his lip. "I can call Mom from the bridge."

"You said you're not a great swimmer."

"I'm good enough. Besides, both of us might have to use the staff."

"Good point." I feel safer with him beside me anyway.

We slowly walk onto the bridge. The moonlight shines on the spaced wooden boards and the water below us glistens. On the other side of the river, the bridge ends in a dirt road that borders Superior National Forest.

Trying to steady myself, I hum.

"Why do you always hum the same song?" asks Jake.

"It calms me."

His tone softens. "Well, do it quietly."

My thoughts drift to Mom's gentle face, her soft inviting eyes, and her playful voice. It's painful, but I don't immediately push the memories away as I have all last year. Images flash through me . . . *something red flies past me and light blinds my eyes. . . .*

"Sam. Samantha." Jake shakes my shoulder and I blink.

We're at the center of the bridge.

Out of the trees on the far side steps Uncle Biggie. In the moonlight he appears even bigger, well over eight feet. His eyes flash gold.

My mouth is dry. "He's a monster."

Charlie whistles. "Add some green and we've got Shrek."

Uncle Biggie's singsong words fill the night. "Wittle children, let parrot fly to Uncle Biggie."

I gesture to him. "Thanks for lying to Magnar to protect us. We can work together to stop him."

"Magnar trying to save all animals. If you don't give me wittle parrot, Magnar say he hurt your daddy more. Give me parrot, then wittle children can go home."

Confident he'll listen to reason, I take a step forward. "Magnar's not a good person, he's—"

"Magnar my father."

"Crap." That definitely puts a kink in my plan.

"He's not going to help us." Jake backs up. "Let's get out of here."

Charlie whistles. "Time to bail, kids."

A growl causes me to pivot. On the other end of the bridge is the crocle-lion, yawning, its huge open snout revealing rows of gleaming white teeth, its eyes bright ovals.

In two strides I'm at the side rail. I climb jerkily, placing one foot on the top, ready to jump. Charlie flutters to the bridge railing, teetering on it as if he might not have enough strength to fly away. But Jake is absent.

I swing around. He's standing at the center of the bridge, staring at the crocle-lion.

"Jake!"

He looks at me, the moon shining in his blue eyes. "I can't swim at all, Sam."

TWENTY-SIX

Capture

EVERYTHING HAPPENS AT ONCE.

Jake dials his cell phone and Charlie squawks.

Uncle Biggie takes enormous, silent strides along the bridge, while the crocle-lion thumps toward us from the other side, growling and wagging its large head with its eyes narrowed to slits.

"Mom," shouts Jake. "We're on the old bridge."

I hustle back to Jake's side as he yells into his phone, "We're being attacked by a nutcase and the crocle-lion. Help! Right now. On the old bridge. North of town!"

I forgot about Charlie. He's still perched on the bridge railing. "Fly away, Charlie!"

He takes off, flying in a wobbly pattern toward Uncle Biggie. What's the crazy parrot thinking? The giant will crush the small bird. "Charlie!"

"Call Tarath." Jake has the cell phone pressed to his ear. "Call her, Sam."

Raising the staff, I face Uncle Biggie.

Charlie flies wide of the big man's charge, circling around to follow him. Maybe the parrot plans to peck him from behind.

I slam WhipEye into the bridge—there's no echo. Still, the Great One's name roars through my lips; "Tarath!"

I'm shocked when the cat's face remains dark on the staff, the wood cold in my hands. I twist to see Jake.

The crocle-lion is six feet away when it jumps.

Pushing me to the side, Jake lifts his hands in a martial arts stance, yelling, "Hiyah!"

The large head of the crocle-lion flies through the air, aimed at him.

"Jake," I shout.

He jumps sideways, chopping at the crocle-lion's neck.

I face Uncle Biggie. He's two steps away and towers over me. With all my strength I thrust the staff forward. But the man swerves impossibly fast to the side, around the end of WhipEye, reminding me of how fast Tom moved.

Before I can strike again, a thick forearm clamps around my waist, lifting me off the bridge. I struggle to thump the staff once more, but Uncle Biggie's massive arm keeps WhipEye immobile in my grip.

My lungs are starved and I'm squeaking, "Tarath. Tarath."

"Screaming not a good thing to do." Uncle Biggie taps the side of my head softly. "Hurts the ears, it do."

Struggling against the giant's arm, I can't see Jake. The crocle-lion is standing to the side, Jake's cell phone held between its teeth. I imagine the beast bit off Jake's hand and he's lying on the bridge, dying.

"Jake," I croak. "Jake."

"Put her down!" He appears from the side, throwing a circle kick, which Uncle Biggie avoids by stepping back.

Next, Jake comes in fast with palm strikes. I'm amazed how good he is, and how brave.

But Uncle Biggie moves in a blur, sweeping Jake's arms aside. With his free hand he pushes Jake's shoulder, spinning him around, then wraps the same arm around his body, clamping Jake's arms to his ribs.

Uncle Biggie heaves me to one side of his massive torso, Jake to the other.

Jake kicks Uncle Biggie's thigh with his heels, but otherwise he's unable to move in the giant's grasp.

The crocle-lion cocks its head as a small voice yells from the phone, "Jake. Jake. Are you all right, Honey?"

"Mom," gasps Jake. He stops kicking. "Mom."

Crunching the phone with its teeth, the monster lifts its head and gulps it. Then it nuzzles against Uncle Biggie's leg.

"Good wittle crocle-lion," purrs Uncle Biggie. He bends his knees to pat the monster's head.

My eyes widen when I finally notice Charlie sitting on Uncle Biggie's shoulder. "Go, Charlie," I whisper hoarsely.

"I'm too tired, Sam. Besides, friends don't abandon friends."

Uncle Biggie's forearm is an iron bar around me, and my legs dangle like a puppet's as he carries us across the bridge. Jake kicks a few more times half-heartedly, and then goes limp.

My body droops too, except for the hand clutching WhipEye. Why didn't Tarath come? How could the compass and my gut both be wrong?

Uncle Biggie has Charlie, but he lied about letting Jake and me go. And I'm sure he plans to give WhipEye to Magnar. I'm going to fail Dad *like I failed Mom*.

That idea's been boiling beneath the surface for a long time. Though he never said it, Dad's silence over the last year felt like he was accusing me of Mom's death. Maybe I did cause her death, and that prevents me from remembering my last moments with her.

But I don't want to hide from the truth anymore, no matter how painful it might be.

On the other side of the bridge the dirt road curves east, but Uncle Biggie steps into the thick woods, heading north.

When we enter the dark forest, the bridge and moonlit waters disappear. Superior National Forest encompasses hundreds of miles. An easy place to hide in.

Uncle Biggie moves smoothly through the woods, not disturbing anything. Originals and Lessers probably don't leave tracks. However, Cynthia will organize a search party and Dad will never stop looking for me.

A short time later, we arrive at another river running north and south.

Uncle Biggie easily jumps from the shore onto a large rock in the middle of the running water. However, instead of crossing the river, he leaps fluidly from rock to rock in the center of the flowing dark liquid, the crocle-lion following. Dogs won't be able to track our scent.

As the glistening waters of the river pass by, I think of Mom. Her smiling face. I miss her more than anything.

Tarath's words come back to me then; *If you strike the ground once with WhipEye, Samantha Green, and call Tarath, I must and will come.*

The bridge runs above ground, so the caracal never heard the staff's call. I hang my head.

We're moving north, toward *Love*, but all I have inside me is emptiness.

TWENTY-SEVEN

Uncle Biggie

I TRY TO COUNT MILES, but the darkness and my sleepy eyes make it impossible to judge distance on the winding water. The river turns into a stream, and Uncle Biggie jumps off the last rock and wades through shallow water.

Eventually he takes us back into the forest, where he moves at a fast pace. Often ducking tree branches, he finds a path around everything.

The crocle-lion trots ahead as if on familiar territory.

My limbs flop like a doll's as the man carries me. I can't see Jake, and Charlie hangs his head, the glow around his body even stronger, as if his life is seeping out of him. It's hard to watch.

After another hour, a high cliff blocks our way. Trees and bushes grow in front of it.

Careful not to step on any plants, Uncle Biggie slips between two of the taller spruce trees. On the other side is a large hidden cave mouth.

The man hurries into the dark entrance, rounds the first corner, and carries us into a giant cavern with a high ceiling, dimly lit by burning lanterns. It's cooler inside, refreshing, and the air is damp. Large boulders litter the floor of the cave and the walls arch far above us into deep shadows.

No one will find us here. Wondering when Magnar will arrive, I clutch WhipEye. I plan to call Tarath as soon as Uncle Biggie releases me.

He sets Jake down first. "Stay here, now."

The crocle-lion lies in the dirt in front of Jake, blocking the exit from the cave, resting its reptilian head on its paws. Jake pales and doesn't blink as he faces the creature.

Charlie flutters to a big rock, wobbling when he lands.

Striding farther into the cave, Uncle Biggie slips WhipEye from my grasp, sending a jolt of panic through me.

"No," I murmur.

The staff is our only way to defeat Magnar, but something else about parting from it hurts again, as though I've lost something important.

He puts me down, straightening to look at me.

Exhausted, I glance at the crocle-lion, then at WhipEye in Uncle Biggie's hand. We're finished.

The big man bends over me, his eyes big as golf balls. "Ya be a good girl, now."

"Right. I'll try," I say hoarsely. Unsure what he thinks a bad girl would do, I dig out my inhaler and take a puff.

"I so sorry." The man leans closer. "Why you not tell Uncle Biggie ya couldn't breathe?"

"You big brute." Jake keeps his arms plastered against his sides, his body rigid in front of the crocle-lion.

Uncle Biggie glances at him.

I exhale weakly and take a step back, unsure what to think of the giant.

He swings back to me. "Aw, wittle girl, is ya scared of Uncle Biggie?"

"Kind of."

"Everything is okay now. Ya can trust Uncle Biggie."

"That's what you told the ostrich and water buffalo."

"Uncle Biggie doing what's best for wittle friends." He sounds hurt.

Without taking his eyes off the beast in front of him, Jake says, "You're a stooge for that monster, Magnar, sent to catch us and turn us over to him."

"Maybe not." Moving my head slightly, I try to gain Jake's attention. Bad-mouthing Uncle Biggie's father isn't a great way to get the big man on our side.

"Nooo," croons the giant. "Uncle Biggie try to warn ya not go in warehouse."

"You did not," says Jake.

Even I wonder if that's true, but the man wags a finger slowly at Jake. "Uncle Biggie not think ya can break chain and get in, so he not run at ya. Not want to scare ya. And Magnar say bring ya there now, but Uncle Biggie don't want him to hurt wittle children, so he bring ya to his secret cave."

He adds, "Uncle Biggie help wittle children escape from big snake in warehouse too. Not tell Magnar."

Sighing, I sit down on a large rock. "It makes sense, Jake."

I'm right about Uncle Biggie protecting us, but it doesn't matter. He's going to hand Charlie over to Magnar, and he has Whip-Eye. Even if he doesn't want to hurt us, he's not on our side.

Fists at his sides, Jake says, "I don't believe you. Anyone who kills animals can't be trusted."

"Nooo. Uncle Biggie never hurts wittle animals. Uncle Biggie loves 'em."

He steps away to a cardboard box big enough to hold a small car. Nestled in shadows behind some boulders, I didn't notice it before.

Setting WhipEye against it, he reaches in and takes out a folded yellow bed sheet, which he flaps open and spreads on the dirt near me. The cloth has many stains on it, some of them dark red.

Wild thoughts race through me, but I let those go. Instead, my gaze rests on WhipEye and the ache returns. But it's too far away. Uncle Biggie would easily stop me.

While he rummages inside the box, I inspect the cave for another exit.

Pencil drawings of animals on large pieces of white construction paper are pinned to the walls with small knives and sharp sticks. A few framed oil paintings hang from spikes. Uncle Biggie couldn't have painted them, for they all have a delicate, professional appearance.

Several of the drawings show a young woman with dark hair in various poses around wild animals, reminding me of KiraKu. The woman has to be Rose, when Magnar loved her. Thinking of her again brings up sadness.

All the artwork has a bright, natural beauty, at odds with the dark walls of the cave.

In different nooks rest pots and pans, a large trash can with a lid, and a crude bed made of tree branches and leaves. Other miscellaneous items like a rubber tire, an old swing set, and pieces of junk lie scattered throughout the cave. Shadows hide the rear of the cavern.

There's no way out except past the crocle-lion.

"Let us have a nice wittle picnic." Uncle Biggie carries two loaves of bread to the sheet, along with large tubs of peanut butter and raspberry jam. The red jam relaxes me about the sheet stains.

My stomach growls.

A butter knife and three cups come out next, which Uncle Biggie sets on the ground cloth. Lastly, he brings two gallon jugs of water and fills the cups.

Sitting on the sheet, he makes two stacks of five sandwiches.

Finished, he gets up again and reaches back into the cardboard box, pulling out two large hams. Walking over to the crocle-lion, he tosses the meat in front of it. At least he's not feeding *us* to the monster.

The animal rises and attacks its dinner, growling and tearing at the hams. Gulping large chunks of meat, the beast keeps its eyes on Jake. I don't think it's as tame as Uncle Biggie believes.

Uncle Biggie returns to the sheet. Grabbing one of the jugs, he empties it with one long drink. Then he plows through the sandwiches.

Watching him reminds me of my gurgling stomach. I slide off the stone to the sheet, moving toward the food.

Uncle Biggie motions me closer while he chews.

Mechanically, I take two slices of bread from a bag and sniff them. They smell fresh, so I make a peanut butter and jam sandwich, and take a bite. It's delicious, but I chew with dulled interest.

Jake glances at me. "How can you trust him?"

"I'm starving."

"He's going to give us to Magnar."

"Maybe, but I'm still hungry."

Charlie flutters to the sheet. I wince when he takes a few shaky steps to my cup to sip some water. The parrot gargles, and says, "Now give me some of that grub, kid. I'm starving."

Breaking off half my sandwich, I put it on the sheet where the parrot greedily pecks at it. I try not to consider that it might be his last meal. Bread crumbs fly everywhere.

Uncle Biggie finishes his final sandwich. "Magnar want Charlie back, because wittle Samantha stole him away."

"Hey." I lift a hand in protest. "I didn't steal Charlie. I *freed* him. Magnar was keeping him prisoner."

His brow knits, then he says, "Uncle Biggie want to know something. Wittle people have a dad and mom?" He sounds sincere.

I take a gulp of water. "Yes." I hang my head a little. "Mom's gone, but I have a dad." I picture him rotting in jail, wondering if I'll ever see him again.

"I sorry your mom gone."

"I am too." Uncle Biggie appears truly sad, and I believe him.

Jake shuffles backward, away from the crocle-lion. Finished with the hams, the animal lifts its head, making him pause. "And when our parents find you, you'll go to prison for the rest of your life."

Uncle Biggie sits back, his face drawn. Then he bends forward again. "Magnar find Uncle Biggie when he all alone in streets in London. People make fun of Uncle Biggie or act scared of him, so Uncle Biggie live in sewers wit rats. Animals like Uncle Biggie. Uncle Biggie help wittle children living in streets. They name him Uncle Biggie."

He pauses. "Magnar like that I friends wit birds and rats and other animals. Uncle Biggie hears them talk. Good ears. Magnar bring me here to help him save all animals. Magnar say he my father, but Uncle Biggie want to find real parents. Learn real name."

Some of my concerns fade away. Uncle Biggie isn't Magnar's flesh and blood, after all. And I understand his loneliness. I lost Mom, and in a way I also lost Dad over the last year.

Jake glares at him. "Who cares what Magnar says? He's a murderer."

Uncle Biggie's face darkens.

I frown at Jake. He needs to ease up on his attack. The big man might have a temper.

Charlie devours the rest of the half sandwich, wipes his beak on the cup, and takes another sip of water. Then he cocks his head at Uncle Biggie. "Magnar's been lying to you, Uncle Biggie."

The giant shakes his head, his singsong voice rising. "No, no, no. Magnar good. He promise Uncle Biggie he save wittle animals, save Charlie, help everyone."

I search for a way to convince him of the truth. "Magnar treats you horribly. How can you put up with that?"

The giant looks at me innocently. "Magnar help Uncle Biggie for long time."

Eyeing the crocle-lion, Jake finally reaches the sheet. He whirls on Uncle Biggie. "What about all the animals you've changed into mutants?"

The big man winces.

"Magnar's making a monster with the animals," I say.

"To save all animals," Uncle Biggie says softly.

I give up trying to prove Magnar's guilt to him.

After watching me finish my sandwich, Jake quickly makes one for himself, shoving chunks of it into his mouth. Maybe he'll stop talking now.

But while chewing, he says, "You belong locked up."

Eyes wide, Uncle Biggie stares at him.

Before Jake can toss out another angry remark, I say, "That might not be true. Are you scared of Magnar, Uncle Biggie?" I wipe crumbs from my lips, ignoring Jake as he rolls his eyes. "Are you worried he'll hurt you?"

"Magnar nice to Uncle Biggie. Help Uncle Biggie draw." He points to an especially good painting of an Atlantic spotted dolphin leaping over a rainbow, pinned to the cavern wall.

"You didn't paint that." Jake motions scornfully. "That's professional artwork."

"Magnar draw it when Uncle Biggie smaller."

Jake says quietly, "Magnar drew beautiful pictures of animals?"

"How could Magnar draw such beauty and commit such evil?" I whisper.

"Uncle Biggie no liar."

"But Magnar is a big, fat liar about some things." Charlie fluffs his feathers. "Stick out your hand, Uncle Biggie."

I stare at the parrot. Uncle Biggie should be able to see methuselahs and KiraKu without a feather. "What for, Charlie?"

The parrot tilts his head at me. "Truth should never be kept for just the few, Sam."

I'm confused.

Uncle Biggie's forehead wrinkles, but he extends a palm. Charlie uses his beak to pull a gray feather from his underwing.

Jake's eyebrows arch and we trade glances. Our red feathers came from Charlie's tail. It never occurred to me his other feathers might have any significance.

Taking a few awkward steps, the parrot drops the feather into the big man's hand.

Uncle Biggie's mouth opens and his eyes widen.

Charlie wobbles back to me, his head hanging. I pick him up and hold him gently. "Oh, Charlie."

Uncle Biggie wraps his fingers around the feather, his face a grimace. He closes his eyes and rocks back and forth.

"What's wrong with him, Charlie?" I ask.

"The feather helps him understand his relationships."

"Why didn't I get that one?"

The parrot sounds as weary as I am. "There's only so much a

person is ready for, Sam, and some things are better learned on your own."

"Sometimes it seems like I'm not learning anything."

"Remember that humility, kid. When you assume you know everything, you can become a Magnar."

"Nooo." Uncle Biggie wails loudly, his cries echoing through the cave. "What has Uncle Biggie done? Nooo."

Crying like a child, his whole body shakes and tears run down his face. It convinces me he doesn't want to hurt anyone or anything.

He continues to wail for several minutes and then stops, wiping his closed eyes. "Uncle Biggie has done wrong. Uncle Biggie a bad person."

"That's right, you are," says Jake. When Charlie and I glance sharply at him, he asks, "Well, he is, isn't he?"

"Everyone can change, kiddo, even a monster like Magnar, if he wants to."

Jake's hands do flips. "Magnar can change while he's spending lots of time in jail."

A surge of energy fills my limbs. "It's all right, Uncle Biggie. You can make everything right again. You can help us stop Magnar."

The giant quiets his rocking and opens his eyes. "Uncle Biggie will help ya."

Those words ring in my ears, filling me with a deep sense of responsibility. Something else occurs to me. With Uncle Biggie's help we have a better chance to defeat Magnar, which means going to the bridge *was* the right thing to do, after all. The compass wasn't wrong. Neither was I.

Jake looks at me. "So what's next?"

Uncle Biggie spreads his hands. "Magnar has terrible shadows. Scary."

Charlie eyes me. "It's your move, Sam."

My gut gives me an immediate answer. "We have to go back to the Endless Warehouse."

Uncle Biggie's mouth forms an *O* and Jake's face scrunches.

Who can blame them? I'm asking them to do the impossible. I look at each of them. "I have no idea how to defeat Magnar or get his rings, but we have to go back."

I also don't say how scared I am, but Dad, the caged animals, and Magnar's cruel experiments won't leave my brain alone.

Charlie claws his way up to my shoulder and shakes his wings. "I trust you, kid. You keep surprising me." The parrot's grip is weak, so I move my palm near his feet in case he falls.

The big man's face steadies. "Uncle Biggie will go, if ya wittle people go."

Jake flips a hand. "We have to stop Magnar."

Though I'm glad for their loyalty, their support also puts more weight on my spirit. What if they're hurt or worse?

The parrot inches across my shoulder. "We're all making our own decision, Sam."

Sometimes I think the parrot can read my mind. "Thanks, Charlie."

"When are we going?" Jakes looks at all of us.

Uncle Biggie yawns and stretches his limbs. "Uncle Biggie need sleep. Tomorrow he carry ya back to the warehouse."

I shrug at Jake. "That settles it."

"I guess so," he says.

"Now let's get some shuteye, so tomorrow we'll at least be half-alive." The glowing parrot floats to the sheet. He closes his eyes, tucks his head under a wing, and promptly falls asleep.

I don't know what time Charlie is supposed to die tomorrow. He never told us. As soon as he wakes, I'll have to ask him.

Feeling calm, for the first time in a year I actually try to remember how Mom died. No memories return.

Uncle Biggie puts away the food, then shuffles to his bed of leaves and branches. "Nighty night." Yawning again, he lies down, quickly sending loud snores echoing through the flickering light of the cave.

The crocle-lion closes its eyes and soon breathes peacefully.

Jake arches his back, reaching high into the air, and then touches his toes. When he straightens, he asks, "You really expect Uncle Biggie to help us? What if he changes his mind? The guy lives in a cave and writes notes with crayons."

"It's kind of cute." The feather sticks out of Uncle Biggie's fist and, despite his size, he does look like a child.

I walk closer to WhipEye. The deep yearning to have it in my hand is gone.

Beside me, Jake motions tiredly at it. "It's not pulling me, either."

"When we don't need the staff, it doesn't respond." But I don't want him to touch it.

He flicks my shoulder. "Sorry for not telling you I can't swim."

"Why didn't you?"

"I didn't want to be alone in the dark."

"Honesty is the best policy." I smile and brush hair from my face. "I figured out why Tarath didn't come."

"Yeah. Stupid bridge." He yawns, triggering a yawn in me.

Sleepily, I say, "If you yawn in front of a dog or cat they'll yawn too. Yawns are contagious between mammal species."

"I'll try it on the crocle-lion." His eyes are bleary. "Where are we supposed to sleep?" His arms are crossed and he has goose bumps.

I take off my coat and hold it out to him.

"You'll be warm enough?" He eyes the coat.

"Yeah. Flannel shirt and jeans."

"Thanks." He takes it and quickly puts it on, zipping it up.

We sprawl on the sheet, the ground hard beneath us. The scent of dirt fills my nostrils.

Lying on my side, I grasp my compass, my mind racing to find a way to defeat Magnar and get his rings. After staring into the shadows for what feels like hours, sleep finally comes. But dreams bring images of Mom and shadow monsters, mixed together with crazy chases in a big cavern.

By morning I'm exhausted, but glad to escape my nightmares. I rub my sleepy eyes.

Uncle Biggie is stretching in his bed, and from a nearby rock Charlie spreads his wings.

"My, my, my. Isn't this cozy?"

I jump to my feet, blood roaring to my head.

Magnar stands behind the crocle-lion.

The resting animal jumps up and spins, growling and baring its teeth. For once, I'm glad it's acting ferocious.

Magnar doesn't look the least bit afraid and his eyes gleam. In one hand he holds a feather, and his other arm is wrapped around Jake's neck.

TWENTY-EIGHT

Defeat

JAKE STANDS STIFFLY, his face pale as he grips Magnar's forearm. His glasses rest crookedly on his nose.

My stomach lurches and panic fills me. Magnar will snap Jake's neck with about as much concern as most people have when they step on ants. After all, he killed Rose, someone he used to love.

WhipEye is only a few steps away, but the distance might as well be a mile. The sudden urge to grab it makes my hands sweat.

"I'm sorry, Sam," gurgles Jake. "I had to go out."

"It's okay," I say softly, and to Magnar, "Please, don't hurt him." I want to fight the creep, but I can't risk anything happening to Jake.

"Ya liar, Magnar." Uncle Biggie jumps up with fists at his sides, his eyes flashing gold. "Ya hurt wittle animals. Ya leave wittle boy alone."

"I'm displeased with you, Uncle Biggie." Magnar frowns. "You were supposed to bring the children to me at the warehouse. Did you really think you could hide your cozy little place from me?"

Gloomily, I realize Magnar planned far ahead of us for every possible path we might take. The man's victory was never in doubt. After all, he only had to outsmart me.

He looks at me knowingly and smirks. "I knew you'd come to me, girl."

Uncle Biggie takes a step forward. I want to yell at him to stop. Charlie doesn't move.

Magnar tilts his head to the big man. "They've told you lies, Uncle Biggie. They want you to believe I'm doing terrible things, but I'm the only one with any chance to save all the animals, to save this planet."

Uncle Biggie takes another step.

Magnar pockets Jake's feather, then rubs his thumb ring.

The king cobra slithers into the air six feet off the ground, rearing its heads and hissing at the big man.

I take small, sideways steps toward WhipEye, unsure what will happen, wanting to be close to the staff. My legs are stiff. I can't watch Jake die.

"If you come any closer, Uncle Biggie, I'll hurt the boy, and you'll learn what one of my shadows can do." Magnar's face softens. "I don't want to hurt you, Uncle Biggie. You're like a son to me, and we have great things ahead of us."

The cobra lowers its heads. "But we're hungry for sssomething to sssnack on."

I stop moving, too far from the staff to reach it. "Don't do it, Uncle Biggie." I doubt an Original is a match for the cobra, and I believe Magnar when he says he'll hurt Jake if Uncle Biggie attacks.

But Uncle Biggie stands his ground, his eyes narrowing as he raises his fists. "Ya leave wittle boy alone, Magnar."

Rubbing several rings together, metal scraping against metal, Magnar aims his free hand at Uncle Biggie.

A golden ray of light streaks toward the big man, but he shields his eyes with his arm. When the light stops, the giant lowers his limb and glares at Magnar.

Magnar seems visibly tired. He drags Jake farther away from Uncle Biggie, and then gives me a fierce look.

"Please, don't hurt him," I say.

His face darkens. "You deserve to pay for what happened to Rose."

"You killed Rose," I say softly.

"You forced her to fight me," he snarls, the veins on his forehead popping out.

Jake lifts a foot and kicks him hard in the shin with his heel, then elbows him in the stomach.

Unaffected, Magnar growls and squeezes his neck.

"Don't hurt him," I shout. *Oh, please don't.*

Struggling against Magnar, Jake barely whispers, "Call Tarath."

Uncle Biggie charges across the cavern, moving fast and smooth like Tom.

The snake wriggles through the air toward him.

Worried Magnar will kill Jake if I don't do something, I run to WhipEye, not caring about anything except my friend.

In those seconds, Uncle Biggie leaps high and grabs the snake below its heads. They crash to the ground, the snake writhing around the big man.

The crocle-lion growls and circles them.

Clutching the staff, I raise it high in the air, Tarath's name on my tongue. The wood resonates in my palm, sending a flame of energy into me. I never want it out of my grip again.

"Don't do it, kid."

I waver. Charlie glows brighter now, as if the light is ready to burst from within him. I want to smash the staff into the ground, but something in his tired voice stops me.

The parrot tilts his head. "Tarath doesn't stand a chance against Magnar."

Magnar scowls at me, while Jake's face turns red. "Rose never stood a chance against me, either. But if you call the caracal, you'll lose the boy, and we wouldn't want that, would we? Especially since you'll be next."

I avoid looking at Charlie. "Please. I'll do whatever you want."

Uncle Biggie holds the cobra's lower neck with one hand, punching its heads with the other. The snake's body slowly coils around his flailing arm. When he can't move it, its dagger-sized fangs inch closer to his neck.

Roaring, the crocle-lion leaps onto the snake's tail, sinking in tooth and claw.

Jerking out of Uncle Biggie's grasp, the cobra hisses and rears back, then strikes at the crocle-lion.

The crocle-lion jumps away from the snake's snapping jaws, allowing Uncle Biggie to seize the hissing cobra again before it can bite him.

Keeping the staff high, my insides go numb. Jake's cheeks are purple.

Magnar bares his teeth like a rabid animal and tightens his hold on Jake. "Charlie, if you want to save your friends, then give me what I want."

Jake falls to his knees, coughing weakly. With quivering fingers he pulls on Magnar's arm.

My insides are jelly. If Jake dies, I'll never forgive myself.

Squawk. "Let him go, you bum. Free Samantha's father, take your worm, and I'll come to you now. I give you my word."

My face grows hot over my silence. I'm glad the parrot isn't looking at me.

Uncle Biggie is in a standoff with the king cobra as they wrestle on the ground. The Original is stronger than I thought, but he can't outlast the snake. Growling and circling them, the crocle-lion is waiting for another chance to attack.

Magnar shakes his head, his voice cold. "No deals, parrot."

"Then you'll have to kill all of us. You'll lose what you really want. Rose was right. You're a madman who murders the innocent." The parrot pauses. "Do you really want to waste energy on a fight now, when you're so close?"

Magnar's face darkens, his lips twisting savagely. "WhipEye too."

"So the great Magnar is scared of a sliver of wood. Even wielded by a girl. The coward shows his ugly head."

Magnar's eyes harden.

Jake chokes, each breath weaker than the last as Pug-face slowly forces the life out of him. I imagine him lying dead at Magnar's feet. It destroys all resolve in me.

"Rose was a fool to believe Great Ones would answer WhipEye, a fool to believe all the lies the Great Ones told her. . . ." Magnar's voice trails off, regret in his words. "But I'm taking the staff. I'll use it to enter KiraKu, and then the reign of the Great Ones will finally end." His tone stiffens. "Otherwise, the boy dies now."

I remember Rose's words, that Magnar must never have Whip-Eye. But I don't hesitate. "You can have it."

"The girl is weak." Magnar's eyes glint. "Is this the price of friendship these days?"

Barely audible, Jake mumbles something and twitches his chin. His eyes roll back into his head and close.

"Jake!" I force myself to look at the parrot. "I'm sorry, Charlie." Tears stream down my cheeks as I slowly lower the staff.

"So am I, kid. So am I. But you're the bravest person I know. You follow your heart, and most don't even know where their true heart lies."

I half hear Charlie's words, because I believe Magnar. I'm selling out my best friend.

"We have a bargain, parrot." Magnar pushes Jake away from him, easing the strain in my chest.

Falling to the ground, Jake curls up, gagging, his glasses falling off his face. His shoulders heave as he clasps his neck.

Magnar quickly rubs his thumb ring. The cobra hisses and slithers from Uncle Biggie's grasp, retreating into the ring in a stream of gray.

Uncle Biggie rolls to all fours, his head hanging. The crocle-lion growls beside him.

Lying on his side, Jake unscrews the canteen cap with shaking fingers. "Don't do it, Charlie." He tries to push himself to a sitting position, falls to his shoulder, then tries again, coughing and falling once more.

It's painful to watch him. "There's nothing we can do, Jake," I say dully.

Ignoring me, one hand bracing his body, he cradles the open canteen, his arm trembling. "Fly away, Charlie."

"It's already done, kiddo. Remember, I love you, and once you touch this world it's permanent."

Jake's eyes show confusion as he looks at the parrot.

Magnar rubs his rings together and a small glow of light appears in his palm. He murmurs and a kinkajou forms in his hand, then disappears again. His shoulders slump. "It's back in its cage in the warehouse."

Without the evidence, Dad will be released, but I don't feel any satisfaction. WhipEye is cold in my hand.

Jake squirms on the ground to look at me. "Don't, Sam."

I don't answer.

Magnar reaches toward me. I lift the staff and throw it vertically to him. He catches it in mid-air, his eyes gleaming.

Quietly, Charlie flies in a low arc to Magnar. Landing on his shoulder, he perches there, his head hanging.

Magnar straightens, his eyes more vibrant, as if Charlie's energy is already strengthening him. A sneer on his face, he rises off the ground, his body floating backward. His outline fades as he soars higher into the dark shadows near the cave's ceiling, his eyes on mine.

Growling and running forward, the crocle-lion jumps, but doesn't come close to reaching him.

Jake wipes his eyes, lowering the canteen.

"Nooo." Uncle Biggie stands and shakes a fist. "Ya weave wittle parrot alone." He charges across the stone floor.

My eyes remain on Charlie as Magnar glides farther away, disappearing around the corner leading to the front entrance.

Shouts, barks, and stamping feet fill the cavern. For a moment I'm wildly hopeful someone will stop Magnar.

Dozens of men and women wearing police and FBI uniforms run into the cave, gripping guns and holding a pack of bloodhounds straining on leashes. The officers skid to a stop when they face the bounding crocle-lion and Uncle Biggie charging them. Raising their guns, they free the barking dogs.

"Don't shoot," I yell.

"Stop." Jake motions feebly.

Uncle Biggie leaps sideways when the first shots explode in the cavern. The big man races across the ground, ducking and jumping over boulders fluidly. Following him, the crocle-lion swerves around rocks as more gunshots echo in the cave. They quickly disappear into the deeper shadows. The howling dogs run after them.

Police call out, motioning to me, while others help Jake to his feet. There's no use telling them that while they were all looking at Uncle Biggie and the crocle-lion, Magnar escaped over their heads. They'd never believe me anyway. But I want to help Uncle Biggie.

When I reach the officers, I say, "The man was a friend. He didn't hurt us."

One of them steps forward. "It's all right, miss. We're going to take you home now."

I can see from his expression he feels sorry for me and doesn't believe me. I wipe my eyes and trudge out of the cavern, my head down, not wanting to talk to anyone else.

TWENTY-NINE

Remembering

ALL THE WAY OUT of the sunny woods I don't say a word. Members of the rescue party offer to carry me, but I refuse. Jake walks nearby, but never once looks at me.

The officers around us talk quietly about the cavern. The shadows and poor lighting didn't give anyone a clear view of Uncle Biggie and the crocle-lion, which everyone describes as "an unusually big man with a deformed wild animal." I'm glad they somehow escaped.

Failure runs through my head. Charlie will die today and become one of Magnar's shadows, and all the animals in Magnar's warehouse are going to die or become part of his claw. Magnar will start his war.

Yet a deeper pain lies beneath all of it.

It isn't until we walk onto the Old River Bridge, three hours later, that everything bursts apart inside.

Dad stands with Cynthia, an arm around her shoulders. Both of them are wearing jeans and jackets. They hurry toward us.

I stumble across the wooden bridge into Dad's waiting arms, while Jake strides into his mother's.

I'm held a long time, and Dad strokes my back repeatedly. "I'm sorry, Sam. I'm so sorry."

"Me too, Dad." Tears fill my eyes and I know his apologies are for the whole last year.

He pulls back, leaving his hands on my shoulders. "The evidence disappeared, so I'm free. They brought me here as soon as they found you."

"Yeah." I wipe my face.

"Honey, this man would like to ask you a question." He motions to a burly man wearing a U.S. Fish and Wildlife Service jacket.

We walk to him, and I'm glad Dad's arm remains firmly around my shoulders.

Pulling a photo from his pocket, the man shows it to me. "Samantha, we received an anonymous tip. That's how we found your kidnapper's hideout. We think this man's dealing in illegal wildlife trade. Do you recognize him? Is he the one who kidnapped you?"

I eagerly take the picture, speechless when I see it's a photo of Uncle Biggie.

Magnar. Always planning ahead of us.

I shake my head. "This isn't the man." Uncle Biggie's photo brings more heaviness to my thoughts. "It was dark, so we never had a good look at the person who grabbed us. But it wasn't him."

The officer stares at me, but I don't budge.

Jake says the same thing when questioned, and minutes later we're all climbing into Cynthia's black SUV.

Jake and I sit quietly in back.

Without Charlie, my shoulder feels naked. I remember the parrot's words when Uncle Biggie first captured us; *friends don't abandon friends.* I put my hands in my lap, gazing at them.

Brandon's and Lewella's comments about the strength of the WhipEye tree float back to me. I never deserved to bond to the staff. Rose and Charlie made a mistake in choosing me. The desire to have WhipEye in my hand is gone, as if it never existed.

Cynthia takes a back road home to avoid the trail of police and FBI cars leaving the bridge. We drive into the morning sun.

Jake's hands wring in short bursts. "Magnar's evil. He's the one who's trading in exotic animals. He's a killer. He wants to take over the world. He's the one who belongs in jail."

I gape at him.

"Where does he keep the animals, Jake?" Cynthia glances into the rearview mirror, pushing blond bangs off her forehead, her lips pursed and her blue eyes wide.

I shake my head, but Jake ignores me. "In his old warehouse north of town. It's huge, Mom. Endless. You'll never believe it once you're inside and—"

"We were inside, Jake," Cynthia says gently. "We investigated Magnar right after you called from the bridge. His warehouse is old and dusty, and doesn't have any animals in it."

Jake talks excitedly. "You went to the wrong building, Mom. Turn around. I'll show you."

While Jake argues, I pull Charlie's feather from my pocket, its bright red hue shining in the light. Guilt floods me.

When Cynthia won't agree to Jake's demands, he sits back, fists on his lap. But when he sees my feather, his eyes light up. "Of course! It's Charlie's feather. You have to hold it to see the animals and the true warehouse. It's magic. Give them the feather, Sam."

I tuck it into my pocket, studying the back of Cynthia's seat.

Jake's eyes blaze. "Give me the feather, Sam."

Cynthia wipes her eyes.

Dad pats her shoulder, then leaves his hand there. I want to yell at him to take it off.

"You should have let me use the water on the stupid snake," says Jake.

I sit rigidly.

Dad says softly, "Calm down, Jake."

His hands move wildly. "Give them the feather. It's the only way to save Charlie."

"We can't," I whisper, twisting away from his grasping fingers.

"The parrots died for nothing," he yells, giving up.

"What parrots?" Cynthia frowns. "Jake, no parrots died. We were at the pet store."

"You betrayed Charlie," Jake continues. "You were supposed to be his friend and you gave him to Magnar."

His words cut me like knives. "I did it for you," I murmur.

"No you didn't. I hate you!"

Dad says firmly, "Jake, you have to calm down."

"You're not my father. I don't have a stupid father! What father would ever want me?"

Cynthia twists in her seat, teary-eyed. "Oh, Jake, it's me he didn't love."

"And if you weren't working all the time, Dad wouldn't have left us," he shouts.

Cynthia blanches.

Through the glare of the sun shining through the front windshield, I see a figure walk onto the road. It stands there, the sunlight outlining it. The glow reminds me of Charlie.

Without moving, the young moose watches us. A small calf, it's probably lost without its mother.

"Look out!" I yell.

Jake shouts.

Cynthia slams the brakes. The tires squeal.

A stiff jolt and *bang!* shoves us forward against our seatbelts and air bags blow out in front. The engine dies.

The moose sails through the air and hits the pavement hard, flopping once before it stops. The front end of the SUV is pushed in, the hood crumpled.

My hands press into my thighs.

"No, no, no," whispers my father.

Cynthia stares out the windshield. "I didn't mean to do it."

"You killed it," Jake says quietly, then louder, "You killed it!" He buries his head in his hands.

I'm the first to open my door. I slowly swing my feet out, as if they belong to someone else.

Shuffling to the calf, I kneel beside it, gently stroking the coarse hair of its neck, the warmth of the body seeping into my palm. "A.k.a. *Alces alces*," I murmur.

I want it to rise and walk away, and when it doesn't, another wrong is added to a world where everything's off-kilter. I doubt even healing water can bring back the dead.

Images fly through me, keeping me motionless. *Mom's walking beside me on a sidewalk, humming the song I'm always humming. A breeze blows her long brown hair. A red ball I'm bouncing flies away from me and I run into the street to get it. The bright sunshine blinds me. Mom shouts and I turn, my compass swinging out from my neck. Things blur. Tires squeal. Mom's eyes meet mine as she pushes me out of the way. I fly backward as the car hits her.*

I release deep sobs. Dad kneels beside me, hugging me tightly for the second time in an hour.

"It's my fault she died, Dad. That's why I didn't want to remember."

"No, Sam. I never blamed you. It was never your fault. Never. It just happened. Your mother loved you too much to let you get hurt. I didn't talk about it, because I didn't want you to feel responsible."

I continue crying, the sadness running out of me like a river at first, slowly easing to a stream, then a trickle subsiding to a distant pain. I sag against Dad, spent, but he doesn't let me go.

"It's her song I'm always humming, Dad."

"I have so much to tell you. I'm proud of you, and I'm so sorry." His voice catches. "I've been silent the last year because I didn't want to admit she was gone. But when I thought I'd lost you, I realized I wanted to be with my daughter who I love very much."

Keeping my head buried in his shoulder, Dad's words sink in and the world stops spinning. I'm not drifting alone on the ocean anymore.

I'm aware of Cynthia talking to Jake about his father.

In a few minutes, I stand with Dad. Cynthia has an arm wrapped around Jake. We all stare at the young moose lying in the road. I can't believe we killed it.

Dad and Jake drag the calf off the road, while Cynthia calls the police, a tow truck, and a friend.

While the police take our statement, Cynthia's friend arrives. We pile into another SUV. I'm unable to look at Jake, unable to think anymore.

"I'm sorry about your mother, Samantha." Cynthia sniffles. "And about the moose."

"Thanks." A finger pokes my shoulder.

Jake has red eyes as he mouths, *I'm sorry.*

I'm glad for that, but the sadness inside crowds out everything else.

THIRTY

Love

WHEN WE RETURN HOME, I pause near the dining room entryway.

The table is empty. Cleared and wiped. Cynthia. My birthday party disappeared like Charlie, along with my hopes for stopping Magnar.

Dad gives me another hug.

"I want to be alone for a while, Dad."

He pulls back, his eyes on mine. "You're all right?"

"Yeah."

"I'm going to talk to Cynthia for a few minutes, then I'll check on you."

"That sounds good."

He smiles.

I try to return it, but my lips won't cooperate. I grab the railing and Cynthia steps next to me. She places one hand on mine, her eyes moist. It's enough.

A voice stops me halfway up the stairs.

"Can I come up to say good-bye?" Jake's standing on the bottom step, his glasses crooked and his blue eyes sad and uncertain. He's still wearing my coat.

"Sure."

Once in my room, I sit on my bed. Jake closes the door before joining me. He brings the swallowtail scale out of his pocket, rubbing it absently with his fingers.

Silence surrounds us until he says, "It was always calling to us, wasn't it? The staff."

"You too?" I don't look at him.

"All the time. Sometimes it was all I could do to not rip it out of your hands." He takes a deep breath. "I'm sorry about your mother, Sam." He pauses. "And I don't hate you. I . . . I really like . . . what you did for me was. . . ." He's unable to continue.

"Yeah. It's still lousy."

"It's cool you hum her song. It's a nice way to remember her."

"I'm sorry about your father."

"Mom said his leaving had nothing to do with me. She says we're staying this time and not moving again. And she's going to be home more."

"That's great." Even though I'm glad for him, and that he's staying, I don't feel any enthusiasm.

"I'm sorry for yelling at you. I just couldn't bear the thought of Magnar having Charlie." He pauses. "What's our Plan B?"

"There isn't one."

His hands are quiet in his lap. "It's horrible." He pockets the scale.

"The worst." I think about Mom, who gave her life for me. And Charlie's words float back to me, about following my heart. I suddenly get what Rose meant about finding north. If you act out of love, then something is always right in what you do, something is always right in the world, and your inner compass has a guide.

When I level my compass the needle points north, to *Love*, and I understand then. *Trust Love. Trust Mom.* I do.

Standing, I pick up the family photo lying facedown on the dresser. Mom's radiant smile warms me, and memories flood me without pain. Mom hugging me, talking to me, walking with me, tousling my hair, helping me with my room mural, and all the other things she did for me every day. Over the last year she was with me in a million different ways. I just didn't let her in.

The journey was never just about saving Charlie and freeing the methuselahs. It was also about saving myself. Remembering Mom without pain or guilt. Charlie wanted that for me from the beginning. The parrot saved me, when all along I thought I was saving him.

My chest heaves. "Anytime I was scared to do something, Mom would say, 'Just do it, Sam.'"

"Sounds like an awesome mom."

"The best." I set the family photo upright on the dresser.

Jake's blue eyes look sad and mud streaks his torn clothing. He was a big part of the journey, and he risked his life many times to help me, to be a part of my life. He never hesitated, even after I tried to get rid of him.

That's when it hits me. "Magnar isn't bonded to WhipEye."

Jake's face is blank. "So?"

"So he can't use it. And at Rose's cabin, Magnar said the largest trees would witness his new beginning."

"So he's taking Charlie somewhere." He bites his lip. "And Magnar's able to move small things short distances, and only if they don't have a will of their own."

"And WhipEye has a mind of its own."

Jake stands, his hands flying. "Charlie's going willingly, but Magnar might not be able to take the staff with him."

We stare at each other.

Jake wraps his arms around me. My hair is against his face, which he doesn't seem to mind.

I whisper, "No matter how things turn out, we make great partners."

"Five-star."

I have a lump in my throat when I pull back. We both smile. I've never had a friend like this before, and it warms my insides.

When I go downstairs and enter the living room, Dad's sitting close to Cynthia on the couch. Surprisingly, I don't feel angry. I'm happy for him. "Dad?"

He leans away from Cynthia, his face a little red. His eyes are bright, like they were when Mom was around. Good-bye and good riddance to the zombie.

"What is it, Sam?"

"Can we all eat here? A late lunch?"

He beams.

Cynthia brightens. "That's a great idea, Sam."

I stuff my hands in my pockets. "Could we have a barbeque out back? The grill's a mess. I could clean it, but I'm kind of tired."

"I'll do it." Dad rises, pulling Cynthia to her feet. "Would you like to help me pick some veggies from the garden?"

"Of course." Cynthia smiles.

Dad walks over and hugs me. "I love you, Sam."

I hold him, knowing I'll never get tired of those words. "I love you, Dad."

"Can I?" Cynthia gives me a warm hug. She isn't Mom, but in time it might feel as nice.

When he passes by, Dad pats my shoulder and winks at me.

They're barely out the back door when Jake bounds down the stairs, the canteen slung over his shoulder. He's no longer wearing my jacket. I grab Dad's car keys off the entryway table, hurry outside, and fling them into the tall grass of the front yard.

In seconds, I'm wheeling my bike out of the garage. Jake takes my father's bike.

I ride into the street. "We only have one feather."

Jake's pedaling hard beside me. "I might not need it. In Uncle Biggie's cave, when Charlie said *once you touch this world it's permanent,* I figured he had to be talking about KiraKu and Magnar's warehouse."

Soon we're racing along the sunlit path in the park.

I have no clue how we'll fight Magnar if he's there.

THIRTY-ONE

Allies and Partners

C HARLIE NEVER TOLD ME what time of day he turns one thousand years old, but my gut tells me the parrot is alive. I trust that.

The image of the small parrot dying alone, with no friends, with no one who loves him, brings a lump to my throat. And the idea of Magnar using Charlie's death to gain more power tightens my fingers on the handlebars.

We ride to the Endless Warehouse and prop our bikes against the building. The door isn't chained, but I hesitate. Jake offers his hand and I grip it, then open the door. We walk in together.

We're facing aisle upon aisle of cages again. Crackling lightning streaks a purple sky and booming thunder fills my ears. Intermittent light again fills the room. The koala bear is sitting in the same spot in its cage. I'm glad it's still alive.

Jake tugs at my hand, and I let go of him. He was right about not needing the feather.

"Magnar could be here," he says.

"We don't have time to search the whole warehouse." I look at him. "But I already know where I want to go."

"I feel it too. What does your compass say?"

When I check it, the needle slowly swings from north to southeast, matching my gut.

We run east down an aisle, the needle slowly swinging. There are more empty cages than before. Jake's frown echoes my disappointment. At the end of the aisle the needle points south, and we run along the wall to the door of the room where Magnar did his experiments.

Jake grasps the knob and quietly inches the door open. We peek inside.

The ceiling crackles with lightning, which reveals the two cages and the glass pen. The computer screen is on the stand, dark, but the globe containing Magnar's claw is gone.

My stomach knots.

We walk in, the door slamming behind us.

"I'm glad the creep is gone," says Jake. "How could he move the claw?"

"The claw follows his will. And Charlie said Magnar would be a hundred times more powerful just by touching him." The compass needle is back on north, but there's a tug on my gut. "It's here."

Jake's hands do circles. "It's close."

I hurry to the computer station. The desktop is thicker than I realized. The pull becomes stronger. My hands twitch as the urge builds.

Slowly, I walk around the metal workstation. "Where is it?"

Jake runs his fingers along the front underside of the desk, glancing beneath it when lightning sweeps away the shadows. A latch clicks, and I move beside him.

He pushes against the front edge, and the top of the desktop slides back along its length, revealing a six-inch-wide shallow depression.

"Brilliant," I say.

Jake smiles.

Flashes of lightning reveal papers, Jake's red feather—which he grabs, and odd objects. WhipEye is nestled on top of everything else. I quickly clutch it, wanting to before Jake does, the urge so strong now it's pulsing in my belly.

The garage door starts to rise, the chain winding like poured gravel.

I raise the staff, Tarath's name on my lips.

Lightning bursts reveal a familiar figure, his bib overalls torn, dirt on his patchwork shirt, and the leather and chain leash coiled over a shoulder. Beside him stands the crocle-lion, its big head wagging side-to-side as it watches us, its cat-like eyes gleaming.

Jake and I shout, "Uncle Biggie."

The huge man steps toward us with long, silent strides, and then we're all hugging each other. His arms gently wrap around us.

My inner compass was right in Uncle Biggie's cave. We're all here, in the Endless Warehouse. Just the timing changed.

"How did you escape?" I ask, smiling.

"Uncle Biggie have tunnel in cave." He pulls back and gently pats our shoulders. "Uncle Biggie look everywhere, but Magnar gone."

Jake sidles behind me, staring at the crocle-lion, which eyes him intently.

"Come on." I run around the computer station to the large open space on the other side of it, where the massive glass ball held Magnar's claw.

"What are you going to do?" Jake keeps me between the crocle-lion and himself.

"Find Charlie, then call Tarath."

"Call Tarath first. Then maybe we can surprise Magnar."

"Good idea."

Uncle Biggie and Jake stand on either side of me, and I bang the staff into the floor of the warehouse, the echo filling the room. "Tarath."

WhipEye warms my palms and my fingers loosen on it involuntarily as it spins once. Above my hand, the caracal's head glows, but nothing happens. Desperation hits me. Maybe the Great One knows we lost Charlie and she gave up on us.

Jake looks worriedly at the staff. "Where is she?"

The staff spins again, clockwise this time, before it again stops sharply. A bear's face glows. I exchange glances with Jake—Great Ones can contact the staff without us calling them.

"Pretty," says Uncle Biggie.

Excitement builds in me as I thump WhipEye again with more strength, and call, "Kodiak bear." Four more times it rotates, and each time I strike the floor with the staff—*boom!*—and shout the name of the brightly lit face. "Rhino. Iguana. Wolverine. Gorilla!"

The chestnut wood shudders and the lit carved faces come to life, changing color. Tarath's eyes open and she snarls, the rhino snorts, the wolverine growls, the bear opens its jaws with a loud roar, the iguana hisses, and the gorilla bares its canines and screams.

They streak from WhipEye in six separate rays of bright light, forcing us to shield our eyes with our hands.

The light reaches ten yards from the staff, then expands quickly, producing six massive creatures that form a circle around us. Like Tarath, each towers over us and has golden eyes.

"White rhino," I whisper. "One of the largest." I nod to the stocky, powerful-looking great ape. "Mountain gorilla. Silverback."

I'm glad the iguana is here, and nod to her, but my gaze settles on the caracal. She bolsters my courage. The gorilla beats its chest as the other animals again give deafening cries, as if ready for battle.

My spirits soar at the sight of them. Six Great Ones. All beautiful and strong. WhipEye has dozens of other faces carved on it, but none of them glow. Maybe the Great Ones think six is enough. That idea steadies me.

Surprisingly, I'm only a little tired from the effort of calling them. I wonder if using the staff strengthens the bearer over time.

"Tarath, we lost Charlie," I blurt. "It was my fault."

"We both lost him." Jake grips my hand. "But we're here to get him back."

The six Great Ones gaze at us, their eyes glowing in the dark.

Tarath growls softly. "You're brave, children."

I smile. "You brought team KiraKu."

"We six believe in you, Samantha and Jake. That your hearts are worth fighting for and that you can make a difference."

"Will the other Great Ones let you return to KiraKu?" I ask.

The iguana lowers her head toward me. "Doing what's right is all that matters."

"We're going to beat Magnar." Jake's hands do cartwheels, but they stop when Tarath's eyebrows hunch.

The caracal bows her head to Uncle Biggie. "Welcome, old one."

"You remember Uncle Biggie?" The big man's face shines.

"Your true name is Altaar, one of the last Originals to leave KiraKu. It's an honor to have you with us."

I regard Uncle Biggie with awe.

Uncle Biggie presses his palms against his chest, his face like an expectant child's. "You know Uncle Biggie's real parents?"

"Zione and Marissa. But I don't know where they are now."

"Zione and Marissa." He straightens. "But Uncle Biggie keep his name for wittle children in London who name him."

"As is your right. Altaar was always thinking of others." Tarath's head swings around to the open garage door, her ears cocked forward. "Others are coming."

I tense, peering into the dark. "Who?"

Jake stiffens. "Friends?"

Tarath doesn't answer.

A distant buzzing grows louder, reminding me of what I heard outside my bedroom window, and in the woods when Tom joined us.

During streaks of lightning, a flash of yellow zigzags through the large door and across the room.

Abruptly a young woman is standing in front of me, possibly in her early twenties, dressed in black jeans, black boots, and a black cotton blouse. In the fractured lighting, Lewella's long yellow hair and impossibly green eyes are radiant. I'm even more curious about what kind of Lesser she is.

"Lewella." I throw my arms around her.

"Samantha," she says warmly, embracing me. "And Jake." She hugs him next.

"It's great to see you," says Jake. "Really great."

Brandon and Tom run up silently on either side of her, Brandon grinning, eagerness in his face, while Tom looks tense. Brandon claps my shoulder and shakes Jake's hand. Tom remains aloof, his arms crossed.

"How did you know?" I ask Lewella.

"Lessers can sense Great Ones coming." She smiles. "We couldn't sit back any longer."

Tarath stamps the floor with a paw. "Originals and a Lesser. All welcome."

"Here to protect my friends, not Great Ones." Tom juts out his jaw, but I'm glad he's here.

"Tarath never wanted Originals or Great Ones to leave KiraKu."

Lewella walks to the big cat and strokes her lowered neck. "I miss you, old friend."

Tarath purrs. "You've been missed too, old friend. KiraKu lost some of its balance with your leaving, Lewella."

I'm surprised after thousands of years they greet each other as if it's been days. It helps me understand even more deeply what KiraKu lost.

Lewella takes one of Uncle Biggie's large hands in hers. "It's good to see you, Altaar."

"Uncle Biggie not remember you." But the big man smiles at her.

"If you're away from KiraKu's water and energy too long, the memory of it fades." Lewella sounds sad.

I'm even more amazed when Tom and Brandon step to either side of Lewella, giving deep bows to Uncle Biggie.

"An honor, Altaar." Brandon winks.

"Truly." Tom's face shows awe.

Uncle Biggie pats their shoulders. "Uncle Biggie happy to meet you."

Lightning sends flashes over us and Tarath hisses. "Children, we're out of time. Do what you must, Samantha Green."

Jake faces me, grasping WhipEye with both hands.

The Great Ones form a tight circle with their shoulders touching each other, Tarath's leg against mine. Inside the circle, Uncle Biggie rests a wide palm on my arm. Lewella and Brandon grasp Jake's shoulders, and Tom places his hand over Brandon's.

Jake and I move the staff in three figure eights, three times calling, "Charlie." Then we strike the staff against the cement floor three times, sending deep echoes off in all directions.

THIRTY-TWO

fighting Monsters

THIS TIME I'M MORE DRAINED, as if I sprinted a quarter mile. Moving everyone took a lot more energy than calling the Great Ones.

Jake appears less tired. The canteen rests on his hip, but I don't want to use any of the healing water to boost my energy. Not yet, anyway.

Wide-eyed, Jake slowly pivots. "Where are we?"

I stare. "California. Sequoia National Park or close to it."

"Wow, two thousand miles." He motions. "The trees are awesome. What are they?"

"Giant sequoias, a.k.a. *Sequoiadendron giganteum*. Some are over three thousand years old. Biggest trees in the world. Mom loved them." I understand why. Silent. Majestic. Giants. Even the Great Ones are small by comparison. The sequoias remind me of the massive trees of KiraKu.

A bank of dark clouds, along with the massive canopy above, blocks any sunlight. Instead of late morning, it's looks like dusk, with lightning streaking over the tops of the trees and thunder echoing around us. Dark-eyed juncos and mountain chickadees chatter nearby, along with one gray squirrel. There isn't much vegetation on the soft ground, and the scent of pine fills the air.

I face south with everyone else. Far ahead of us in the dim light shines a small blaze of gold. *Charlie.* My mouth is dry.

"Magnar knows we're here," says Tarath.

Jake adjusts his glasses. "So much for surprise."

"Will you kill the methuselah shadows?" I ask.

Tarath doesn't reply.

We walk, the Great Ones spreading out through the trees in a wide line, Tom and Brandon near Lewella, Tarath and the iguana walking on either side of Jake, me, and Uncle Biggie.

Jake reaches into his pocket and pulls out the swallowtail butterfly scale. Pressing it against his sternum, he squints as if he's concentrating.

Astonished, I watch as a film of yellow, orange, and red seeps out from beneath the edges of his hand, slowly covering his chest, shoulders, torso, and back, from his neck to his waist. I gape, and our friends stare at him.

Jake grins and raps his knuckles against his form-fitting armor. It sounds solid.

"How did you figure that out, Einstein?" I ask.

"From you. The way you imagine things when you use Whip-Eye. I visualized the armor and figured it was worth a shot. When Lewella said the scale was strong, it made me think of the butterfly's words again. He said it was a gift. It didn't make sense that it was just for show and tell."

"Cool." My attention is drawn east through the trees, to a small meadow. A man dressed like a park ranger stands in the middle of the waist-high grass, open-mouthed with a camera in hand, staring our way. He turns and runs.

I hope he saw Magnar and called for help. It couldn't hurt.

As we draw closer, Magnar's black suit is visible through the trees. The cobra and buffalo shadows bracket him, but my gaze is drawn to the large glass globe on the ground behind him.

Trapped inside it, Magnar's claw is easily twice as large as before, the monster's dark skin pulsing with shapes that rise and fall beneath it. I don't want to think about how many more animals lost their lives or how many more chimeras Magnar created. One finger is still scarred with fine lines.

Charlie perches on Magnar's shoulder, glowing like a golden sphere. His bright aura almost hides his body. The sight of the parrot lifts my spirit. We're not too late. "Oh, Charlie."

"Charlie." Jake waves to the parrot.

Tarath and the others halt sixty paces from Magnar, and we stop with them.

Charlie spreads his wings a few inches, barely lifting his head. "You came for the birthday party, kids. I knew you would." His voice is weak and he wobbles on Magnar's shoulder.

I want to shout at the creep, but I say, "Charlie, we're going to set you free."

The cobra heads rock back and forth, their four gray eyes glassy. "Finally, I'll have a sssnack."

Jake pales, his hands curling into fists.

In front of Magnar, a three-foot-high, flat-topped boulder has a single gold ring resting on it. The ring Magnar intends to use to capture Charlie's methuselah energy.

I clench WhipEye. "We won't let you do it, Magnar."

Pug-face bares his teeth, bright against his skin. But he's a younger version now, less wrinkled, his forehead veins gone. He's already benefitting from Charlie's energy.

Tarath hisses, and the other Great Ones drum, roar, growl, and snort their defiance.

Magnar glares at me. "Do you think I was stupid enough to leave WhipEye where you could find it, girl?" I'm confused until he adds, "I knew you'd bring the staff to me, and I wanted you to bring a few Great Ones for my claw. You and the boy will join them."

Again, he's one step ahead of me. Worried I've led the others into a trap, I look at the caracal, but she's already gazing at me.

"Magnar counted on me coming, Samantha, not six Great Ones with three Originals and a Lesser." She turns back to him. "Besides, this fight can't be avoided any longer."

Magnar laughs. "You're too late. Charlie's mine. All the methuselahs are mine." He gestures, and twenty feet to the side of him floats a giant digital clock showing 11:53 a.m. "At noon Charlie will die, and there's nothing any of you can do to stop it. He's given his word he'll stay with me."

Tarath and the others stare at him quietly.

Uncle Biggie clenches his hands, his thick shoulders hunching as his eyes flash gold. "Let poor wittle parrot go."

Magnar says harshly, "You dolt. You should have stayed in your cave."

"Charlie!" Uncle Biggie runs at Magnar in fast, blurring strides.

Tarath hisses. "The battle begins."

Magnar rubs one of his rings and from it grows a colossal shadow, a cross between a sperm whale and giant squid, with tentacles coming out of its massive whale head.

Streaking through the air, the shadow beast wraps itself around Uncle Biggie and the snarling crocle-lion. The three of them fall to the ground and roll to the side into a tree.

"Nooooo." The big man thrashes his arms. "Charlieeeee!"

"Altaar!" cries Tom.

Uncle Biggie continues to struggle wildly, gripping tentacles and squirming until he breaks free. The growling crocle-lion chomps on the end of a tentacle, also freeing itself.

Shouting, the big man takes his leash and in a flash wraps it around a writhing tentacle. Pivoting on his feet, with both hands he swings the creature in a wide circle, releasing it so it sails toward a distant tree.

Thwap! Falling to the ground, the shadow rolls out of sight.

Uncle Biggie watches, not moving.

My heart pounds. I hope it'll be this easy.

But a flash of gray swerves through the trees, headed toward Uncle Biggie. Three thick tentacles wrap around him, and the shadow monster smashes him to the ground. Roars and shouts fill the air as they roll away into the forest. Growling, the crocle-lion runs after them.

"Altaar," murmurs Tom, his face strained.

Brandon rests a palm on his brother's shoulder.

My fingers throb on WhipEye and I wait, hoping more of its carved faces will shine.

"Good riddance." Magnar laughs. "I've waited ten thousand years for this, Tarath. It's too bad Rose isn't here, but all of you will witness the beginning of a new world. My world. Humans will answer to me, and I'll decide everything."

"It's not noon, Magnar." Tarath hurtles forward.

Magnar doesn't move.

The caracal's words drift back to me; *Remember, Samantha Green, never show your true strength until it matters.* Maybe she wasn't just giving me advice. Hopefully, she was also trying to tell me that she'd held back with the buffalo shadow in their first encounter.

The buffalo shadow strides forward, its feet punching into the ground, leaving deep impressions. Bending toward the caracal, the shadow clutches air as Tarath darts around the monster.

I tell myself it's not luck.

With bunched legs, the cat leaps onto the shadow's back, her bared claws sinking into it. Both creatures roar, twisting away to the side of Magnar.

The gorilla beats its chest and the wolverine growls.

Jumping seventy feet onto a tree trunk, the primate leaps to another tree, then to the shoulders of the buffalo shadow, while the wolverine races ahead and rams it from the side. All of them fall over and roll away in a wild struggle.

Shouts of encouragement fill my throat, but I wait.

"Yeah!" Jake raises a fist, but he sees my frown and becomes quiet.

The buffalo shadow struggles to its feet, throwing off Tarath and the other two Great Ones. Bending over, the monster lifts a section of a massive fallen tree trunk, which dwarfs the beast in size. The shadow hurls it at the gorilla, but he catches it, spins, and throws it back.

Swinging both arms, the buffalo shadow deflects the log into the forest, where it crashes against trees, disintegrating in a shower of splinters that rain onto the soil.

Tarath leaps at the buffalo shadow from the side, and the wolverine springs onto the monster, toppling it backward. Growling, the gorilla hurtles into the fight again.

The creep's voice is ice. "That's two shadows. I have seven left. Is this the best you can do, girl?"

Gazing at the remaining Great Ones, I'm silent. There aren't enough of them to defeat Magnar's shadows, much less his claw.

Lewella's expression is hard, and Tom grimaces. But Brandon smiles.

Jake bites his lip as we watch WhipEye. But the staff remains dark.

The Kodiak bear growls and charges next, its paws thumping the ground.

Flying through the air, the cobra shadow wraps around the bear's neck and front legs, causing it to lose its footing. I wince when the bear crashes to the ground. Both beasts roll past Magnar with thunderous growls and hisses. It's hard to watch, but I can't turn away from my friends.

The rhino snorts and hurls itself forward, its hooves making hard crunches.

Another shadow leaps from Magnar's rings. This time it's a giant tiger with six legs. The cat swipes a paw at the rhino, but the rhino is quicker, ducking its head and catching the feline with its horn. The tiger is thrown upward, spinning end-over-end. It manages to extend one claw to grip the thick hide of the rhino. Pulling itself down, the cat straddles the Great One's back.

Leaning sideways, the tiger topples the rhino with a crash, and the two of them skid in a spray of dirt past Magnar, careening off trees.

The creep laughs again. All of it numbs me.

Leaping onto a nearby tree trunk, the iguana jumps from tree to tree, moving to Magnar's side, then around him, forcing him to turn. From a trunk twenty feet away, the lizard springs at him.

I'm hopeful until a monstrous raven with a toothed beak and spiked wings flies out of Magnar's next ring. Flapping hard, the bird catches the iguana in mid-air with its talons and the two tumble away into the woods.

Yellow, insect-like wings grow from Lewella's back. Barely moving them, she rises into the air beside us, her black-clothed body expanding to twenty feet in length, her wings just as wide. Her green eyes surround gold pupils and her golden hair lies in long tresses over her shoulders.

I stare at her. "A.k.a. *Anisoptera*. Ancient. Five-thousand species. Fly thirty-eight miles per hour. They can see in all directions."

"Dragonfly." Jake is wide-eyed.

Lewella is stunning, reminding me of childhood stories about faeries, but she looks too fragile for Magnar's monsters. I take a breath.

"Please, Lewella, don't." I can't bear to see her hurt.

Sadness fills her eyes. "We all must have the courage to do what's right, Samantha. You've shown us that."

Moving much faster than any Great One, she flits toward Magnar in a zigzag pattern. Tom and Brandon run impossibly fast below her.

Magnar releases a shadow woolly mammoth, which stands on two legs, whirling its unnaturally long trunk like a whip.

Reaching the mammoth in a blur, Lewella swings the soles of her feet forward into the monster's body, sending it flying backward. Surprised at her strength, I watch intently as the Lesser chases the falling shadow. Brandon and Tom run after her.

The mammoth smashes into several trees, crashing to the ground where it slides on its back into another trunk. Rolling to its feet, the shadow methuselah whips its trunk around Lewella's legs, impossibly catching her.

A shout rises in my throat.

"Lewella," cries Tom.

"To battle," yells Brandon.

The two brothers leap from forty feet away, crashing into the behemoth's legs. All four of them fall to the ground. I crane my neck, but trees block my view of them. I swallow, worried for Lewella.

Magnar's eyes gleam.

Helicopter blades whir to the east, but trees hide the aircraft from view.

Magnar sweeps a hand over the outer surface of the glass sphere. Stirring inside, the creature looks like a giant, awakening spider, its six appendages unfurling, revealing that it's much larger than I thought. It dwarfs the Great Ones and methuselah shadows.

The claw presses against the glass until cracks appear on the globe's surface, running around the whole sphere. Grating, the breaks expand until the glass shatters, sending millions of small shards dropping to the ground, leaving the monster floating free.

Jake blanches. I grip the staff.

Magnar points east, and the claw rises a dozen feet, speeding quickly toward the meadow. I step with Jake around trees to watch.

Two army helicopters are flying across the meadow toward us. The park ranger must have made calls when he saw Magnar's monster. Small compared to the claw, the helicopters still should have a chance against it, giving me hope again.

When the claw bursts through the trees into the meadow, one of the helicopters fires two missiles.

Shooting forward, the shadow closes around the bombs. I cover my ears as muffled explosions fill the air, the shock wave reaching us. When I look, the claw is knocked back in the air, curled up.

But in moments it unfurls, even larger now, showing no damage. Horrified, I realize anything Magnar's monster captures will increase its size and strength. Human weapons will never be able to defeat it.

Darting forward, the creature grabs one of the passing helicopters by its tail. Moving in a circle, it flings the aircraft away with little apparent effort. Spinning, the helicopter falls to the ground in a deafening crash.

I wince. People are dying, and Magnar's just warming up. He'll kill thousands, millions, if necessary, to achieve his new world.

The claw rises higher, chasing the other evading aircraft.

Jake turns to me. "Sam."

Raising WhipEye with him, we thump it into the ground, sending a deep echo far into the distance. But the staff chills in our hands.

"Call them," cries Jake.

I look from one carved face to another on the chestnut wood. "Monkey. Turtle. Leopard."

Jake says, "Zebra. Baboon. Bat."

On and on we call names, but no faces glow.

My voice grinds to a halt. I can't pretend anymore.

"They have to come," whispers Jake, staring at the staff.

"No more Great Ones will answer." Magnar smirks. "Humans have killed and hurt animals for centuries out of selfishness, so why should Great Ones risk anything for a pathetic girl and boy?" He loses his smile. "The two of you aren't worthy."

Charlie slumps on his shoulder.

I can't bear it: Charlie near death, Magnar smiling as if death and suffering have no importance, and the corrupted methuselahs forced to fight Originals and Great Ones.

"Forget you, Pug-face." I yank WhipEye out of Jake's grasp and charge.

THIRTY-THREE
Saving Charlie

SAM!"

Ignoring Jake, I watch the glowing parrot as he falls. "Charlie!"

I look sideways at the clock and stumble when I read it. Noon. The clock fades away and I run harder.

Magnar ignores me. He's waited ten thousand years for this and won't allow anything to distract him. With one hand he catches Charlie as he falls. With his other, he removes the ring from the stone, then places the parrot on the pedestal. Carefully, he sets the ring on Charlie's exposed wing.

When I'm a dozen strides away, Magnar finally notices me, his eyes tightening.

I hear steps behind me, and call, "Jake!" Without thinking, I extend WhipEye out to my side so he can see it and toss it vertically ahead of him, as if we've practiced this maneuver a thousand times.

Jake flies past me and catches the staff in the air on the run. Before Magnar can call another shadow monster, Jake jabs Whip-Eye at him.

Almost casually, the creep sidesteps the blow, moving faster than he should be able to, even for an Original. Grasping the staff, Magnar jerks it out of Jake's hands and tosses it to the ground where it rolls away.

Shouting, Jake hits the creep with his fists and feet, moving fast in martial arts stances. "This is for Charlie!" he yells.

Magnar stumbles back several steps, wide-eyed, showing more surprise than injury.

Strangely, chickadees and juncos chirp nearby, flitting through the trees on both sides of me. When I reach the rock I silently send my wishes to them, hoping they understand. I'm frightened for Jake and know he's buying me time.

"You creep!" Jake keeps swinging at Magnar, his armor flashing in iridescent hues that change in the light. But Magnar moves faster, his hands blocking the blows.

Finally, Magnar spits, "Foolish boy." His hands blur and he catches Jake's wrists. Flesh sizzles and Jake screams.

"Jake!" I shout.

Chirping harshly, the chickadees and juncos dive at Magnar, pecking and scratching at his face until he's forced to let go of Jake and raise his arms protectively.

Bright, golden light shimmers around Charlie.

I make myself turn away from Jake, the light from the parrot heating my face like a hot fire. Jake yells again, but I bury a shout in my throat. I have to focus on Charlie.

The light from the parrot expands farther, moving in a bright circle several feet past me, where it pauses, forcing me to cover my face with my forearm. In a moment, though, the light recedes back toward Charlie. I follow the edge of it as it shrinks toward the parrot's wing.

Inside blinding rays of light, the ring glints like a small gem. I reach in, my fingers curling around the metal. Grasping it, I bring it out and press my fist against my chest. My palm burns as if I'm holding a red coal, and the light seeps from my hand in a thick stream back into Charlie's body.

A bright flash erupts as the parrot's body glows like a star.

Magnar yells.

I lift both arms for protection and glance away.

Light sweeps past me in an expanding circle, bathing the trees and forest, going over them and streaking for the horizon in all directions. It's as if the sun is shining on me with its full force. I close my eyes, but it still hurts.

When the brightness fades, I lower my limbs. Sunlight streaks through a break in the clouds above.

Jake lies on the ground near Magnar, gasping, his face twisted, his armor shining. I glare at Magnar. The hot ring sears the palm of my right hand. Somehow, I don't mind the pain.

Charlie's body lies on the pedestal.

Shrieks, growls, and roars fill the forest. Tarath and the other Great Ones continue to fight Magnar's monsters.

"You'll pay, girl." Magnar rubs all three of his remaining rings, bringing forth more shadows.

I straighten shakily, but my voice is steady. "My name is Samantha Green, my father is Bryon Green, and my mother is Faith Sommers. And you're nobody."

Magnar throws back his head and growls inhumanely at the sky, his cry quickly becoming a deafening roar in the forest.

Machine gun fire erupts from the meadow, where Magnar's claw pursues the other helicopter.

"Sam." A few paces past Magnar, Jake is crawling, grimacing. Wobbling, he rises to his knees, arcs his arm, and sends the canteen flying.

I raise my left hand, my fingertips barely catching the strap. I trap the canteen under my right arm, and with shaking fingers unscrew the stopper.

"Please don't leave us, Charlie." The parrot might already be beyond help. Or maybe he can't live without the methuselah energy. I don't care. I have to try.

I tilt the flask, but something knocks it from my grip, sending it flying several yards from me where it bounces once and stops. Healing water pours out over the forest floor.

"No!" I cry.

A giant wild boar shadow stands on two legs, hulking over me with bared claws and enormous, curved tusks.

When it reaches for me, I throw myself to the ground beneath its shaggy limbs, banging my knees. Crawling wildly, clutching the ring, I watch the clear water run out of the canteen. I reach for it, but the beast grabs my ankles and drags me back.

"No." I stretch my left hand as healing water pools on the dirt.

Heavy weight presses my torso into the ground until my head lies against cool soil. I can't move. I hear Jake shouting to the side.

He's making a dash for the canteen while dodging the cobra. One of the snake heads hits him in the back, slamming him down. He lands on his armor, bouncing off the ground.

"Jake," I gasp.

Without pause he rises, looking unhurt, and continues running. This makes no sense to me, unless the armor is somehow making him stronger too. The cobra strikes him again, knocking him within a few feet of me. He thumps the ground hard, but again rises to his knees. This time the snake pins him, pressing its weight into his back and pushing him down to his belly. His glasses are twisted on his face.

One of the snake's heads hisses and Jake gives a muffled yell.

Something pulls my gaze away from him. A dozen feet from me, WhipEye is calling—not with sound, but in my gut there's a tremendous urge to grab it.

Jake quiets and reaches for it.

Impossibly, the staff rolls a few inches toward him, but one of the cobra heads strikes his arm. He jerks it back, covering his face with his hand.

WhipEye stops.

I consider reaching for it, but the other cobra head lowers near me, its large eyes inches from mine.

From somewhere nearby, the creep says, "You're going to pay, girl. My claw will take both of you alive."

Trying to ignore him and the snake, I look for help. A short distance from us, Tarath is swiping at the leg of the buffalo shadow, tripping it backward.

My chest is compressed by the shadow monster atop me and I can't fill my lungs. All I can manage is a whispered, "Tarath."

The caracal's head whips around.

Roaring, the buffalo shadow regains its balance. Tarath faces it, and from each of her eyes a golden ray shoots out, striking the buffalo shadow torso like heavy punches that send the beast reeling into a tree. I stare in awe, wondering what else Great Ones can do.

The cat blurs toward me in great leaps.

Recovering in moments, the buffalo shadow gives pursuit. The gorilla shoulders the shadow from the side, but the buffalo keeps moving. Jumping on the monster's shoulders, the gorilla grabs the buffalo freak's horns, yanking its head back. Reaching up, the beast finds the great ape's arms and flings him away.

Twirling in mid-air, the ape lands on a tree trunk and leaps back onto the buffalo monster.

Tarath paws WhipEye on the run, sending it rolling toward me. But I can't try for it with a cobra head hissing near my face.

Spinning around, the caracal crouches and snarls at the charging buffalo shadow. A flash of yellow and black slams into the buffalo shadow's side, sending it stumbling away. Lewella. The wolverine rams the shadow's legs, finally toppling it.

The cobra heads rear up to strike the cat.

"Watch out," I croak.

Tarath spins, growling, her claws flashing at the cobra, keeping it at bay until a massive foot lands near the far side of Jake's head. I'm staring at the gorilla's leg.

Grasping the cobra just below each of its heads, the ape frees Tarath to harass the boar holding me down. Brandon and Tom yell from somewhere nearby, but my pounding gut focuses my attention on the staff.

WhipEye stops rolling, just inches away.

I quickly transfer the ring to my other hand, and my fingers curl around one end of the staff so tight they ache. Jake clutches the other end and we pull it in close. None of the faces we called earlier light up.

A tear rolls down Jake's cheek. The sight of him pinned by the snake, Charlie dead, and our failure to defeat Magnar even with the Great Ones who answered is too much to bear. Tears streak my face. There isn't anything left in either of us. Magnar will crush everyone we've brought.

I rest my cheek on the staff, watching the tear from Jake's cheek drip onto the wood with mine.

When our tears strike the chestnut staff, a small flicker of light flashes from both ends of it, quickly spreading to its center until the whole length of it glows brightly. The wood is hot and jumps out of our hands, spinning in front of us. First clockwise, then counterclockwise it rotates near our heads, in moments coming to an abrupt halt.

I seize it near the bottom. "Stand it up, Jake."

"Get the staff," Magnar yells to his shadow monsters.

My fingers tighten around the hot wood, which is brightly lit. Searing heat pours into my palm. Jake grabs the staff above my hand and gasps.

Slowly, we bring WhipEye vertical.

My wrist throbs. Jake grimaces.

Tarath and the gorilla prevent the wild boar and cobra shadows from interfering. Beyond them, the rhino, wolverine, and Kodiak bear pound other attacking shadows. Lewella slams into the buffalo repeatedly with flashing speed, keeping it from charging us.

Snarls and wild cries fill my ears, but I concentrate on the staff.

Once we have WhipEye vertical, we strain to lift the end of it a few inches off the soil. My shoulder stings.

Jake gasps and our eyes meet. It has to be enough.

Loosening our grip, we let the staff fall, keeping it upright.

When the end of the chestnut staff strikes the earth, there's no echo. My heart sinks. Jake's chin drops to the dirt, his lips trembling.

The rumbling begins beneath us, escalating until a deafening *BOOM!* erupts beyond us in the surrounding forest.

Bulging under our bodies, the surface of the ground rises and then ripples like a wave flowing away from us in all directions. Simultaneously, the soil around us cracks in narrow seams resembling the spokes of a wheel that run a score of yards.

Shadows and Great Ones lose their balance or leap out of the way of the moving earth.

I cry out over seeing all the Great Ones' faces shining on the staff.

Jake and I shout the names of the illuminated animals as fast as our lips can move, the words tumbling out of us; "Turtle, panther, badger, mongoose, hawk," and on and on.

Great Ones streak from the staff in golden rays. All are huge, like Tarath. As they arrive they roar, shriek or hiss, and then leap forward to fight Magnar's shadows. They keep coming until every lit face on WhipEye has responded.

My wrist aches and I release the staff the same time Jake does, allowing the rod to fall to the ground.

An oversized bonobo and brown bear pull the boar shadow off me, freeing Tarath to help elsewhere. The gorilla and a red-tailed hawk drag the cobra shadow away from Jake.

We push to our feet and wipe our eyes. Jake adjusts his glasses, which remain a little twisted, a sad smile on his face. I understand. I also remember Rose's words, that survival or love might bring the Great Ones out of KiraKu. Maybe it took both.

I stumble to the canteen, which is tipped into a crack in the dirt. Picking it up, I rush to the pedestal and tilt it over Charlie's body. Waiting. Not a single drop falls onto the parrot.

I toss the container away, feeling dull inside.

Jake's beside me and grasps my hand.

Magnar's shadows quickly fall in defeat, each held captive by a number of Great Ones, a half dozen on the buffalo shadow. Tarath and the iguana advance on Magnar, but pause when he raises his rings toward them. I wonder how powerful he is, to make even Great Ones hesitate.

"Come to me," Magnar yells, fury in his eyes.

In the meadow, the claw breaks off the tail of the second helicopter, which spins out of control. Without pause, the monster flies toward the creep. I can't take my eyes off it.

A jarring crash makes me hunch reflexively over Charlie. Jake throws himself over me.

The falling helicopter careens into nearby trees in a shower of sparks, breaking against trunks until it thuds into the ground. Tarath and the iguana leap out of the way as splintered parts of the aircraft fly through the air. One hits Jake in the side, knocking him off me.

"Jake!" I know this time he'll be hurt.

He rolls through the air, hitting the ground hard on his side. But he's somehow quickly on his feet again, running to me.

The claw swoops through the trees, giving me shivers. Tarath roars and charges Magnar, the iguana running beside her.

Magnar raises his hands and sends golden streams of energy at both Great Ones, which freezes them in mid-stride. It reminds me of how Rose froze Magnar in the park when he chased me. Worse, the claw is flying directly at them.

"Tarath!" I yell.

Tarath's and the iguana's eyes shine bright gold until a film of light flows over their bodies. Their legs drop, and they jump back from the monster's reaching fingers.

Still, Magnar's claw darts forward and flicks out two digits, sending Tarath and the iguana flying through the air until they smash into trees and fall to the ground.

Hissing, Tarath scrambles to her feet, her head lowered. She stalks the claw, which hovers protectively over Magnar. The iguana shakes itself and walks beside the caracal.

Magnar scoffs at them; "Great Ones are no match for my creation, but they can feed it."

His confidence worries me. Even with this many Great Ones present, he doesn't look concerned.

Led by a snarling honey badger, half a dozen Great Ones leap on the floating claw, but Magnar's monster shrugs them off, sending them flying into the forest.

I don't want to believe it, but Magnar is still going to win.

Over a dozen Great Ones, led by Tarath this time, circle the claw. When the caracal hisses, they leap atop the monster, hanging on with claws, teeth, and fangs. Slowly, the creature sinks, forcing Magnar to crouch beneath it.

More Great Ones join in, piling atop the monster. I want to cheer them on, but I'm spent.

Just before it touches Magnar, the claw seems to adjust to the Great Ones' size and weight. Shaking itself like a wet dog, it throws off Great Ones like cockroaches, sending them flying into tree trunks or farther into the forest.

Wanting to do something, anything, I feel helpless as the claw rises and Magnar stands and laughs. An urge fills my gut, and Jake turns with me.

WhipEye spins once more on the soil, the last image on it illuminated. A huge pull to grab the staff assaults me.

I pick it up, and Jake grips it. We lift it and slam it into the ground, calling the name of the last glowing image; "Crocodile!"

Blinding light flashes and the fifty-foot saltwater crocodile lies on the dirt behind us. We're standing between the croc and Magnar, and for once I see Magnar's face tighten. He didn't expect this Great One to show.

Magnar motions to his claw. "Kill it."

Great Ones jump on the monster, forcing it to fight them before it can follow Magnar's command.

The croc hisses and his eyes glow bright gold. The Great One's words, that he would never leave KiraKu to help humans, make his appearance stunning. Yet I doubt one more Great One, even a ten-ton crocodile, will make it possible to defeat Magnar's monster.

"You have to give us energy," I say. "Now."

"Everything you've got," says Jake.

The eldest Great One glares at us with narrowed eyes—most

likely from receiving orders from a girl and boy. Moving his head side-to-side, the croc takes in the whole battlefield. Then he roars, "Come to me."

While some Great Ones keep Magnar's shadow monsters captive, and others fight the claw, Tarath, the iguana, and a handful of others run, hop, fly, and canter next to the croc. They form a half-circle, facing Jake and me, their eyes shining bright gold.

"Take off the armor, boy," grumbles the croc. "Hurry."

Jake presses his hand to his sternum, and in moments the bright body armor melts into his palm. He pockets the scale.

Rays of light from the Great Ones' eyes flare out, bathing us.

"Stop them!" cries Magnar.

White-hot heat flows into my skin, filling my body. I release Charlie's ring, which falls to the dirt.

Power.

Energy that can do anything courses through my veins like a warm liquid. I feel unbreakable. I've never felt anything like it before and want more.

The heat inside me increases until sweat covers my face and back, soaking my flannel shirt. Abruptly, it's nearly unbearable, as if it will burn me from the inside out.

Jake's face scrunches and I cry out, "Stop."

The light ends and the Great Ones sink to the ground, heads hanging, their bodies slumped in fatigue.

Gripping WhipEye together, Jake and I turn to face Magnar's claw. It floats toward us, free of Great Ones. I want to scream and run.

Walking beside it, Magnar beckons his creature toward us, his face red with rage.

The monster floats closer, a few feet in front of us. My numb hand tightens further on WhipEye.

Opening like a monstrous spider rearing to attack, the claw pauses above us. I want to shout, but my throat and vocal cords won't respond. Instead, I stare at the monster's pulsing skin as dark shapes push against it and then sink back into it.

"Let's hit it, Sam," says Jake.

I want to, but I shake my head, my face tight. "Not yet."

The beast strikes, its six monstrous pointed fingers thudding into the earth behind us and curling toward us. Above, its black, oily skin throbs.

"Now, Sam."

"Wait."

Cutting us off completely from the others, the monster's membrane quivers three feet over our heads, while the claw closes in around us on all sides, blocking out the light.

Jake bites his lip, whispering, "Sam."

"No." It lowers further and I can't breathe. Can't think. Can't move.

Everything's dark.

"Now!" I yell.

In one smooth motion we slam WhipEye straight up into the center of the monster. A flash of golden light streaks along the staff and crackling energy flies across the undersurface of the claw in jagged lines. It's like a fireworks display, with sizzling light running over the black skin in pulsing bursts.

The monster pauses.

Jake and I lower the rod, too tired to move. Watching. Waiting. Hoping.

I take a deep breath and hold it.

A web of cracks begins in the creature's palm where we struck it, quickly spreading over its entire surface. Then the crawling lines of WhipEye's energy fade into darkness.

Silence. I fear the claw will recover even from this blow.

A garbled sound like ripping fabric fills the air, and the claw's skin ruptures all over. From the monster's wounds pour gray shapes of animals, their forms visible for a flash before they evaporate into the air. Zebras, lions, snakes, antelope, and so many others I can't keep track of them. Hundreds—quickly becoming thousands, fly out of the claw for several minutes. Many chimeras are among them. We watch in wonder until the stream slows to a few last animals escaping into the dark.

Then, deflating like a balloon, the claw descends toward us.

I crouch with Jake, an arm over my head, waiting for its weight to hit my shoulders. But the skin of the monster fades away into nothing, never quite touching WhipEye before it's completely gone.

Sunliight bathes us again.

The ring intended for Charlie rests inches from my feet. I grab it and pocket it.

When we stand we're facing Magnar, crisp clear air around us. His face is haggard and deeply wrinkled again. Veins bulge on his forehead as if the strain is too much. I realize he lost some of his own strength when we destroyed his claw.

He falls to his knees. "Don't do this."

Some Great Ones streak back to the staff in rays of gold, but most remain. Tarath and the iguana move quickly to pin Magnar's limbs to the ground.

Magnar cries, "Leave me alone, you idiots. You dolts. You fools!"

The caracal calls over her shoulder, "Children."

Balancing the staff against the rock, we stumble to her.

"You're as blind as all the other humans." Magnar's eyes are nearly closed. "Ruining a beautiful planet. Killing everything. Do you think anything will change by stopping me? At least I had a solution. What have you got?"

Swallowing thickly, I don't have an answer. I pull on a ring and it comes off hard, as if unwilling to leave Magnar's finger.

Jake works frantically on the other hand.

"The Great Ones haven't told you everything," Magnar says weakly.

"Shut up," says Jake.

I glance at Tarath, but keep working. I don't trust anything Magnar has to say, but I remember the Great Ones' treachery with the Originals, kicking them out of KiraKu.

Magnar continues, barely able to talk, his voice a halting whisper. "Before Rose died, she said, 'I won't forget you. I hope you find peace.'"

I don't look at his face as I pull the ring from his index finger. As we tug off his rings he slowly melts away, his flesh wrinkling like a shriveled apple. It sickens me. Not just his body, but what a waste his life has been. He's quiet, unable to say another word as his skin and muscle thin to nothing until all that remains is a skeleton.

"Gross." Jake keeps working.

When I pull the last ring from a bony finger, the hand it's attached to crumbles into dust. The rest of the skeleton begins to disintegrate.

Jake struggles with the thumb ring, but the digit breaks off with the ring attached, falling from his jerking hand to the dirt. "Geez!" he exclaims.

In a flash, a stream of shadow flies into the ring. The thumb bone dissolves and the ring disappears.

"What?" I murmur.

Jake stares at the ground, gaping.

With a sigh, I straighten, glad it's over.

The iguana bobs her head. "I was proud to help you, Samantha and Jake. Thank you for caring." Before we can reply, the Great One streaks into the staff.

"The boulder," says Tarath.

We take the rings to the rock.

Uncle Biggie gently lifts Charlie off the stone and sits with his legs crossed, cradling the parrot in his lap. The crocle-lion lies nearby, panting, its head drooping.

Silently, we put the eight rings on the pedestal. When finished, I look at Tarath.

"WhipEye," she says tiredly.

I grasp the staff. Warmth floods my arm and I sense what to do.

With both hands, I hold WhipEye vertically over the rock, my right palm burning. Jake grips the staff with me, wincing. Red rings mark his wrists where Magnar grabbed him. The weariness in his face matches mine.

With all the force we have left, we ram the end of the staff against one of the rings. Light flashes from the bottom of WhipEye as it pounds the ring to pieces.

Simultaneously, the buffalo shadow floats above us in the air, freed from the Great Ones restraining it on the ground. Those Great Ones immediately streak into the staff.

The shadow monster quickly melts, shrinking in size until it reaches the shape of a true buffalo, which then disintegrates in a splash of blinding light that sweeps to the horizons. We're forced to duck and close our eyes.

When we open our eyes, the cracks in the ground have disappeared and all tree damage from the fight has faded away. I'm happy about that.

We destroy the rest of the rings one by one, and each of Magnar's shadow monsters streaks above the rock, floating in the air where they shrink into the shape of the original methuselah. Ostrich, woolly mammoth, sperm whale, tiger, kangaroo, wild boar, and lastly raven, bursts into brilliant light flowing to the horizons.

The king cobra doesn't appear. It has to be in the ring that escaped.

"Ugh." Jake shakes his head. "Stupid snake."

"Yeah." I look around. All the Great Ones have streaked into the staff, except for two. I kneel by Uncle Biggie and wipe my eyes. Jake's beside me, his hand on my shoulder.

Large tears run down Uncle Biggie's cheeks. "Poor wittle parrot."

Lewella stands nearby in human form. She's supporting Tom and Brandon, their arms draped over her shoulders. Tom looks sad, but a weary looking Brandon winks while clutching his side.

Lewella appears tired, but she has a soft smile on her face and her green eyes are bright. I'm glad she's all right.

Behind us there's a low grumble.

The crocodile, which fell to the dirt after giving us energy, slowly rises. He labors a few steps forward, then opens his mouth, revealing gallons of clear water sloshing in his lower jaw.

I'm not sure what the reptile wants, but I have to try. "Can you heal Charlie?" I motion to Lewella and the brothers. "And give them some healing water?"

The reptile swings his head toward Lewella, then back to me, then to Tarath, his eyes flashing gold.

"The water was for the methuselah shadows if they needed to be destroyed," says Tarath. "He's never tried to save a methuselah, but he'll do what he can. Put the parrot in his mouth."

I gently lift Charlie from Uncle Biggie's lap.

The crocodile keeps his jaws open, while I place the parrot

inside. I watch the bird sink into the clear rippling water. For an instant it looks like Charlie opens an eye.

"Charlie," I murmur. But perhaps it's the sunlight reflecting off the water.

The crocodile brings his teeth together loosely and faces Lewella, Tom, and Brandon. Gold light flashes from the reptile's eyes into the eyes of all three. Lewella and the Originals fall to the ground, lying in peaceful slumber.

Without a word, the crocodile streaks back into the staff.

Numb, I look at Tarath. "Now what?"

"Yes," she says. "Now what?"

THIRTY-FOUR

A New Beginning

THREE DAYS LATER, Jake and I walk through the sun-drenched park. Tarath told us to come to the park bridge at noon, and to bring WhipEye. I eagerly look ahead, hoping, my feet moving fast.

We have three hours on our own today. Dad and Cynthia are watching us closely, saying we're earning trust. We don't mind.

After the battle, we used WhipEye to move Lewella, Tom, and Brandon to their apartment. But when we visited them two days later, the door was unlocked, their apartment empty. Their disappearance disappointed me, but Tom was probably glad to leave. Uncle Biggie returned to the Endless Warehouse to care for the animals.

There hasn't been anything in the news about our fight with Magnar.

We celebrated my birthday last night. That one meal and warm evening made everything normal again. Jake and Cynthia cooked lasagna and homemade bread for us, and we had the pumpkin bars.

Dad's gift, birding binoculars, is strapped to my belt. I'm wearing Cynthia's gift: an aquamarine T-shirt with a surreal picture of a dolphin on it. It's something Mom would have given me. I also have new shorts and tennis shoes.

I laughed when Jake gave me a bracelet with a small jade elephant hanging from it; a reminder of crossing the river in KiraKu on dolphins.

The compass hangs from my neck and I never take it off. Two days ago, a sliver of gold appeared in Jake's pupils, and in mine. It's a little freakish. Our parents are going to take us to our doctor in town. We haven't told Dad or Cynthia anything about what happened, though sometimes I want to. Without Charlie here to talk to them, I'd just be admitting to stealing the parrot.

WhipEye hasn't called to me or Jake since the last battle. I'm glad. And if Tarath needs it, I want her to have it. But it saddens me that the last door to KiraKu will close.

When the park bridge comes into view, I crane my neck. The disappointment on Jake's face matches mine, but maybe the Great One is hiding in the forest, because a young woman is sitting in the middle of the bridge bench. She's wearing tennis shoes, jeans, and a white blouse, with a red flower in her long, brown hair.

She watches as we approach, her face bright and youthful.

After some hesitation, we sit on either side of her. I hope she'll leave. When she doesn't, I steal a glance at her.

Realization hits me and my jaw drops. "You're the woman in Magnar's paintings."

"You recognize an old friend, do you?" Her voice is familiar and her pupils flash gold.

"Rose?" Jake leans forward for a closer look.

I throw my arms around her.

Pulling back from me, she tousles Jake's hair.

"I wondered why we never saw your body, and just the dress." I quietly set WhipEye against the bench beside her, settling my hands on my lap. "Someone moved you from the buffalo shadow's arms, like Magnar moved the kinkajou."

Rose nods. "There's an ancient energy source in KiraKu, the same one that enhanced Magnar and me long ago. It rescued me."

"Wow." Jake studies her. "You're really young."

"I lived in your world for a long time, so it took a lot of energy to reverse my age, and there was a price."

"Did you know you'd be rescued?" I clasp my fingers.

Rose shakes her head. "No." She gently grasps Jake's forearms. The wrist burns from Magnar are still red.

"No armor on my arms." Jake smiles. "It felt soft inside, like a cushion."

"I wondered why you weren't hurt," I say.

"I heard you took some hard blows, Jake," says Rose. Next, she inspects my right hand, looking at the red circular mark in my palm. "Battle scars." She smiles at us. "Heroes always have them."

I sit with that for a minute, and then can't wait any longer. "What about the animals in the Endless Warehouse?"

"I'm sure Uncle Biggie will take good care of them. Tarath wants me to check on him."

"But most of those animals can't live in Minnesota." I remember the koala bear and dolphin.

"We'll make sure they go home or to KiraKu." Rose pats my leg. "So don't worry."

"And the crocle-lion?" Jake gives a small wave. "I mean, it scares me, but it helped us at the end, and it was kind of cool, in a way."

"It'll stay at the warehouse with the other chimeras for now. People aren't ready to see them, yet."

"What about the snake?" Jake's forehead furrows. "Someone took the ring."

"Maybe Magnar had a secret partner," I say. If true, I wonder what that partner might be planning next, and how angry he might be that we destroyed Magnar.

"Maybe." Rose pauses. "I'm searching for the cobra. I have to clean up Magnar's mess."

"You don't have a choice?" asks Jake.

Rose is quiet for a few moments. "If you find your true path in life, there isn't a choice."

I understand that, but there's pain in her eyes. "I'm sorry about Magnar."

"Thank you, Samantha." Her expression softens. "At one time he had a good heart and was the love of my life."

"You can never go back to KiraKu, can you?"

"The crocodile won't allow it." It's obvious from her eyes that she wants to.

"He's punishing you," I say.

"Idiot," says Jake.

Rose sighs. "I broke a lot of rules, and the crocodile sets them."

Jake slashes the air. "That's not fair."

"I have no regrets."

Swallowing, I can't hold it in any longer. "I miss Charlie."

"Well, don't get all misty-eyed on me, kid." The parrot flies out of the trees, heading for my shoulder, landing and clutching it tightly.

At first I can't speak. Too many words are scrambling in my mouth. I'm amazed by the brightness in the parrot's eyes and feathers, and I blink, to make sure I really have my friend back. I smile, but it's a few moments before I'm able to say, "Charlie."

Jake's hands do loops. "How?"

"Toothy's not all bite, kids. Healing water saved me, and the croc allowed me to come back to your world. But this time around I'm just a smart-talking parrot." He cocks his head at me. "And you know what I want to do, Sam?"

I'm happy for him, but my throat thickens. "Fly through a jungle."

Squawk! "I'm thinking the Amazon for starters."

The four of us sit together, enjoying the gurgling stream.

After a while, Charlie rubs his head against my cheek. "You're the reason we're all here, kid. And I don't mean on the bridge."

"Well, I had a lot of help from friends and you, Charlie."

"My pleasure, kid."

Jake returns my smile.

"Mom's compass guided us too," I add.

I wait, but Rose just stares at the brook, her eyes bright, and Charlie remains quiet. Even though I don't have all the answers, I have enough to think on things.

"The journey wasn't so bad, was it?" asks Charlie.

Jake's hands fly up. "Are you kidding? It was scary." He pauses. "And fun sometimes."

I continue smiling. "I think I'm ready for summer vacation."

Charlie clucks. "Remember, the journey never ends, and all that matters is how you live it."

I get that, and like it. "Did you know how it was all going to work out, Charlie?"

"I had a hunch, but I'm not a psychic." The parrot tilts his head. "It would make a good movie, though, wouldn't it?"

Jake holds up five fingers. "Five-star."

"Will things get better now?" I ask. "Will people treat animals and the planet differently?"

"The methuselahs' energy is free, as the Great Ones intended all along, so there's hope." Rose looks at me warmly. "If love is in one of us, then it can spread to others."

After a bit, I ask, "What about the gold in our eyes?"

Charlie squawks. "You've both breathed KiraKu's air, tasted its healing water, and Great Ones gave you energy. Nobody knows what that means."

Jake gives an awkward chuckle. "As long as we don't mutate into monsters." He frowns. "We won't, will we?"

"Let's hope not." Charlie clicks a few times. "Any favorites?"

When our time ends, Rose hugs Jake, and then me. Charlie hops to her shoulder. I smile at the parrot, not wanting to say good-bye. I give one last look at WhipEye, but stuff my hands in my pockets.

When we turn to go, Charlie whistles sharply. "Hey, kid, aren't you forgetting something?"

When I face Rose, she's holding WhipEye out to me.

I want it terribly, but don't reach for it. "It's yours, I can't take it."

"You've earned it, Samantha." She shrugs. "Most of my powers are gone, anyway. After the warehouse is straightened out, and we find the cobra ring, I want to do some traveling with Charlie. I was a guardian a long time and I just want to live my life now. If I need help, I can call Tarath by name alone."

The desire to grab the staff grows stronger. "What about the Great Ones?"

"WhipEye is mine to give," says Rose. "And Tarath liked the idea. So did the other Great Ones."

Charlie fluffs his feathers. "Even Toothy didn't argue, Sam."

"Way cool." Jake pumps his fists.

My fingers curl tightly around the warm chestnut wood.

"There's one condition." Rose doesn't let go of the staff.

I keep my grip on WhipEye, looking at her uneasily.

"I knew it." Jake's hand flops. "There's always a condition."

Tension creeps up my throat.

Rose's voice is serious. "The WhipEye tree has a very strong spirit. It can survive almost anything life throws at it. Whoever holds WhipEye has to be ready to do the same. Both of you must pledge to be guardians of this world, KiraKu, and any future methuselahs."

"So we share the staff?" I glance at Jake.

"Can you?" Rose regards me curiously.

I smile crookedly. "Sure."

"What do we have to do?" Jake grasps the wood, his eyes flashing gold.

Something about that knots my stomach.

"For the moment, nothing," says Rose.

Jake rolls his eyes. "Yeah, right."

"It's not a bad gig, kids."

I look at all three of them, but in the end I trust Charlie, as always. "Okay." It's not a choice for me, anyway.

Jake shrugs. "Why not?"

Rose releases the staff, and Jake's fingers slowly slide off it. I wonder what other secrets the staff has that no one explained to us. Somehow, that doesn't bother me now.

"Safe journey," says Rose.

"Stay out of trouble, kids."

I grin. "Right, Charlie."

"We probably won't." Jake beams.

Charlie adds, "And don't talk to any strange parrots. It could get you into a mess."

As we walk away, for the first time in a year my mind and heart are completely free of worries and sadness. "Guess what?"

Jake's bouncing in his stride. "What?"

"I haven't used my inhaler for the last few days. I think my asthma is going away." Maybe it's the healing water I drank in KiraKu, Great Ones giving me energy, or having Mom with me again. Perhaps all of it. I hum Mom's song.

"You know what I was thinking?" Jake's hands do little patterns. "If Bryon and Cynthia get married, we'll be brother and sister."

"No way." My forehead wrinkles. "Stepbrother and stepsister."

He checks his watch and taps my shoulder. "Ten minutes to get home."

We round a corner, and bushes rustle near the side of the path.

I stop, every muscle tense. I clench WhipEye and Jake goes into a martial arts stance.

I imagine the fifty-foot two-headed cobra slithering at us.

A deer pokes its head out of the vegetation.

I gasp a chuckle. "Whew. I'll take a deer any day."

Jake smiles, lifting both arms high into the air. "A.k.a. no more monsters!"

I laugh, and for once flick his shoulder.

We jog down the path. Cardinals are singing and sunlight glistens on the green leaves of the trees. I want to go for a walk in the woods, which reminds me of KiraKu.

Don't miss the next
exciting adventure in the

WhipEye Chronicles
BOOK TWO

Gorgon

To receive updates on Gorgon go to

www.geoffreysaign.net.

Acknowledgments

MRS. STIFTER, my high school creative writing teacher, started my writing journey early by giving me praise. I'm also fortunate to have friends that don't complain when I occasionally become a hermit with my computer.

Pamela Klinger-Horn provided insights early on, and was gracious enough to find three young readers, Austin R. Bray, Christian A. Bray, and Hannah Flom, who gave feedback; as the first young readers of *WhipEye*, they also provided inspiration. John Graber had good advice. Steve McEllistrem gave valuable critiques and helped with writing basics.

Jillian Bergsma helped with copy editing and removing fluff. Ashley and Kassity Davis, Emma and Theresa Vaske, Karin Vaske, Rachel Vaske, Connie Saign-Piché, Cari J. Cordova-Sandstrom, and Dennis Grubich all helped with cover design and the trailer. Connie also helped trigger the process that led to the current title. Carl Brost, Alexander Nordstrom, Krystin Novitsky, GeNae Blomberg, Rose Kranz, and Grayce Grohovsky, gave suggestions, help, and support. Cathy Pinkosky allowed me to run many questions by her. Ken Epstein took my photo.

Patrycja Ignaczak created the fantastic cover.

John Harten, who gives the best overall critiques I've ever had, lifted the book to a higher level with his understanding of story, character, and his amazing knowledge of trivia and stuff.

Dad gave constant support, read all my drafts, and gave common sense advice, as always. And Mom, who reads all my writing, gave ceaseless and invaluable suggestions and feedback on every aspect of the book throughout the revision process. Over the years, we've probably had a thousand discussions. Without her help, this book wouldn't be what it is today.

Geoffrey Saign can often be found looking for interesting critters, and magic, while swimming, snorkeling, sailing, or hiking in the woods. He has assisted in field research with hummingbirds and humpback whales, and sailed as far away as Australia. He lives in St. Paul, Minnesota. To learn more about Geoff, visit him at www.geoffreysaign.net.

CPSIA information can be obtained at www.ICGtesting.com
Printed in the USA
LVOW11s0904250215

428303LV00004B/228/P

9 780990 401308